The Ultimate Pleasure

The Ulltimate Pleasure
and Other Stories

by
Renée Dunan

translated, annotated and introduced by
Brian Stableford

A Black Coat Press Book

TABLE OF CONTENTS

Introduction

La Dernière jouissance by Renée Dunan, here translated as "The Ultimate Pleasure," was first published in Paris by France-Édition in 1925. *Kaschmir, jardin du bonheur*, here translated as "Kaschmir, the Pleasure Garden," was published in the same year by Éditions Henry-Parville. The short story "Le Métal, histoire d'il y a vingt mille ans," here translated as "Metal," first appeared in three parts in the 13, 20 and 27 November 1920 issues of the socialist weekly *Floréal*, to which the author was a regular contributor of articles and book reviews; it might well have been her first-published work of fiction.

Dunan appears to have written very prolifically, in a wide variety of genres, between 1920 and 1925, when she published several books, as well as contributing to a number of periodicals. If the supplementary material in the books can be believed, she wrote a great deal more than was actually published—or, at the very least, she intended to. In the introduction to the earlier Black Coat Press sampler of her work, which features the four stories in the collection *Baal, ou La Magicienne passionnée* (1924; tr. as "Baal; or, The Passionate Sorceress") and the short novel *Les Amants du diable* (1929; tr. as "The Devil's Lovers")[1], I included a list of all the books advertized in the former volume as "forthcoming," most of which never appeared or were long delayed, and *Kaschmir* also includes a detailed synopsis of a novel

---

[1] Black Coat Press, ISBN 978-1-61227-046-3.

advertized as forthcoming from the same publisher, *La Confession cynique* [The Cynical Confession], although the abrupt demise of the publisher resulted in a four-year delay before it appeared via another outlet.

Most of Dunan's early work appeared from small, rather marginal publishers, and much of it might well have been written some time before publication—comments in the pages of *Floréal*, for instance, imply that the stories included in *Baal* were already works in progress in 1920, and it seems likely that *La Dernière jouissance* had already been completed when it was advertized in *Baal*, probably having been started while she was working for *Floréal*, although the abrupt change of direction part-way through the text suggests that it was not finished until she had become severely disenchanted with revolutionary socialism.

As this somewhat hit-and-miss record suggests, the author did not have an easy time in making an initial impact in the literary world of post-Great War Paris, in spite of a relentless energy and a willingness to experiment with all kinds of materials. There is no doubt that she was ambitious, and also well-informed. One of the most interesting ventures of those early years was a series of *Lettres intimes* featured in *La Revue des Lettres* in 1925, which couches articles on various topics in the form of letters to imaginary correspondents, the longest of which, addressed to "Monsieur le Professeur J.-D. Prettywhore à Dayton, Ohio," offers an elaborately sarcastic and admirably detailed account of the current literary coteries of Paris, diversifying from the solid foundations of romanticism (allegedly the most flourishing), naturalism and symbolism to take in various "new schools," including Jules Romains "unanism" and surrealism—described, in complimentary terms, as the grown-up bastard child of Dadaism—to conclude with an answer to the hypothetical question of where she would place herself among the "schools, groups and chapels."

"Truly, nowhere," is her reply. "I am of that special sort of novelist who directs lived adventures in accordance with a philosophical rule. Three bases are indispensable in order to comprehend the range of my writings: the Neo-Platonism of Bergson, the Relativism of Einstein and the Pansexualism of Freud. As, especially in the milieux in which letters are judged, abstract knowledge is not much in favor, I must resign myself, just as Rabelais passed for a mere humorist, and Flaubert for an insipid bourgeois, to passing for a simple pornographer..."

Although the false immodesty of this reckoning is not entirely serious, it does illustrate the fact that, although Dunan was already being written off by some contemporary critics as a mere pornographer, she did have much larger ambitions, and the explicit eroticism of several of her early works really was guided by an intense interest in the psychological functions played by sex in human affairs rather than by a simple determination to titillate her readers. Subsequently, having been forced into the role of hack pornographer by the pressure of popular demand, she did go in for vulgar titillation on a considerable scale, under various pseudonyms, but always remained ambitious to do other things as well, as illustrated by such erotically-charged exotica as *Les Amants du diable, Papesse Jean* (tr. as Pope Joan) and *La Masque de fer ou l'amour prisonnier* [The Iron Mask; or Love Imprisoned]—all of which were published in 1929, although they has probably been written earlier, at intervals.

The full extent of her writings remains unknown, some of her pseudonyms probably remaining undiscovered or undisclosed; a sensitive inspection of the pages of the short-lived *Revue des Lettres* suggests that several of the variously signed contributions in each issue were actually by the same hand, and that Pierre Nézelof and André Steeman, to name but two, might actually have been Dunan in other guises.

The possibility remains, in fact, that "Renée Dunan" might have been a disguise herself—such, at least, was the claim belatedly made by one Georges Dunan, who claimed after Renée Dunan's supposed death in 1936 that he had actually written all the books signed by that name and the others associated with it. If so—and he might have been lying, although the only photograph of the author reproduced on the world wide web does look suspiciously like a man in drag, and the plot and title of *La Confession cynique*, describing the travails of an effeminate young man in heartfelt terms, might well give rise to pause for thought—then it was a remarkably extreme and consistent imposture, given that Renée Dunan maintained an extensive correspondence with numerous real individuals as well as fictitious ones.

Whatever the truth of the matter, there is no doubt that the elusiveness and mercurial quality of Renée Dunan's identity, which saturates her work as well as her personal history, makes her an exceedingly intriguing author. Although her work is a trifle rough-hewn, the relentless propensity for the melodramatic demonstrated therein, in rare combination with blackly comic sarcasm, ensures that it always possesses an admirable vitality and is often fascinating. The three stories included in the present collection, belonging to very different genres, illustrate both the spectral range of her work and the nature of its underlying consistency—which, if not really possessed of Bergsonian Neo-Platonism and Einsteinian Relativism to the same extent as a conscientiously Freudian Pansexualism, is nevertheless not entirely devoid of such pretentions.

La Dernière jouissance is a very peculiar addition to the tradition of dystopian fiction, not least because of its curious even-handedness, although that might be partly due to a reversal of opinion while the work was in progress. In its depiction of a future absolute tyranny it is remarkably stark. The manner in which it designates its initial heroine, B 309, is reminiscent of Evgeny Zamyatin's *We* (written, in Russian, 1921; published, in English translation, in 1924), although it is highly unlikely that Dunan could have had any awareness of that work, and her novel offers a far more conventional image of ruthless oppression. What is unusual even about the novel's first half, however, is its explanation of the origins of that oppression as a deliberate Terrorism, imposed by a small technocratic elite in a desperate attempt to preserve the last remnant of the human race from a worldwide disaster precipitated by a massive disruption of the San Andreas Fault.

Following the orgasmic conclusion of that first part, the story becomes much more peculiar in ideological terms, and also in respect of the similarly-orgasmic conclusion to the entire plot, and its eccentric relationship to the story's title. (It is arguable that I ought to have rendered *dernière jouissance* more brutally as "last enjoyment" rather than "ultimate pleasure," but the judgment call had to be made, and I felt sure that the author would have sympathized with the more pretentious rendering.)

It is not easy to figure out, as the narrative develops, where the author's sympathies actually lie, and what conclusion it is actually groping for; some readers do not like that kind of uncertainty, preferring to know exactly where the author is trying to position them, but those who appreciate more open-ended prompting will undoubtedly find a certain chemical aliment of thought in the combination, especially if they are able to draw comparisons with other notable accounts of dystopia and its destiny.

Kaschmir belongs to a curious subgenre of the rich French tradition of *femme fatale* stories, the "female Bluebeard" story, pioneered by Eugène Sue in *L'Aventurier ou La Barbe-Bleue* (1842; partially translated under various titles, including *The Female Bluebeard*) and most memorably extended into the twentieth century by Pierre Benoît's Rider Haggard-inspired *L'Atlantide* (1920; tr. as *The Queen of Atlantis* and as *Atlantida*). It is not improbable that Dunan read the latter book—indeed, given that she was such a prolific literary critic in the early 1920s and that it attained both commercial and critical success, she would have had difficulty avoiding it—but her own take on the theme, lightly dusted with anthropological spice and strongly flavored with a typically-French fascination with the Orient, is markedly different and engagingly idiosyncratic.

"Le Métal," which must have been one of the author's earliest literary endeavors, is understandably less fluent than her later productions, but is of considerable interest within the rich tradition of French prehistory fantasy inspired by local paleontological discoveries. It probably owes part of its inspiration to the works of J.-H. Rosny, with which Dunan was familiar (he is one of the authors favorably referenced in her letter to J.-D. Prettywhore), although a more proximal prompt was probably Edmond Haraucourt's epic *Daâh, le premier homme* (1914; tr. as *Daâh, the First Human*)[2], some of whose key themes and imagery it echoes, albeit with reference to a much later period of prehistory. Interestingly, it was not the only work of speculative fiction published in *Floréal*; the periodical rapidly followed it up with a futuristic utopia, *La Résurrection du Docteur Valbel*, in 1921, which was reprinted by the publisher of *La Dernière jouissance*, France-Édition, in the same year. It bears the dual signature of Lucien Deslinières and J. Marc-Py; the former was a well-known socialist who published several non-fiction books, while the latter is credited with several novels of an amorous nature.

Like the other two stories here included, as they eventually unfold, "Le Métal" is fundamentally a violent, lurid and fast-paced action-adventure story, but like them, it has pretensions to be something considerably more ambitious, and is fueled by a genuine sense of intellectual curiosity. All three of the stories are, in fact, primarily interesting for their exploratory nature, to which their insistent eroticism is secondary—an aspect of a quest rather than a vulgar means or end. Their principal virtue might, in retrospect, lie in their peculiarity rather than their literary or philosophical achievement, but they remain eminently readable as well as endearingly eccentric.

The translation of *La Dernière jouissance* was made from a copy of the France-Édition version inscribed by the author to "M. de Bourbon." (If that inscription can be taken at face value, I might now be the proud possessor of smudges and stains imparted to virgin pages by a one-time pretender to the defunct French

---

throne, but who can tell?) The translation of *Kaschmir* was made from the copy of the Henry-Parville edition reproduced on the Bibliothèque Nationale's *gallica* website. The translation of "Le Métal" was made from the version reproduced on Steve Trussel's ElectiCity site at trussel.com.

Brian Stableford

.

THE ULTIMATE PLEASURE

Introduction

I. The Fault

It was thirty years earlier that the great misfortune had occurred. Before that, for a long time, wars and massacres seemed to have thrown humanity into an endless cycle of destruction. One day, however, a definitive peace appeared to have arrived; the era that had opened then had been named the Great Fraternity.

It was then, by an atrocious irony of destiny, that the prodigious cataclysm had occurred.

Soon, social life was no more than a memory.

Time went by. The terror gradually decreased. People attempted to restart the old governmental machines that surprise had dislocated. Soon, there was hope that relationships between the peoples might be renewed. France attempted to find out what had become of America—for all the cables had been destroyed and wireless telegraphy received no response.

Missions were organized. Aircraft and balloons reached the West, where it was hoped that they would find life in the process of adapting to the new and tragic circumstances.

At that moment, frightening news spread. Near the Fault, and increasingly further away, in accordance with an inexplicable progression, people were dying in a new and strange manner.

Blood, suddenly becoming too fluid to remain imprisoned in the vessels, was oozing from their bodies like sweat.

Fear gripped the word tightly. The epidemic extended. Scientists set forth to attempt to investigate, confront and circumscribe the new disease. During weeks of anxious waiting, terror anguished four hundred million civilized people.

Before the key to the monstrous mystery could be discovered, however, the Bloody Sweat appeared in the old world. It was first seen in Spain, and then Algeria. Shortly afterwards, the Eastern Mediterranean fell victim to the atrocious disease. The Balkans were depopulated in a matter of months. In November it reached Holland and England, and it was learned that the central Plateau was beginning to perish too.

It was then that a few of the scientists sent to the source of the evil returned. Only sixteen out of the two hundred and nine who had departed returned to their homeland. What they said was even more terrifying than the reality already seen.

The terrestrial crust, ripped to its depths from Peru to the Far North, constituted an immense volcano. But the most horrible thing was that an unknown gas was emanating from it, whose penetration into the human lungs produced the quasi-gaseous fluidity of the blood that caused it to spread from the vessels like sweat.

The gas had been given the terrible name of Necron.

That was not all. The viscous metallic mass of the subsoil, laid bare, was producing immense quantities of cyanogen, carbon monoxide and free chlorine. The terrestrial atmosphere was destined to become unbreathable, even for those that the Necron did not kill. So rapid and powerful was the oxygenation of these toxic gases in the light that the depletion by the Fault exceeded oxygen production.

In sum, the quantities of oxygen absorbed had already disrupted the proportion of the atmospheric constituents. The terrified people saw some mediocre plants becoming enormous, and others dying. Under the strange influence of these vital changes, nettles grew with a vertiginous haste and vigor, sweeping over the world. Some were already seen that were as large as oak-trees.

It was the End of the World.

Labor ceased everywhere. The last relics of civilization disappeared. In parallel, the frenzy of pleasure-seeking and the fury of asceticism increased. Their partisans massacred one another.

The lands where life persisted took on the aspect of forests full of wild beasts. Only France still had scientists, who maintained the struggle against the Necron, the Fault and the end of everything with a desperate will. The coasts of the Mediterranean had sunk into chaos. Nothing more was heard from Germany, but no one was unaware that the Balts were putting all foreigners to death. The inhabitants of shores isolated themselves as in lacustrian times.

Still, however, hordes of the wretched fled toward Siberia, without knowing where it was, as the crusaders of the year one thousand had set out for Jerusalem.

It was thought, suddenly, that the respiration of chlorophyll would ensure the purity of the air in forests, and there was a desperate flight toward regions where trees were abundant. Soon, however, the sylvan over-population terrified the first to arrive, and they murdered the newcomers.

Cannibalism reappeared. Rural populations occupied woods like fortresses, and millions of unfortunates prowled the roadsides like wolves.

In Paris, a special terror reigned, ferocious and concentrated. The crowd there was so nervous that not a day passed without bands of people putting others to the torture who were suspected or accused of being carriers of the bloody sweat. Rich and poor confronted one another in pitched battles. The rich accused the poor of propagating the disease; the poor accused the rich of hiding and monopolizing "the remedy."

Hundreds of dreamers and intellectuals were burned, having been suspected, because they did not appear to fear death, of "knowing the secret." Communal suicide became commonplace among people of feeling. In memory of Socrates, twenty philosophers and highly cultured individuals poisoned themselves with a decoction of hemlock and died while one of them read the *Crito*.[3]

---

[3] The core of the dialogue in question, between Socrates and Crito in the former's prison cell, is the argument that Socrates sets out for his refusal to escape, even though his friend promises to facilitate that eventuality, and the great man's determination to accept the death sentence passed on him.

But the bloody sweat invaded the Languedoc. A crazed and disheveled population flooded toward the center, destroying everything. The defense of the Ile-de-France had to be organized against those people, deprived of everything human.

It was then that a formula against death by Necron emerged from a laboratory, It was the fruit of labors long pursued by Jacques Landève. That scientist had already isolated the vital gas that he called Bion, and he won the immense but ironic glory, at the moment when the end of the world seemed nigh, of having created, based on the chemical series of the albimunoids, a protoplasmic body that lived, reproduced and excreted.

At that time, in Paris, retrenched in three blocks of buildings in Passy, guarded and defended by negroes, there was a combative group of intellectuals who were also in search of "the remedy." They included all the branches of constructive intelligence: chemists, engineers, physicians, physicists and physiologists. Incapable of despair, those men already possessed a kind of extended occult power. They recruited adherents for all possible purposes, seeking arms to serve them.

Jacques Landève submitted his discovery to them. A powerful laboratory trial hastily studied the possibility of sanitizing determined spaces. It was concluded that, given certain superhuman conditions, it might be possible to preserve a fraction of humanity.

Humanity survived.

II. Survival

The leader of the Society of scientists grouped around Jacques Landève was named Tadée Broun. He was a man of indomitable energy. He gathered together nearly a thousand people, who would be the masters and leaders of the new society. They were subsequently named the Thousand by the people.

One unique duty was imposed on those sovereigns. They were not to take account of any individual life among the few million unfortunates submissive to them; only the struggle against the Necron and the atmospheric poisons was important.

Time was pressing. They drew up a plan for the necessary measures. They had to create monstrous chemical factories to produce millions of tons of the products of salvation so far only obtained in grams in laboratories. That required iron and coal. It required giant dynamos of copper, lead and nickel. All of that, or substitutes, had to be extracted from the earth locally—where else could they find millions of arms except in Paris, the last refuge of dying humanity? And what efforts, on the part of all those individuals, hurling themselves without distinction of sex or age into fearful, frantic, titanic labor, would be indispensable!

In addition, it was necessary to nourish that host. With what? They would, in consequence, have to fabricate chemical aliments from immediately obtainable substances: oxygen, nitrogen and carbon. Not to mention clothing those flocks; the effort of creating primary industries alone surpassed the largest possibilities. They did not recoil. The raw material of labor was there: thirteen million people! They would be subjected, like steel being shaped into a piston-rod.

It was done.

That living paste was manipulated, like a metal melted in order to be poured into a mold. Tadée Broun already had five hundred thousand serfs, better nourished and cared for than the Thousand themselves. With that small army he took possession of a power that no one, in any case, disputed with him. There was a fight to the death against the universal depression, fatalism and obstinate indifference of all those who believed that the end of the world had come.

To bring those amorphous masses into the factories, to enslave them to an urgent and gigantic task, seemed an insane enterprise, but Tadée Broun was not discouraged.

Because it was necessary...

After vain attempts, the decision was made to act by means of terror. Tadée affirmed that it would galvanize the mass, and that nothing would stand up to it.

What he imagined then surpassed in atrocity the great misfortune itself. First, he gathered together sixty thousand people and took them to a vast plain not far from Paris, under the "protection" of eight hundred machine-gunners. He left then without food for two days and then, on the third, had sixty people chosen at random sawed in two, alive, on top of immense scaffolds.

The alarm of the crowd quickly attained what he called a "motivated" degree.

He fed them that evening, and the next day he made them file past the active machine-guns. Then they drew lots to select one person in every hundred, who would be crucified by the ninety-nine.

A horror soon reigned in their souls that surpassed in power the terror of the bloody sweat.

On the fifth day, Tadée Broun had forty thousand dehumanized serfs at his disposal, which he was able utilize in the abandoned factories. They began work on the combination of Titanium, Bion and Geocoronium that would make the Necron disappear.

For a month, Tadée Broun softened up his workers. He recruited others by varying his methods of terrorization.

Soon, there were twelve hundred thousand.

Then, the great work made progress.

Later, it was forbidden to mention that redoubtable era in public conversations between members of the Thousand. It retained its power to terrify through time, even in the hearts of grim and pitiless leaders.

The subsoil around Paris was emptied, and was soon as hollow as a sponge. Iron, coal and copper were discovered there. In the sixth year, an enormous deposit of oil was found. Vertiginous factories were created. In the second year, six million human beings were working. By the fourth, the totality of known living humanity belonged to Broun's factories.

That total was eleven million individuals.

To nourish and clothe that enslaved mass, fabulous enterprises emerged from the earth. The famous chemical aliments produced a mortality of four per cent in the first year. They persisted...

The death toll rose to eight per cent in the third year, the most terrible. They did not have time to worry about it. The Necron in the atmosphere was nine thousandths below the mortal dose. The mortality decreased thereafter, doubtless spontaneously. Tadée Broun was victorious.

In the fifth year, the département previously known as the Seine was no more than a Babelesque factory in which, in pitiless activity, and in unspeakable suffering, terrible masters permitted life to overcome its destiny.

That struggle against death finally came to an end.

Although human life had virtually disappeared from the terrestrial surface, it persisted there. Devoid of morality, pleasure and desire, an atrocious life was obstinately maintained, in spite of everything.

In the seventh year, the mortal gas seemed to decrease in virulence.

It was a strange thing, that Society created by Tadée Broun and his companions. It no longer knew either smiles or joy. The two castes that it contained, the people and the Thousand, were further apart than any previous aristocracy had ever been from those it commanded.

Twenty years after the Fault, one might have thought that geological epochs had constituted the physical and mental abyss hollowed out between the mass and its masters.

The Thousand were the serfs of the scientific idea, and knew nothing else. They were aware of pleasure, and even its perversities, but everything outside of their duties was sad, somber and negligible so far as they were concerned.

The people had not forgotten laughter and joy, but everything in them was frightfully debased. An uncertain mysticism, a dolorous anticipation of the Messiah, and the obstinate desire to deceive the masters was all that maintained their souls. Dragged into the factories for sixteen hours a day, between electrified fences, brought back and forth under the constant mortal menace of

Necron bombs, they lived a precarious and vegetable existence. The disciples of Old Broun had gradually rendered automatic all the means of defense against the proletariat, of whom it was necessary to anticipate occasional revolutionary desires.

Paris had, therefore, been abandoned by the Thousand. A complex and scrupulous police force, using turncoats and women, kept watch of the dwellings of those millions of unfortunates. Paulin Vialy, who directed that delicate organism, was the second person in the Thousand. Methodical organizations of tunnels and telephones constituted a perfect network of surveillance.

In Paris itself, a kind of popular Municipality had regulated questions of accommodation, the distribution of food and fabrics for clothing. A single cloth for ten million bodies was retailed in special well-defended shops that were in communication with the factories where it was produced, and with the City of the chiefs. The latter had been built when the Necron had become less dangerous. It was situated to the north-west, and a barbed-wire fence defended its borders. Charming, and comprised of dwellings build in accordance with the most varied caprices, it was now a subtle and secret nucleus of debauchery, whose actresses were drawn from the factories. Sometimes, with the aid of Vialy, hunts for beautiful girls were carried out in Paris.

There was no longer any ordinary commerce, since the mass received, in return for work tokens, nourishment, clothing and the right to shelter in some house or other, perhaps sumptuous or ruined, the former always being preferred.

Nothing, therefore, was manufactured for sale. An immense black market persisted, however, both among the Thousand, who were beginning to treasure old things from before the Fault, and among the people, where a sentimental value was obstinately attributed to innumerable useless or ridiculous objects.

Alimentary foodstuffs were also traded, which the Thousand pursued ardently, and in spite of their vanity, a mysterious attraction was still exercised on minds by the wealth of old: gold coins or jewels.

Thousands of insubordinates were hidden in Paris, and even crossed the defenses of the city, although they were redoubtable. Their remembrance was a kind of tradition and constituted the words of numerous popular songs. Everyone hoped for the advent of "the hidden one" whose arrival would liberate the enslaved people. A considerable number of secret societies and criminal associations added a leaven to that living and obscure dough.

The laws imposed by the Thousand provoked a muted and stubborn resistance, especially the one that condemned old people incapable of working to death. The most shameful compelled the immediate fecundation of every nubile female.

Jealousy between all those wretched people, however, helped to maintain them in their misery. Spontaneous denunciation was rife. In the corridors, the access stations where workers were embarked to take them to the factories, with such precision that they were not allowed a single free moment, grilles disposed between rotating doors and right angles, isolating each individual, ensured an inviolable discretion for thrown pieces of paper that dropped into the tunnels. By means of anonymous confessions thus obtained and stimulated by the secret operations of Vialy's police, everything concealed was discovered. A system of disguised bastions within Paris itself, armored shelters and tunnels capable of bringing negro police to any part of the vast city, forced the tranquility of the mass, which remembered with terror mobs drowned in their own blood.

Besides which, in the case of a decline in production or absence from the factories, a terrible system of collective responsibility sufficed to master troublemakers completely.

Thank to all of that, thirty years after the Fault, the sovereignty of the Thousand seemed indestructible. Sensualists now, and vicious without ceasing to be devoted to their work, they sought beautiful mistresses above all else.

There was always much talk of Revolution in Paris, and, in spite of many vain attempts, the crowd still hoped to succeed in vanquishing their rulers. Like a threat, however, at the height of Sacré-Coeur, an immense dial in the center of the city indicated the proportion of Necron in the air. The gas was mortal a level of one part in ten thousand, and everyone knew that only hard labor and science could maintain the proportion of the gas below that redoubtable figure...

That day, the dial indicated one in seventeen thousand. It was five o'clock. The heat was heavy, at the start of spring.

Over shaft 104, in the east, where the damned worked at a depth of three thousand meters, the smoke sketched a monstrous cypress in the air.

The sun was shining upon the dwellings of the Thousand and caressing with gilded brushes the tenebrous dirt in which Paris lived.

The sky was the color of pure water. In the distance, beyond the grim circle of immense factories, where the Necron was doubtless master, the new verdure reigned...

Part One: Pleasure

I. The Masters

Between ancient Paris and the aggregation of giant factories, all the marble of the sumptuous dwellings of the Thousand gleamed in the light of the declining day.

A flattened and carbonaceous cloud oscillated on the horizon, to the south of the setting sun. To the east, the age-old city displayed its decrepit and illustrious monuments: Notre-Dame, the Panthéon, Sacré-Coeur, church bell-towers and spires. Surrounded by an enormous wall that dominated the vast defensive glacis in which metallic disks and networks glittered, however, overlooking and keeping watch on the thousands of dwellings and gehennas of labor, the bright columns and sculptures of the palaces of the Thousand seemed to be smiling.

It was 19**. The fissure in the terrestrial crust that had almost wiped out the human race was already thirty years old.

After having known the nudity of their laboratories for a long time, the Thousand now lived in delicate luxury. Following no law other than their omnipotent caprice, they had edified that original city without any other intention than satisfying the whims of variable and voluptuous moods.

Their palaces were secret, full of unknown riches and armored like fortresses. The people referred to them

generically as the Louvres. There was not a single labor-
er who did not vomit incessantly the worst insults
against the Louvres. Nor was there a single young woman in the factories who did not dream, her heart beating
with desire, about their sumptuous, soft and perfumed
dwellings, where Asiatics served you in silence, and
where it was only necessary to desire to have. Those
whom the Thousand had adopted excited the envy of
their peers, when those of the mass thought about their
perfect happiness. That also motivated the hateful verve
of the men, who could never dream of that issue from
their torment.

There were, in fact, in the homes of the Thousand,
more than two hundred women of the people, including
the famous B 309, the former rebel of the great textile
mill, who had become the mistress of old Tadée Broun,
now almost a septuagenarian.

In the speeches of revolt preached in the depths of
cellars or the secret refuges of the insubordinates, it was
always one of the most powerful verbal alcohols to re-
call those unfortunate women, who were imagined to be
weeping day and night in their servitude, and submissive
to abominable vices.

And they believed, naively, that if they were free,
those vanquished women would return to the factories.

That evening, the various roads linking the mines to
the protective glacis of the Louvres carried a few of the
Thousand returning to their enclave after being relieved
of their managerial duties. Two men were conversing on
the long footbridge 14, which ran over bare, dead ground
for five kilometers.

At the summit of tall, slender pylons, between two
narrow rails, the automatic carpet was transporting the

two "white-coats." They were generally in a hurry to get home, but the two belated travelers, instead of accelerating the progress of the carpet, had reduced its speed. They were contemplating the somber and metallic landscape.

"I wonder, Pierre," one of them said, "how important any hypothesis regarding the present state of the Fault can be..."

Those words emerged from the mouth of a red-faced and clean-shaven quadragenarian, who was indolently smoking a cigarette of some highly-perfumed artificial herb.

"Someone could go and see," replied the other, a nervous dark-haired young man who was casting an attentive and curious gaze all around.

"Of course—but the rules and our duty demand that we should not occupy ourselves with the rest of the world, and I think that very appropriate."

"However..."

"Life consists of eliminating its torments, my boy. By watching the behavior of the people who live before your eyes, and nothing else, you obtain knowledge of the greatest wisdom accessible to us: to limit one's concerns!"

"I'd prefer not to cultivate that ferocious egotism any longer, and to think about that which escapes me."

"Well, Pierre, I believe that the books from before the Fault that affirmed the psychological opposition of generations weren't so stupid. Your father, Tadée Broun, thought about nothing but Necron throughout his life, while you're perhaps thinking about negroes living, if there are any, in some inextricable forest in Africa, who had doubtless never seen Europeans before the Fault."

"Yes! I'm curious to know what extends beyond the circle of factories in which we live enclosed."

"Before the Fault, if I can believe their novels, they would have said that in order to be afflicted by that inexplicable anxiety, a man must have some secret torment."

Pierre Broun blushed, and asked, in an embarrassed fashion: "What do you mean?"

The other started laughing, and gazed at the landscape momentarily before replying.

"Oh, yes—you don't like reading those intoxicating books. They're being rediscovered, now that nobody down there has a taste for them any longer. I have my agents seek them out, and I find them very diverting. People weren't stupid in those days! Scientifically speaking, they were sentimental, and somewhat fond of their ignorance, which often seems very curious to me as a state of mind—but their social life was complex, and their mental condition was curious. It developed rare psychological talents. Given your reverie about the Fault and the rest of the world, they would unfailingly have declared that you're in love..."

"Love?" said the other, with suppressed irritation. "What's that?"

"Not the vice of Sigliaresse, evidently, but a kind of vague and tender aspiration that turns the mind away from facts to direct it toward dreams—perhaps pleasant, in sum, and which makes one sees life as beautiful."

"Bah! With whom do you think I'm in love?"

"Isn't B 309 capable of inspiring sumptuous sentiments?"

"You know that my father has forbidden calling her that," Pierre Broun murmured.

Vialy shrugged his shoulders. "It's the only name she likes. Then again, Tadée's prohibition is only aimed at jealous adolescents and the other women from the factories who'd like to wound the Master's mistress. In any case, he was wrong to give the order."

"You don't like B 309 very much?"

"Me! Certainly, if I'd anticipated that your father would take her out of the factories, I'd have prevented it."

"You'd have killed her?"

"Yes, and given her to the rats in the great shaft to eat. I have dungeons where I execute dangerous subjects—by which I mean the most intelligent."

Pierre Broun seemed to be in a bad mood. "I can't abide your kind of mockery, Vialy. It's too obvious that you're scornful of everything and suspicious of everyone."

"It's the only wise attitude to adopt."

"Isn't there something grandiose and noble in our mastery of the Necron, and our great hope of creating a kind of superhumanity?"

"Yes, we have mastered the Necron. Perhaps humankind will live for another fifty years or two hundred...a drop in the ocean. But your hope of seeing the birth of the superman is a chimera, with no connection with reality. We're still similar to those people down there, and thirty years hasn't given us even the superiority that one race of monkeys has over another." He indicated Paris. "Perhaps there are more men of genius there than among us."

At that moment the footbridge passed over a profound cutting, through which a long train was traveling carrying factory-workers back to their dwellings. An innumerable crowd was crammed on to the platforms that were the only kind of carriages that existed.

Vialy leaned over to see. Pierre Broun did likewise. Immediately, a clamor of hatred rose up toward the two men, a furious multiple cry that filled the air with countless insults. Ten thousand pale faces, mouths open, vomited abuse and scorn.

Vialy started laughing. "They're singing!"

Angrily, Pierre Broun straightened up, his cheeks pink.

"I suppose you're going to do something about that rabble?"

The other shook his head. "What do you want me to do?"

"But if you let them insult us, isn't it to be feared that they'll do worse one day?"

"It's not the desire that they lack. My role is to make sure that the desire remains a desire. I'm not aiming for absolute realization, as in the time of monarchies, but for the equilibrium of a relative utility: that of confidence and force. If they shout, so be it—provided, of course, that they work and that I know what they're doing at home. I don't require any more than that to give our power the value of perfection. It's necessary not to forget, in any case, that there a chance that we might be carried away, one unforeseeable day, by a wave from the depths of that human ocean."

"You're content with very little, it seems to me."

"No—the necessary isn't trivial. In fact, it's everything. The monarchs of the world before the Fault tried a thousand methods to secure their power, and none of them succeeded. They endured by chance or the play of circumstances, not otherwise. Think about this: however great our defensive faculty—which is enormous and frightful—might be, we'd be defeated by those people, if they consented to the necessary sacrifices."

"I don't understand. What about the blood-sweat bombs, the toxic gases, the electrified networks, and many other mortal inventions, the mere listing of which makes one dizzy?"

Vialy shrugged his shoulders. "All that's theory. Just remember that there are eight hundred of us and ten million of them. We have ten thousand servants, it's true, but put the two figures in opposition: eleven thousand, in round numbers, and ten million!"

"But..."

"Do you really think that we could kill nine million of them?"

"Perhaps not."

"Well, even if we did, there would still be enough remaining to kill us all. I've calculated that if they were prepared to sacrifice twenty per cent of their manpower in a rapid attack, they'd have a chance, for what would be left of our defenses when we'd killed two million of them?"

"However..."

"Our means of defense are limited by the possibility of deployment and direction. We could obviously destroy everything—ourselves included—by igniting the sixty thousand tons of klazzite we have in store, but I don't consider that operation to be intelligent. In any case, rid yourself of the idea that if ten million human beings attacked out little city we could destroy more than fifteen or twenty per cent of therm. Even if we destroyed eighty per cent, which would blacken the entire region with cadavers, we'd eventually be defeated. Syster's great operation can kill a million at a time, but it takes six months to set up, and once the first million had been asphyxiated, another million would find us dis-armed."

"They wouldn't dare attempt such an attack."

"Of course not! Not soon, at least. But the soul of a crowd is a mysterious thing. If some such ambition is born in certain brains, my job consists of discovering it, and dissolving that enthusiasm. In sum, I know how our power could be threatened. Government isn't, in my view, a matter of sanctions, dungeons, executions and terrors. Those means tend toward absurd ideas and pure vanity. It's uniquely a problem of proximal but sufficient solutions, applied when appropriate. When they seem no longer applicable to the reality, one chooses others, equally transitory. In the meantime, at present, there's a danger. The people are agitated, and insubordinates are preaching a kind of holy war. They're beginning to wor-ship the famous Messiah Diavide, for whom I'm search-ing, and who will come to a sorry end, I swear..."

"Oh!"

"Yes. He must even have accomplices among us. I need to investigate that carefully."

"Who do you suspect?"

Vialy smiled. "Do I really need to tell you?"

Pierre Broun turned toward the darkening décor of the sunset. B 309, his father's beautiful mistress, was evoked in his imagination like a magnificent phantom, terrible and fascinating.

In order to change the subject, he murmured: "Do you think that people were happier before the Fault than they are now?"

"They were already complaining before the Fault. They always thought they were unfortunate. But they cultivated a tender sentiment that seems to have disap-peared from our world: Love."

"You really think that that alone colored all existence?"

"Undoubtedly. They sought Love from the cradle to the grave, and that desire, for them, was a passion full of charm, even when they complained about it in their books. And they grafted on to that kind of material mysticism a desire and a determination for sensual pleasure equal to that which our friends with the greatest propensity for such games have reinvented. Love was then able to reign without being mingled with cruelty. How can you expect it to be the same here? Our mistresses count for so little! Down there, don't they hold sexuality in horror—those, at least, who follow the propaganda of Diavide?"

"How strange they are, these mental transformations of human beings!"

The footbridge came to an end. The two men found themselves on a platform. Moved by a counterweight, it descended into a shaft in the center of the last pylon. They were on the edge of the glacis, strewn with secret defenses, which separated the empty anterior terrain from the wall of the city of the Thousand. Very deep, the glacis could only be crossed underground. They found a corridor with a rolling floor that carried them through a metal tunnel. Vialy carefully commanded the doors by means of complicated mechanisms. He passed through the apron of the footbridge the electrocuting current that only a member of the Thousand who knew the commutation code could interrupt. The four-button password was changed three times a day.

Soon the two men were in an elevator cage, which took them upwards when Vialy had manipulated various levers and handles. The two men then found themselves in a garden filed with rare plants and monstrous flowers.

Thick walls protected it, and it could not be seen from anywhere.

Vialy pointed at a distant form lying on a kind of divan amid the vegetation and the carpets.

"One senses that those howling crowds are far away when one comes in here," said Pierre Broun.

Vialy shrugged his shoulders. "Perhaps." He followed his companion toward the recumbent woman, who watched them without moving.

She had a satined oval face, dull and sad. Two large blue eyes perforated that melancholy mask, dominated by tenebrous hair. She seemed to be crouching like a hunting tigress, but when the two men reached her, her body relaxed. She extended a hand to Vialy without speaking.

The policeman kissed her fingers without ceasing to direct his harsh gaze at the azure-tinted irises.

A blush rose to B 309's cheeks.

Pierre Broun, stirred, and sensing the charm of the woman enter into him like a needle, tried to master himself. "Marie," he said, "We've been insulted by the shift returning from the Geocoronium factory. I'm going to drop Necron bombs on them tomorrow. What do you think of that?"

The face, having become pale again, turned to the young man. The eyelids lowered part-way over the blue irises. She made no reply.

"Pierre," said Vialy, loudly, "you're a madman. When one comes in here, one only ought to talk about love."

In a soft and hesitant voice, with a hint of hoarseness at the end of each word, B 309 said: "Love? What's that?"

Vialy held on to the slender fingers of the tremulous hand. "Pierre will explain it." He added: "I'm leaving for the Council of Order. Do you know, Marie, whether Tadée is in."

"He is."

"Good! *Au revoir!*"

As he went away, Vialy murmured to himself: "Far from the people in revolt here? One is never closer to them." He added: "Love is not being able to perceive that..."

II. The Passionate B 309

"That man frightens me!"

B 309, her face slightly haggard, watched Vialy move away along the tortuous path he had taken. His clipped footsteps could be heard on the sand. The tall silhouette outlined a faint shadow behind a Japanese tree, transparent and twisted. Finally, the sound of the curt closure of the door leading to Tadée Broun's apartment was distinctly perceptible, and silence fell once again in the garden.

The young woman and Pierre Broun looked at one another. He held out his hands in an uncertain gesture of supplication and desire. Her face ardent, she took hold of the two muscular wrists and pulled them. The son of Old Broun tottered, and almost fell on to the recumbent body. As he tried uncertainly to maintain his equilibrium, his hand brushed the feminine shoulder, involuntarily seizing the multicolored silk that dressed the supple form, and laid bare B 309's firm bosom. She blushed, and made a strange movement of her hips.

Scarlet in his turn, Pierre Broun saw the beautiful breast rise up toward his lips. He tried to straighten up. His hazardous gesture extended him over the abdomen of the woman, who quivered nervously.

Troubled, and having become almost unconscious of his own actions, in a vehement desire no longer to be self-contained, the young man le himself go. B 309 had taken his head between her palms and lifted the congested young face to her red mouth. Strong, ardent and feline, she kissed him. He was no longer anything but a plaything between the fingers of the perverse and strange seductress.

In a low and halting voice she said: "My darling!... My darling!...."

Meanwhile, the magnetic blue gaze kept watch on the garden.

Soon, Pierre Broun felt his body captured, as was his mind. Ingenuous and frightened, he was the Daphnis of that expert Lycénion.[4] Had she not once satisfied the overseers of textile workshop no. 22? The brightly-colored silk garment that dressed her, open from the neck to the knees, revealed a body the color of pink amber, with harmonious curves and lubricious movements.

He felt possessed by a solar power. Tadée Broun's mistress strove to create unforgettable sensations in that young and new organism. Her mouth caressed the closed lids of his ecstatic eyes softly. Meanwhile, he could feel two sharp breasts weighing upon his swollen chest. His hands did not know where to clasp, and descended incessantly on to the bare torso only to withdraw immediately, as if something had burned them. B 309 divined that, and smiled.

Soon, Pierre Broun was no more than an adolescent vanquished in amorous combat, on the very day that it had been revealed to him.

Sprawled on the divan next to the woman, who had pulled away and was rearranging herself with a king of arrogant coldness, Pierre Broun attempted to recover

---

[4] In the Latin prose narrative by Longus, *Daphnis and Chloë*, the innocent Daphnis does not know how to make love to his beloved Chloë physically until he is lured into the forest by the lascivious Lycénion, who obligingly educates him.

consciousness and recognize himself. It seemed to him that an entire epoch separated him from what he had been an hour before what he sensed he had become.

Superior to his filial love and his devotion to the Thousand, a kind of bewildered gratitude shone in his face, engraved by joy.

Impassively, B 309 folded the multicolored and luminescent silk around her body again.

Entirely given to his pleasure and desirous of loving the whole world, so much joy possessed the fibers of his being, he said: "Why are you afraid of Vialy?"

She smiled nervously. "I know him. Oh, if they could reach him, there are two thousand men down there who would sacrifice themselves to kill him!"

The strangeness of that response struck Pierre Broun. He looked up anxiously.

"I assure you that he's a conscientious and strong man, but he's also a good friend."

With a grimace of hated, she said: "To you."

"To you too, Marie. He's one of the pillars of our society. He was talking about you just now as we came back from the shaft."

Her gaze became sharp and attentive. "Ah! You came over footbridge 14?"

"Yes, the one that cuts through the Titanium factory."

She coughed furiously. "He often passes over it— but it costs dear, that footbridge!"

Pierre Broun looked at her uncomprehendingly.

She kissed him ferociously on the lips. "Ah! My lover!"

"What are you saying, Marie? *Costs dear?*"

"I love you," was B 309's only reply.

"But tell me..."

She made a dismissive gesture. "Don't you know that more than a hundred men have tried to lie in wait for him, because he's hated, and people know which way he goes...?"

"Well?"

"Oh, he can defend himself. You can count on him. All those who have tried to reach him have been electrocuted. He has frightful means of defense."

"But it's only just that Vialy should defend himself," said Pierre Broun, embarrassed before that new fury.

B 309 looked at him as if he were appearing to her for the first time. She took hold of him again. With a seductive gesture she took the adolescent's head again and lowered it between her breasts. The perfumed robe opened. Pierced by an unknown odor, nicotinic and toxic, he was intoxicated as if by alcohol.

Her face, out of sight, took on a slight rictus of scorn. Her beautiful mouth twisted desperately while a harsh gleam filtered between her eyelids.

"What did Vialy say about me, darling?"

"I think he foresaw that I would fall in love with you. I divine his irony now."

Two tears emerged from B309's eyes and ran slowly down her pale face. "Ah! He divines too much," she repeated.

Naively, Pierre replied: "He's very capable, certainly. But he loves you too, as I do."

She shrugged her shoulders with a somber regret. "According to Manya, the one that Vialy will love hasn't been born."

As if to defend his friend, Pierre murmured: "He has such a great responsibility, you understand."

She laughed sardonically. "I know, I know. He's the Master of everything."

"No, Marie! My father counts."

She extended her naked arms, in a gesture that might have been a plea or a threat.

"Your father doesn't know what Vialy knows. He's the possessor of all the secrets. Your father doesn't do anything without asking for his advice." She added, as if to herself: "And he hates me."

Astonished by a despair so unexpected and so disproportionate, Pierre wanted to prove to his mistress that no one could hate B 309 as much as he cherished her. He suddenly desired to give her a proof of his love so complete and so powerful that life would henceforth seemed desirable and joyful to the young woman—but having been a lover for only ten minutes, he remained embarrassed and hesitant, for lack of amorous science.

Finally, he hugged the woman such total ardor that she perceived a gift superior to anything words could express, and fell silent. He would have liked to be a god before a mortal woman, but was tempted to be a devoted and humiliated lover.

The young woman gazed, with malice in her eyes, at that manifestation of love, which moved her in spite of everything. However, she did not lose sight of the doors and pathways of the garden through which someone might come. A kind of cold and calculated wisdom was manifest in all her gestures.

Weary, puerile and happy, Pierre Broun straightened up in order to contemplate with a satisfied gaze the flesh that he thought exhausted by joy. She smiled at him, and all deception was enclosed in her red and swollen lips.

"I'll make Vialy love you," he said.

She started, evoking all those that the terrible Chief of Police had "loved," and who had died, no one knew where, in the mysterious prisons linked to the phosphate factory. If the famous lesbian Sigliaresse, who was also the wife of Mairal, Tadée Broun's secretary, had not taken her out of the workshops, she too would doubtless have disappeared.

She saw once again the somber sloping corridor through which she had passed in handcuffs from her rebellious factory to the mysterious underground dungeons. But Mairal knew her. He had mentioned her beauty and renown as an ardent woman to Sigliaresse, and the mathematician, the daughter of the Thousand's foremost engineer, had wanted to see her. When Vialy had arrived, B 309 was already in the lesbian's house.

He kept silent. The caprices of the Thousand were sacred. Tadée had caught a glimpse of her, and soon after, had asked Sigliaresse, already weary of her conquest, whether she would consent to surrender her to him. Thus, so ironic was destiny, the rebel of the textile factory, whose inflammatory words had cost the lives of twelve hundred unfortunate workers, had found herself the mistress of the sovereign Master in the society born of the Fault and the fears engendered by the Bloody Sweat.

"Vialy would love me," she said, "as he pretends to love the invalids whom he electrocutes to spare them suffering."

Pierre Broun found that quite natural. But he said in his turn. "He gets on very well with Sigliaresse, who loved you, and still retains affection for you."

B 309 pulled a face.

"Sigliaresse loved me like a bitch. It was necessary for me to bend my knee before her, and she never called me by my name..." She laughed, angrily. "I am, however, as beautiful as she is, and more so than Manya, the skeleton-thin woman that Vialy loves."

"You're more beautiful!" said Pierre Broun.

She stifled her anger. "Your love is sufficient for me. It will protect me."

"Don't worry, Marie. Look, Vialy told me that he knows about a plot, and that he was going to the Council of Order to take the necessary measures against it. Are they all mad down there?"

B 309 had a kind of convulsion. Her legs stretched and her neck folded. She went the color of oil. A frisson agitated her jaw and a ripple of fear passed over her charming features. She struggled, without Pierre Broun perceiving it, against the threat of fainting. Finally, she raised a paper pellet to her lips, which she had removed from her hair, and swallowed it. Her emotion was so strong that she remained there, having gulped it down, extended like a corpse, devoid of strength and movement.

"Are you tired?" said Pierre, sympathetically.

"No," she said. "Sit down here, beside me. I love you."

So, Vialy had said that...

III. The Council of Order

When he left B 309, the Chief of the Thousand's Police and Judiciary went rapidly along a secret corridor, which descended inside the wall all the way to the subterrains. He stopped half way and opened a small door. There was a small telephonic apparatus there. He gave figures and brief instructions to four individuals, then closed the door again as he emerged.

The Louvres had been built solely for the comfort of their masters. They were, in consequence, a series of edifices with no unity of appearance or order of construction. The majority were surrounded by gardens. In others, like Tadée's, invisible gardens were found in the center of the block. Friends' dwellings were sometimes side by side, connected by suspended passageways. Others were isolated, devoid of external windows. Leoncel, the meteorologist, lived in a high tower. Syster, the chief of the defenses, possessed a Venetian palazzo surrounded by a minuscule lagoon. Laboratories raised up enormous pylons next to little châteaux with pointed roofs, themselves adjacent to concrete cubes with glazed terraces. Between the houses the majority of which were isolated, the streets were paved, without sidewalks. There were no means of locomotion except for moving strips situated in the middle of the streets, unequal in velocity, covered with glass arcades.

From everywhere, one could see the shadow of the city's protective wall: the famous wall that the rebels had never been able to breach. It gave the extraordinary, apparently sumptuous City a grim and martial aspect. In addition, the near-total absence of windows and the mute heaviness of the rare doors, always oddly situated, gave the lie to the occasional gaiety of its architecture.

Vialy went to his own home. His house was adjacent to the surrounding wall. It was a vast, squat building reminiscent of a fort. Antennae ornamented the roof, along with a miniature watch-tower.

When he got there, he placed himself carefully on a protruding steel plate bolted to the door itself, which formed a step. Then he inserted a commutating key, an ebonite tube containing a platinum wire that operated the electric lock. The door moved inwards, and a mass of steel crashed down on the spot where the entrant had been standing a quarter of a second earlier. Anyone apart from him, the only person who knew where it was necessary to stand and insert the key, would have been crushed like a dab by the steel plate.

Once inside, Vialy changed the entrance code by rotating six buttons. Then he went through multiple corridors whose walls were charged with pigeon-holes containing millions of files. He went through a circular room, in which thirty telephones were arranged in a circle around a table, and then a rectangular room, with hundreds of plans rolled up along the walls. Finally, he reached a library of sorts, with a glazed ceiling. Three men and a woman were working there.

The woman, tall, slim and supple, with the face of a Greek goddess, stood up when Vialy came in. It was his secretary and mistress, Manya, Tadée Broun's niece.

"Bonjour, Ma."

She nodded her head with a sharp smile.

"What's new?"

"Unfortunate developments. Three men murdered down below, two of them ours: 806 and 1312."

Coldly, he said: "The whole quarter isolated, until the denunciation and death of the guilty parties."

"Three threats against you transmitted in writing."

"That's of no importance."

"Sixteen insubordinates pinched by the Chinese patrol."

"Good. All of them to the deep shaft."

"Political meetings in which the Messiah is announced."

"Where is he, this Messiah?"

"Nine reports on him. All estimate that he lives in the forest zone, near the old chalk quarries.

"Throw thirty Necron bombs into the zone every day for a week."

"Rumors of revolt. 107 has sent us a sample of speech."

"Let me see it!"

"Today's blue sheet?" Manya demanded, imperiously.

One of the assistants stood up and brought a sheet of blue paper. Vialy read:

Comrades, the allies we have among the brigands of the Louvres assure us that we shall soon be masters of all their secrets. I've received a message saying: Courage! The hour of victory is in preparation. The great secret of the automatic machine-guns and the electrocuting currents will be known tomorrow. *Let us swear, comrades, that not a single one of the Thousand will be spared. We shall have them, and those who are suffering for us in the accursed city will be liberated in a matter of days. For the holy revolt! For our happiness! For justice!*

Coldly, Vialy said: "Any nocturnal signal will bring death: electrocution at a distance. Set up the apparatus on top. Transfer the commutators to the post designated in plan 3. Keep watch on the access tunnels. Triple the current in the networks."

With an undulation of her hips, the woman extended an ophidian arm. "What, you think…?"

"Nothing—but it's necessary to be watchful. Sigliaresse doesn't have a new mistress?"

"No, only Josèphe Broun."

"Nothing from the factories down below?"

"One woman who said: 'Patience, my friends, we have friends who are preparing our liberty.'"

Vialy pulled a face.

"Sent down to dungeon Omega."

"Good. What's the name?"

"The file of the last Omega," Manya demanded.

A man went out without saying a word, and returned immediately.

Vialy read the folder that was handed to him. "*B 400, Jacqueline Rabotte, Charonne…etc…*"

He smiled. "B 309's sister. Set her free and search her six times a day, including the organs. Change her clothes every midday and bring them to me. Put networks around the dormitory where she sleeps. Keep me informed.

"Anything yet from outside Paris?"

"Yes. Detachment of five negroes discovered human footprints in the sector where I thought I saw signals, and the debris of a fire. Twelve cylinders of Necron disposed."

"In the workshops?"

"Nineteen dead, one fewer than average."

"Good!"

Vialy consulted his watch. He said to the three men: "Messieurs, you're free until seven, except for V 9, who'll hold the fort until the next shift. Where are your comrades now?"

"On missions," Manya replied. "Reports at midnight."

Vialy went out, followed by his mistress.

At that moment, a telephone bell rang. Vialy went to the apparatus. He heard: "It's Jacques Aldyr, 76-W. Origin, gallery B.P. fourth floor. Heard this at insubordinate meeting, ex-Metro station Bolivar: 'On Sunday, I'll be in charge of the control-panel in Tadée Broun's house.'"

"Perfect," Vialy replied. "Kill the man as soon as possible. Continue investigations of his contacts."

The Chief of Police and his mistress finally went out and went up to the top of the house by means of an inclined rolling carpet. There, in a kind of blue and gold drawing room, Vialy sat down on a divan.

"They're obstinate, these idiots, Manya."

"Bah! We'll calm them down for a year."

He laughed. "How beautiful you are today!"

She burst out laughing. "How do you know?"

He reached out and grabbed her by the hips. "As you casting doubt on the evidence of my senses?"

Her laughter had an equivocal ring to it. She pulled away with a thrust of her buttocks,

He became serious again. "I'm irritated by the folly of luxury that the underground workshops are creating every day for our sole usage. Here's another three hundred typographs from Paul Landève. They're shrewd in that métier. That's where all the threats are coming from today."

"Bah! You like me to dress up like the women from before the Fault, my friend. Without workshops we'd be poor and devoid of luxury. And it's necessary to love books...."

"You're just as beautiful without ornaments, Manya. As for the printing-press, it's a stupid invention!"

"But we're protecting civilization by making the tailors make garments, the weavers weave, the sculptors sculpt, the upholsterers upholster, the embroiderers embroider... If the Necron disappears, it's necessary that all that isn't forgotten..."

"Don't assume, Manya, that if the Necron disappears, we'll be able to liberate the proletariat. They'd cut our throats immediately. Our power can only endure in its present form. Attenuated, it would collapse. There's nothing to ameliorate..."

He paused for a moment's reflection, and went on: "Which is to say that the arts we're protecting, as you imagine, are utterly vain."

"But they embellish our life."

"Indeed. Nevertheless, there are already eighteen thousand people down below. Soon, there'll be a hundred thousand. Then we'll be living on top of a mine whose fuse will already be lit. How are we going to keep watch, search and discipline all that?"

"Don't you think," she murmured, that it will be precious for us to be able to live outside our torments a little henceforth. The Thousand can't become weavers, or swineherds."

He approved, smiling. "Luxury and security are mutually exclusive, Manya!" After caressing his mistress' breasts, he added: "I'm going to the Council. They must have been chatting at their ease. I'll have the conclusions."

Manya smiled tautly. "Not before having proved to me that in frequenting your proletariat, you..."

"How could I forget you?"

"Ah...B 309. She makes heads turn."

"I'm going to make hers fall."

Manya was half-lying on the divan. Her elegant and slender contours were outlines by a fabric of infinite softness.

Vilaly leaned over the proffered body. With an amused gesture, she removed the fabric in which she was clad. With a click of opening metallic fasteners, the robe opened, and the bare flesh appeared, mat and carefully depilated. High and scarlet, the virginal breasts bulged imperceptibly.

He felt the blood rising to his face, and his features hardened.

Satisfied with having demonstrated that her power had not weakened, the young woman closed the garment again.

"Go see Tadée. I've put you to the proof."

"Ah, Vialy! We've been waiting for you."

Tadée Broun, clean-shaven, wrinkled and robust, greeted the Chief of Police in that fashion as he came into the Council chamber.

There were six men there. Three were very old and two in their forties. Only one was young. He was the son of Landève, the man who had discovered the remedy for the bloody sweat.

Vialy sat down and said, categorically: "No need for torment. Administratively, everything's going well.

No significant changes since our last meeting. We're living in the relative, and our relativity is excellent."

"Relativity, so be it—but not in matters of security," said one of the old men.

"In security as in everything," Vialy retorted.

"Yes," said Tadée Broun. "Who knows..."

A man with the face of a gorilla, intelligent powerful and affirmative, proffered: "Exactly. Everything human involves a flotation, a more-or-less, in the expected realizations. It's a matter, for us, of knowing whether, in terms of our present flotation, we're close to a point of rupture, or whether, on the contrary, we're holding our position..."

"That's the situation," said Vialy.

The other continued: "As far as I know, the deficiencies of production are still oscillating close to the established average. Popular hatred is scarcely budging, and our control is still as sure."

One of the council members raised his arms in the air. "There's too much talk of revolution down there."

"There always has been, said Old Broun. "Before the Fault, they were free and happy compared with that they are now, but they dreamed of nothing but bloody revolt. Against whom and against what, I wonder? Certainly, those men of old who ate what they liked, worked when they liked, traveled and lived wherever the pleased, dressed themselves and got out of bed in accordance with their caprice, were happy, although there was less justice than there is today. The circumstances were propitious to felicity. And yet, they wanted to overturn I don't know what. They're incorrigible..."

Vialy took the floor again: "In any case, my opinion is that we shouldn't augment the workshops any further for three years. They're a dangerous nucleus, too close to us."

"That's not without prudence," murmured Tadée.

"Bah!" said another. "They're a good thing. The objects they make are agreeable. With strict surveillance, one can guarantee..."

"Our number is insufficient to occupy ourselves as fully as is necessary with both the factories and the workshops. Some are presently in the charge of men who are reliable, but all the same, aren't ours. Eight hundred of us can't be everywhere."

"That's true," said three of the Council members.

"That's not all. I ask the Council to order a minute check of the defenses and a tripling of the stock of Necron bombs. It's necessary to change all the workers at the big electricity generator and put them in transformer no. 2. We need to keep watch on the walls and glacis of Paris, on Syster's behalf. The cables need to be guarded and a permanent squad of thirty of ours ready to take over the machines if I forward any suspicions. I'll communicate any further measures, if there are any."

Finally, he said to Tadée Broun: "It's known that you have a control panel in your house. It's necessary that it should be moved tonight and that no one goes near it until I say so."

Astonished, Old Broun opened his eyes wide, but he knew that Vialy never said anything unnecessary. "You have fears, Vialy?"

"It's necessary to have fears. It's my job."

Everyone nodded.

IV. The Beautiful Dream

The night possessed Paris, the city of the Thousand and the unknown world extended to infinity beyond human sight: a night similar to those whose praises poets had sung before the Fault, for their sweetness and melancholy. In the sky, the stars displayed their patterns of light, as they have ever since there have been humans on earth, on which so many dreams had been suspended over the millennia. The galaxy unrolled its immense fluid scarf on high. The air had the softness of the time when lovers dreamed among odorous flowers...

Before the open window overlooking Tadée Broun's garden, which the obscurity filled, silent and half-recumbent in a red armchair, the latest word in the new art of furniture, B 309 was somberly thoughtful.

Old Broun came into the room and approached. He kissed her on the forehead, paternally.

"Aren't you coming, Marie? I have an original reception tonight."

She turned her blue eyes toward him, depended by the roseate light of the lamped.

"I'll be there in a minute, my love."

He passed his sinewy hand over her supple spine, and then into the gap of the polychromatic robe. He caressed her like a pet animal. Frowning, she endeavored to tolerate that irritating contact. When he took hold of a breast, touching the sensitive nipple with his horny hand, it was so disagreeable that B 309 experienced a surge of anger and an involuntary movement of recoil.

"Did I hurt you, Marie?"

She controlled herself and smiled. With a desperate energy, she opened her robe and bared her torso.

"No, my love, do as you please."

But Tadée, not wanting to do more or better, stood up again. "I'm expecting you downstairs momentarily."

"Yes—I'll be there."

"Vialy and Pierre will be there."

The woman felt another twinge of anger, but kept silent.

Tadée went out.

Alone, B 309 stood up, with a smooth thrust of her muscles. She circled the room several times, ardently desirous of calming the intimate rage that had stirred her up.

Finally, she took off her garment abruptly, and went into the next room in search for the dress she wanted to put on before going down.

She came back trailing, with a disdainful expression, the long black sheath that Tadée liked. Disgust swelled the beautiful red mouth. So, after having prostituted the body that she loved and had wanted to reserve to her own kind, it was now necessary to put herself on parade in the social life of those she covered in a powerful and secret scorn.

She was naked. She touched her skin cautiously, on the shoulders and the abdomen, as if she were a leper. Horror! Not one place that had not been touched, or even loved, by one of her enemies. She admired her body nevertheless, smiling at the somber and dense tuft it bore. She was proud of that, because it signaled her humble origin.

All the women of the accursed race of the Masters were depilated. Even the mistresses they recruited in Paris, once they got used to their new life, removed their body hair, even though it was technically forbidden. But B 309 remained the rebellious worker, only brought into the world of the Thousand by force, and with the sole desire to discover its most redoubtable secrets in order to reveal them to her brothers.

She already knew a great deal. When she knew everything, the sacrifice of her body would become the masterpiece of her grim and tenacious work. Then, thanks to her, the proletariat would succeed in overcoming its enemies. Millions of her own people would come to cut the throats of the inhabitants of the accursed city. That blood would efface the memory of those that B 309 had been obliged to know, in the heart and in the flesh.

If she died in the defense, no one would mistake her cadaver for one of the Thousand. She wore the shameful fleece that, among the fortunate, maintained her voluntarily among the wretched.

She thought about Vialy then: the Vialy for whose death millions of mouths had been calling for many years. The strange and sarcastic individual was hated as no human being on earth had ever been hated before. Without knowing whether she detested the man by virtue of some secret jealousy, for he alone seemed scornful and suspicious of her, the young woman came to picture in her reverie the mistress of the Chief of Police. B 309 detested that long serpentine body with the thin wrists and the tapering fingers frenetically. A flame of violence passed through her as she imagined that magnificent gliding gait, that indolent and seductive expression, and the cynicism and artistry of the tailoring that made everything that Manya wore a form of perfection.

The patent and manifest aristocracy that signed Manya's slightest gesture was, for Tadée Broun's mistress, a constant insult. She tapped her foot on the floor as she looked at herself in the vast mirror. She knew full well that her ankles were thick and her fingers stout. For four years she had worked in the textile factory. She was not unaware, no matter how string her desire was to forget it, that she had satisfied many males once. She loved them as brothers in misery and blood, but they had placed a kind of seal upon her flesh of mediocre and popular sensuality, and she was jealous of perverse individuals like Sigliaresse, who knew such vertiginous voluptuousness. B 309 did not experience anything in all that claimed to produce pleasure by new ways. She suffered from it...

That made her think of the man she venerated, without knowing, without knowing whether it was an amorous flame that tightened her throat at the mere pronunciation of his name: Daviade, the Messiah, whom she had only glimpsed once in a meeting of insubordinates, and the memory of whom still burned within her.

Thanks to Diavide, the revolution would burst forth of the first day...

It was in order to transmit them to him that she was striving to penetrate the mysteries of the Thousand.

She thought for a moment about what would happen if Vialy discovered the mysterious shaft in the third subterranean level of the house, to which she sent in haste, as soon as she knew them, the scraps of all the secrets of the defenses. Three hundred meters underground, in their incapacity to get any closer because the Thousand had disposed defenses within the soil, there was a gallery excavated by Diavide and his men.

B 309 had heard mention of that tunnel when she lived in Paris working in the textile factory. A vertical shaft descended into the gallery, and no one knew where it ended. Hazard, which is one of the grandmasters of extraordinary things, which contrives the most improbable encounters, had brought into Tadée's house the one woman who, in the midst of wealth, still hated her protectors. She had found the vertical shaft, and was able to send a message down—then two, and then ten. She then gave advice about possible luminous signals. One night, in conformity with her desire, she saw a flame born and extinguished beyond the factories, to the north, at the summit of a distant hill where the Necron was believed to be prevalent. Thus, Diavide lived outside Paris, and that was the reason why Vialy could not find him—but he received messages from B 309 without her knowing how.

Since then, B 309 had been able to believe herself to be the queen of the impending revolt, especially when she had seduced Pierre Broun. As for Tadée, he considered the famous hole to be a convenient orifice into which to throw ordure; each of the Thousand's houses had a kind of special waste-pipe whose contents were burned at a great depth in a factory created for the treatment of coal-tar derivatives.

B 309 thought about all of that. She recalled that, by means of signals and the numbered letters of the alphabet, she had been asked the day before for the location and trajectory of the central cable controlling the electrocution networks and for the secret of the defenses of Vialy's house. The latter, she would doubtless never know, but the plan of the defenses, she would get from Pierre Broun.

Oh, if she had been able to seduce Vialy! That would have been an enormous and superhuman sacrifice, but one of exceptional value and doubtless decisive. But he had the celebrated Manya...

B 309 shivered. She suddenly felt an irresistible desire to go up to the roof to see Paris and the landscape overlooked by the house.

She put on the dark silk sheath, which was thick and soft upon her skin, and then headed for a corner of the room, where there was a stairway as narrow as a ladder, which led to the little corner turret. She went up briskly. She detested the sybaritic rolling carpets, preferring anything that demanded an effort and a deployment of will.

Having arrived at the top she inserted herself into a little round cabin and lowered the curtains that sealed the circular viewport.

The young woman suddenly tasted the soft and sugary air that floated over the city of the Thousand. She imagined the putrid air that reigned above Paris, and her hatred increased. To her right, she could see Sigliaresse's flowery terrace, and remembered having given her the most humiliating caresses amid the cushions in the southern corner. Behind it extended the secret pavilions constructed for Old Broun's personal work. They covered the roof, only leaving one cross-shaped passage. Facing her was the defensive wall, enormous and massive, thirty meters wide and as many high. There reigned the terrible Syster, the director of Death. Everything mortal that was fabricated belonged to the Wall, factory and arsenal, terrifying the people of "down below."

There was no moon. The stars were describing their slow curve around the terrestrial axis. The silence was absolute. Behind the wall, B 309 glimpsed the glacis—the mortal, insurmountable glacis. Momentarily, she imagined the host of her own people rushing madly toward the accursed city. The porcupine with a thousand metallic needles that gave the Wall such a strange appearance by day was vomiting millions of bullets. The Necron tubes were pouring the horrible gas over the inflamed crowd.

What did it matter? In the end, they would reach the wall, they would get over it, or blow it up...and then...

Oh, to cut the throats if the women of the Thousand with the queenly bearing, and the men who...

But could it be done?

B 309 felt a painful doubt born within her. Then, as she leaned forward, believing, in her hallucination, that she could already see hundreds of thousands of her people dying, she heard a whistle overhead, and saw a kind of parachute pass over, scarcely less dark than the night, but which described a slow curve over Paris toward open country. Its movement could be followed against the backcloth of the Milky Way. She felt a sharp emotion. That must be some new method of putting the slaves of the City in communication with the Messiah Diavide.

The thing had disappeared, but B 309 was still gazing. She searched in the north for the patches of the usual signals, but it was not the appointed time and she could not see anything. In the direction of Paris, however, glimmers of light were perceptible that sprang up and immediately disappeared. Other communications, undoubtedly, between rebels who, in spite of Vialy and his police, had not renounced the pursuit of their holy work of salvation and liberty...

Now, her nerves taut and aggravated, the young woman perceived the muffled vibration of the enormous machines beneath the city of the Thousand, which generated power and light, for the defense and luxury of those who were amusing themselves in Old Broun's drawing room, and whom it was necessary to go and meet... She felt the ground tremble under the effort of the dynamos and motors for which the damned cared, under the hard and inflexible eyes of the members of the Thousand on duty.

One cable cut, and the profound caverns would be isolated; one tunnel blocked, and perhaps the power of the masters of the world could be annulled at a stroke...

She recovered hope. Everything that had permitted those men devoid of humanity to dominate the planet and keep death at bay when it had seemed to be the universal sovereign still remained fragile.

One woman might...

At any rate, other men were on watch around her...and young Pierre Broun had not yet told everything...

Afterwards? Bah! It would be necessary, subsequently, to protect themselves from the Necron; the People would take care of that, too, as well as the masters. They would create a great fraternity in which everyone in his place would work for all of society. And the lubricity of the Thousand, their cruelty, their vices, and their scorn for all other human beings, would be abolished forever.

B 309 thought that it was time to go down to Old Broun's reception. It was an honor that the Thousand were doing her, accepting her as one of their own. Nevertheless, there were places and drawing rooms where those men met with their wives and depilated mistresses to which B 309 was never invited.

She felt simultaneously revolted by and desirous of the honors granted by those proud individuals. She was jealous of being sometimes kept apart from the society that she hated...

V. The Homes of the Thousand

Since the Thousand had reconstituted the social gatherings of the world before the Fault, sumptuous and original salons had been organized in almost all their houses. It was also in consequence of that innovation that the workers specializing in objects of luxury had been sought out to operate in the new workshops.

Aristocratic gatherings implied grace and wit, so they had begun searching manuals of ancient elegance at the same time. For one entire winter, that had been the dominant passion of men previously submissive to enormous labor, who found therein a bright interval in the darkness of their formidable responsibilities. They set forth, therefore, in quest of paintings, and then of books. Since the Fault, the only books reckoned worthy of printing had been scientific treatises; those indispensable had been mechanically reproduced, but literature had completely disappeared. As soon as it was admitted that that frivolous and mundane books—especially illustrated books—were precious and desirable objects, a ferocious hunt had been organized for old print.

Those hard men, absorbed in technical meditations, and who, since thirty for the old men and puberty for their children, had only known pure science, had discovered that they were children with regard to the pre-Fault arts.

Libraries were created whose possessors, taking all kinds of risks and disguised as man of the people, sought to enrich them by rooting around at random in Paris. It was thus that Léopold Vernus, the great physicist, had been murdered. He had got his hands on the most astonishing thing in the world: before the war, a bookshop selling obscene books had fitted a hiding-place into a wall in order to avoid the seizure of its stock of costly works sought after by purchasers but proscribed by a rather puerile law. Vernus discovered that treasure. He wanted to take it away in its entirety and had been noticed dragging a sort of prehistoric wheelbarrow laden with volumes, which he was taking toward one of the Thousand's houses, from which a subterranean tunnel would have allowed him to transport everything to his own home. The people found that extraordinary. In sum, recognized as one of the detestable masters, Vernus had been killed.

It ought not to be thought that books, so abundant thirty years earlier, survived in appreciable quantities in a city in which, since then, the poor warmed themselves exclusively by burning things. The Bibliothèque Nationale had passed in its entirety into the fireplaces of the populace, along with all the public libraries. Only a few rare individuals still kept their old treasures, hiding them away carefully. People went crazy over odd volumes from the collected works of Victor Hugo.

Nevertheless, the Thousand gradually enriched themselves. Seven families had been released from the factories in return for having offered their contents of their bookshelves to Tadée Broun. He possessed an illustrated Rabelais, the only one known to exist. Sigliaresse had acquired an Aristophanes, a Marcus Aurelius and Mirabeau's *Le Rideau levé*.[5] It was said that Mairal pos-

---

[5] *Le Rideau levé, ou l'Éducation de Laure* (1786) is a kind of sex manual framed as didactic fiction, by the author of the Declaration of the Rights of Man that was adopted by the 1789 Revolutionaries as the basis for their new constitution.

sessed the second volume of a work that had already been rare before the Fault, *Contes de La Fontaine*, illustrated by a certain Eisen;[6] it was known as the Fermiers Généraux edition—a designation that no one understood. By virtue of a precious play named *Agésilas*, an author named Corneille was known.[7] Voltaire was renowned as the author of *Entretiens avec le cuisinier du Roi de Prusse*, a book that must have been very common, as several examples of it had survived.[8]

It goes without saying that only young people and men who were unfamiliar with pre-Fall society—who were now the majority among the Thousand—amused themselves with that curious game. Their elders, like Old Broun, would have been able, although their memories were already very distant, to inform them about the celebrities of old, but they had always been scornful of literature. They had not changed. The Necron remained, in their eyes, the only thing worth talking about. Thus, among the five hundred people whose youth had not been cradled by any romantic education, those unknown books came as an extraordinary revelation, which testified to a subtle and improbable knowledge of vanished things and souls. Those ingenuous readers marveled on

---

[6] The painter and engraver Charles Eisen (1720-1778). The "Fermiers Généraux" edition of La Fontaine, which he illustrated lavishly, was published in 1762

[7] *Agésilas* (1666) was generally reckoned to be the least meritorious of Pierre Corneille's plays.

[8] *Les Soirées philosophiques du cuisinier du roi de Prusse* (c1785) was an anonymous satirical work claimed by Antoine Barbier to have been largely but ineptly plagiarized from various works by Voltaire, but it was certainly not written by him (he died in 1778) or by Frederick II of Prussia.

observing that the cosmos did not date from their arrival in the world...

Along with the fashion for libraries came that for elegant wardrobes. Women began to ornament themselves with a delicate primitive taste. Then it was realized that before the Fault people had known how to dress. From there to seeking out old people once competent in that delicate art, and then confiding sumptuary labor to them, was only a single step. Workshops had been created for couturiers, and then for the weaving of fantastic fabrics. Afterwards, jewels had been sculpted, and an aged bootmaker of sixty-six had become one of the individuals most highly-esteemed by the society of the Thousand. Indeed, he provided the feet of women with pure marvels, as respectable s works of art.

But the researches extended. It was discovered that some children had been educated in secret in certain paternal professions once in honor, with the result that the traditions of lost métiers had been conserved in spite of the factories and the Necron. There was delirium. All the people who knew how to make pretty and useless things were swept up; their parents were given exemptions from labor and various favors. Luxury was reborn.

At that time, a group of typographers had set to work. They had reprinted the first work that the Thousand had published for their usage; they had dared to print forty copies of it, illustrated by an artist. The volume in question was Paul Adam's *Lettres de Malaisie*.[9]

---

[9] Paul Adam's *Lettres de Malaisie* (1898) describes a fictitious colony in the Philippines established by followers of various French utopian writers, including Fourier, Saint-Simon and Cabet. The communist state in question can be seen as the absolute antithesis of the society designed by the Thousand.

A marvelously skilled embroiderer, who ornamented the robes of elegant women in the Japanese fashion, was the first person since the Fault to be granted the right to work unsupervised in the city of the Thousand.

Thus, the society created for and by the struggle against the end of the world threatened by the Necron began to follow the gradual slope that all civilizations travel, decaying esthetically, and mortally refining the desire for pleasure.

When B 309 appeared in Tadée Broun's drawing room, a large number of aged notables and young people were conversing in groups with the lack of ease that characterizes meditative minds in society. Some thirty faces, uniformly clean-shaven, with strong features, firm chins and staring eyes, greeted Old Broun's mistress without a smile or a bow. Pre-Fault politeness had not yet returned to society.

The young woman knew that. Her teeth clenched and a familiar chill passed down her spine. At a slow pace she traversed the vast room, hung with a silk as artificial as all those who employed it, inevitably, but which the magnificence of its colors and its luster made magnificent. Red and gold, that décor gave a curious impression. The carpet, also silken, thick and crackling underfoot, gave the faces a strange coloration, green and pink.

The majority of the eyes followed B 309 and her fingernails dug into her palms, so tightly did she clench her fists in the rage, shame and hatred she felt at being scornfully admired in that fashion.

She finally sat down in an armchair that had been reserved for her. Then, she recovered her composure.

Not far away, Vialy was conversing with Syster, who was nodding his head. Next to them, three other silent men were following their conversation without saying a word. Vialy's gaze suddenly met B 309's. Tadée was talking to two young men and attempting to prove to them that before the Fault, books signed by Népomucène Lemercier had been devoid of any value.[10] They refused to believe it.

Facing Broun's mistress, Manya was in discussion with five men, one of whom had thought it a good idea to dress in pink silk. However, that did not make anyone smile.

To B 309's left, eight women were debating the merit of the high-point embroideress and another countrywoman, discovered no one knew where, who could make lace. They could not get over the fact that such intellectual labor could be realized so perfectly by an extremely old person who had never been able to read or

---

[10] The poet and dramatist Népomucène Lemercier (1771-1840) had considerable success during his lifetime, although his supposed masterpiece, the tragedy *Agamemnon* (1795), also attracted fierce criticism. The admiration of the young men of the Thousand might be inspired by his diehard opposition to Romanticism in general and Victor Hugo in particular, although the latter succeeded him in his chair at the Académie Française. The antipathy in question did not prevent Lemercier from writing the utterly bizarre and thoroughly Romantic epic poem *Panhypocrisiade* (1819, but written during the Consulate), which includes debates between a worm and Death, Martin Luther and the Devil, and Reason and Rabelais, while various characters from French history are seen undergoing torments in a Dantean Hell. Dunan's attention might also have been attracted by *Les Quatre métamorphoses* (1799), a deliberate attempt to take subjects normally deemed indecent.

write and appeared to be almost an imbecile. Tétrille, the sub-directress of the Titanium factories, a metaphysician of high repute, was theorizing about the esthetic unconscious and imagining an entire explanation, agreeable to the Thousand, of subconscious intelligence and activity mechanized by the absolute.

Five women of the people, the mistresses of a few important individuals, in the same situation as B 309, were also there. Two of them were talking to one another; the others, isolated and sad, were waiting for someone to pay attention to them. The proudest of them, very brunette, was wearing a dress so transparent, and displaying herself in such a fashion that everyone could see that she was depilated like a true woman of the Thousand. The "numbered," although they were all beautiful and attractive, were nevertheless almost always left alone in society.

The groups broke up and reformed. Two of the numbered were finally engaged in conversation, including the depilated woman. She left shortly afterwards with her lover and a woman who was pressing herself against her hip. No one seemed to pay any attention. When she reappeared, no one turned to look at her.

Vialy came over to B 309.

"Serious my dear? Smile at your people, then!"

The young woman sketched a smile.

But Pierre Broun came in. Vialy took possession of him, and seemed to be reproaching him. B 309 shivered in her seat.

Meanwhile, Manya crossed the room. With a burning hatred, Broun's mistress saw the tall and slender form pass in front of her. The ankles that could fit inside a ring, the supple legs, almost naked to the knee, the imperceptible sway of the hips, the bearing of the head emerging from the shoulders, the breasts sticking out and the gliding stride all caused B 309, jealous and wound up, to suffer. In her pale green dress embroidered in gold, Manya fascinated those men as a magnet attracts iron filings. People gazed at her with passion.

Finally, Pierre Broun approached his mistress. "You're adorable, Marie."

She laughed, hatefully. "You tell me that, but you're looking at Vialy's mistress."

He laughed, without understanding the secret torment of that ardent heart. "Impossible to be insensible to that charm!"

She bit her lips.

Meanwhile, Tadée was giving orders. A certain yellow statue, motionless since the beginning of the gathering, was revealed as a human being. It was the chief of Broun's Chinese servants.

Bottles of liqueurs were brought out, and then tea. The cups had been discovered still packed away, as the Asiatics had elected to do thirty years earlier, in a wrecked truck where the crate containing them had been conserved intact since the Fault.

The gilded infusion was poured. Pierre Broun had brought B 309 close to his father, whose smiling welcome consoled her slightly for the scornful hatred she divined everywhere else. She was suffering, being accustomed to chemical aliments, and her taste-buds being too sensitive to vegetal beverages, from being constrained to drink the tea, which caused a redoubtable constriction of the viscera. Alcohol, above all, horrified her—but was it not necessary to drink it, like all these individuals who appeared to find such perfect satisfaction in it?

The great luxury of the Thousand's salons was the possession of those ancient bottles of strong liquor. That taste, critical for the party of "primitives" that counted a third of the Thousand, was dominant in the Broun household. The serving of liqueurs was nowadays the central ritual of elegant gatherings.

An unbearable itch irritating her mucous membranes since she had drunk the cup of tea, B 309 found herself in the presence of an strong-smelling opaline liquid issued from a bottle bearing the label *Chartreuse*. She gathered all her courage to confront the torture.

Three paces away, Sigliaresse, in a musical voice full of secret rhythms, was explaining a paradoxical theory of human parthenogenesis. She laughed, showing her bright teeth. Her long voluptuous face took on an expression akin to desire. Broun's mistress finally saw the lesbian pour a long column of green liquor into her glass. She raised it to level of her dark eyes and looked at it obliquely.

"Read the future, then, in that transparent and secret chlorophyll," said Vialy, laughing.

"I'm reading it," Sigliaresse replied. "Does all life not resolve into a fermentation with green tints?"

She laughed too, and her breasts appeared beneath the white silk in which her torso was clad. Then she drank, without a grimace and without a gesture.

B 309, offended by that ease, lifted her own glass in her turn and swallowed the contents angrily. With her free hand she clung to the arm-rest of her chair.

She thought that her mouth was filled with a violent corrosive. Her stomach burned as if it were stuffed with ardent coals. A red blade followed her esophagus and sliced delicately through its walls. She suffered a prodigious torture. Her eyes wide, her teeth parted in order to let air refresh her mucous membranes, she thought that death was taking her at that very instant. Two large tears ran down her cheeks.

She would never, never be like those people! There was an unbridgeable abyss between them and her. She searched with her eyes for another numbered.

Some distance away, Z 4 had just drunk too. She coughed convulsively, tetanized by the cognac that was torturing her.

Further away, D 38 did not seem to be suffering, but she, the daughter of one of Vialy's agents, had always drunk alcohol.

"It's delicious, this product," Pierre Broun said to her, "isn't it, Marie?"

She nodded her head, red in the face.

"Before the Fault, there was some joy in living when one was rich."

"What did 'being rich' mean?" asked a blond and effeminate young man: the terrible director of the factories of the Gamma aliment, a pitiless sadist and admirable leader of men.

A shriveled old man who was talking to Tadée replied: "Being rich was one of the extravagances of the comical society of my youth. One was rich when one could pay for all joys."

"What joys?" asked Pierre Broun.

Tadée took over. "In those days, pleasure was a commodity, capable of being traded.

"But pleasure is within us," said Pierre Broun, anxiously. "One can't get it elsewhere."

The old man laughed. "Imagine, Pierre, a very clever social organization that studies pleasure, and prepares it, like that alcohol, in a fashion to render it saleable."

"I don't understand."

"Come on—you like alcohol. Good. Well, there were specialist merchants who manufactured that alcohol. If Sigliaresse wanted a maidservant for her bed; someone found her. The pleasure of possessing some agreeable object or other was, therefore, at everyone's disposal, since all pleasures were for sale."

"For sale? I don't know what you mean. I know that we manufacture everything that provides joy, but the workshops are obliged to do as we wish and furnish us with as much as we want. Now, you often say that in those days, everyone was free..."

"That's what I'm saying. Pleasure was for sale—and I added that the rich could have everything..."

"By what means? Was a 'rich' man a man like us, disposing of absolute power over someone and remaining inviolable? If not...."

"Not the same. The strength of the rich man was that he possessed money."

"Yes! I've seen that. They're metal disks."

"Precisely," said Tadée Broun. "Well, there was a commonly accepted convention: the person who possessed a great deal of money handed over a determined or variable quantity of it in exchange for the pleasure provided to him."

"But what did the others do with the metal disks, and where did the rich man get them?"

"Ah! That was the entire social organization of the day, which it would be necessary to explain."

"In any case, the man who had a disposable joy was making a fool's bargain in exchanging it for roundels, or little figures on paper, like those I've seen."

"Not at all, since everything necessary to life was the object of exchanges of that sort. He made use of the metal disks that were give to him to 'buy' pleasure himself, using it in accordance with his tastes and the abundance of disks at his disposal."

"Everyone had as many of them, then?"

"No! That's the problem posed by the question. The rich man had a lot."

"Where did he get them?"

"A convention those people called 'the law' determined that possession was entitlement. It was thus sufficient to procure a lot of money."

"But ultimately, where did it come from?"

"The State manufactured it."

"All right—and it gave it to its friends or indifferent individuals, just like that, out of affection?"

"Something like that—but you need to understand, above all, that those who had little money could be deprived of it. They had less and were unable to defend it. In carrying out that operation, therefore, it was accumulated; notoriously, from laborers who, working for the pleasure of others, could always renew their stock by selling the fruits of their labor."

"They were a band of brigands, then, stealing from one another, the wise men before the Fault?"

"They dressed it up, Pierre. Their theft had become a game. It was played according to precise rules. One could do *this*, but *that* was forbidden. The revolver was forbidden, but eloquence was allowed. One couldn't extort money from people by threatening them, but by assuring them that they could trust you with their money one gained a great deal and then refused them a just return. Magnificent and very honorable riches could be acquired in that way, because people were credulous. In principle, money was supposed to be the result of labor, but over the centuries, the idle had perfected very skillful methods of theft, which had the appearance of being within the admitted rules, although they were brazen violations of them, deep down."

"What happened, then?"

"Nothing. Before the Fault, being a criminal was of little importance, provided that one had the key to certain affirmations that transformed the appearance of an action."

Sigliaresse burst out laughing. "They were good mathematicians. They changed a minus sign into a plus sign, and a shameful action became estimable. It's a charming trick."

"It required a great deal of mastery."

"Obviously. Then again, the money acquired served to make friends—important friends for preference, who could be useful to you in consequence."

"Now," Pierre Broun exclaimed, "I understand that civilization, which intrigued me so much! So, having a great a great deal of money, people had a great many desires, and they made the manufacturers of agreeable things provide for them. The money circulated, and in spite of the imbecility of the organization, everyone tried to accumulate it for himself alone. Consequently, they lived in that hope, so that the State endured by virtue of that psychological mechanism."

Old Broun nodded affirmatively. "That's right."

Revolted, B 309 said, courageously and fearfully: "All the same, the person who made the pleasure of the possessors of money, and had to live unhappily, was a human being like them."

Tadée nodded his head, but in a fashion that caused his mistress' blood to boil. "Obviously, the organization of those days was absurd. The person who disposed of money was in possession of unlimited power over those who were deprived of it. Today, that has disappeared. Our society is much more rational and just..."

"However...," B 309 started to say.

Broun continued affirmatively: "In our day, only mental superiority makes people superior. Do we not employ the best from down below?"

His mistress, her eyes closed, completed the thought: *Yes, provided that lips are soft and their bodies expert in voluptuousness, the women of the people can hope to be employed...and what employment!*

VI. The Beautiful Slaves

Suddenly, there was a stir in Tadée Broun's drawing room. A group formed near the door, and a voice rang out: "I fear that there's no relief..."

"Fortel!" called Tadée Broun.

The man who had spoken came to sit down casually beside Broun. He brushed B 309's arm, and she snatched it away peevishly.

"There. I don't believe that there's any danger, but in the well I inspect, there was a deficit of thirty per cent in the relief shift. If that continues, tomorrow..."

Vialy said, softly: "I'll starve them out and close the aliment distributors."

"Obviously," the man said. "But it's a setback. You aren't taking action against the revolt that's fermenting, and perhaps even exasperating it."

"True," said Vialy.

"Do they have weapons?" asked Broun.

"Certainly!" relied Vialy. "My reports mention a dozen machine guns and four hundred rifles that I can't find."

"Might as well say none," sniggered the man.

Coldly, Tadée concluded: "I've seen it before. Nothing to do. We'll put the picturesque into their lives, since they insist. The workers live and are happy, the rebels end up in the phosphate factories. Take precautions, Vialy. Fortel, go see Syster."

The little circle broke up Vialy drew away, pensively.

So, once again, it would be necessary to electrocute a few thousand of the wretched. They had no hope of doing anything but offer themselves to death, for it would require, to create a great revolution, a universal and monstrous fever: a demonic fever; a mystical and self-sacrificial state of mind that was not remotely close to realization.

He pictured the famous electric machine guns scything deeply into that human mass, leaving narrow and terrified files between their tracks of death, while the reflux of the spared threw disorder into the surge from the rear. Every mob was eventually reduced to work-gangs to remove the cadavers...

How stupid the people were!

Tadée came over to him. "This evening, I have a new kind of amusement recovered from the olden times. We need to organize a circular track in the middle of the room."

Armchairs were moved, and groups gathered around an empty circle to which entry was gained by a passage departing from an arched doorway to the left of the main door of the drawing room.

The arched door opened. Silence fell. Indistinct forms could be seen moving in the narrow opening, violently illuminated.

A white silhouette, and then another, and two more, were framed in the luminous gap: four women. They had been chosen by the Thousand's old Arab, Oulam Bab Ahr, an admirable slave-driver, who had sold them before the Fault and had always attested an infallible mastery. Today, he directed the spinning of mineral fibers, in which thirty-five thousand women were employed. These four graceful children were of that race. A vigorous health was manifest in their gestures and the coloring of their faces. That was rare. The light ankles and wrists, the fine facial features and the large and tender eyes were calculated to please men hardened by science and care. Thus, under argent gazes, the four young women were trembling like hinds at bay. Having arrived in the middle of the room they stopped. Their uniform vestment was a white stola, one bordered with red, the others green, gold and blue. Their feet were bare. A tragic emotion hollowed out their faces, causing hearts to race, haws to flutter and knees tremble.

They knew that they were in the lair of the master of the Thousand himself. They had suckled hatred for the men who surrounded them with their first milk. So, furtively, they searched the visages for the pitiless cruelty that they had been told a thousand times over was the common soul of the Thousand. Pretty and made-up, with tragic expressions, they moved the entire assembly, except for B 309, who suddenly detested them.

They were aware of an unknown sentiment that was giving more charm to their poses. They could be seen curiously interrogating the masks for the promise of the torture to which they had believed they were destined five minutes earlier. They had never thought they would emerge alive from that terrible dwelling, where they were being offered to Tadée Broun as to a devouring monster—but now they only perceived sympathetic attitudes around them, in which no malevolence could be divined. There were even amiable men. They resisted the impulse to faint. Having arrived with their little hearts full of heroism, they had an urge to beg for mercy before that attentive cordiality.

On the anguished faces, Manya read a tragic emotion of incomprehension. She stood up and went to the four children.

They watched the svelte and supple form approach, admiring the fact that she could be so extraordinary and so beautiful.

"Are you going to dance?" said Manya to the one wearing the gold-bordered stola.

All four replied with one voice: "Yes, Madame."

"Don't tremble. Do I scare you?"

They laughed.

Manya passed her hand over the face of one, with a smile, and then went back to her place.

They danced.

The troubled memory of the lessons they had been given was sometimes treacherous, but a charming naivety soon enabled them to improvise instinctively feminine steps forgotten since Rome had conquered the sacred land of Hellas. The light dances of the pre-Christian era, which expressed thoughts better than words, were reborn.

Holding one another by the hand they danced in a circle; then the circle broke, was duplicated, recomposed and deformed.

They had the puerile charm of virgins. Undoubtedly their chastity was subject to a caution, but the novelty of the décor, the bizarrerie of the actions demanded of them, and their own wonderment and youth created an authentic renewal in those simple souls.

They finally stopped, somewhat bewildered by the silent attention that surrounded them. A pride invaded them, young factory-workers, in now being the center of attention of those emphatic and admiring gazes.

Tadée summoned them. They came toward him and knelt down.

"I'm glad to liberate four such charming girls from labor. You'll be the Dancers of our City."

They knew that the old man's words were definitive. They were, therefore, henceforth exempt from the crushing labor of spinning. They would be dancers among the Thousand...

One of them kissed Tadée's hand devotedly. Two of them sobbed.

Manya leaned toward the four delicious little rags.

"It's necessary to go on, children!"

They went back to the center of the room. They no longer had any idea what they were supposed to do, and a charming confusion played over their faces.

Suddenly, the wearer of the red-hemmed stola remembered. She made a sign to her companions. Three of them formed a closed circle around the fourth; then the circle opened and that one emerged, naked.

A slight murmur flowed around the room. Two adolescents still imprisoned the third, who emerged naked in her turn. The remaining two then came gracefully to deposit their robes in front of Tadée, and all four resumed dancing.

Now accustomed to the drawing room and its spectators, they found themselves sufficiently at ease to improvise a series of harmonious steps, as dancers habituated since childhood to play between the hours of labor with primitive chorus-leaders—for the pre-Fault dances had been faithfully transmitted by tradition. The Argentine, Brazilian or Californian steps of old had been modified by organic spontaneity, but they were still recognizable, seasoned by the habit that women had of dancing with one another. They therefore rediscovered before the Thousand, who were unaware of them, the amorous mimes of beautiful rhythmic form: the slow, geometrical and calculated form of the tangos of old.

From the place from which they had emerged came a capricious and languid music. The Thousand had never heard that dolorous moaning of a violin, mingled and married to the liquid quavering of a flute.

And since the Fault, the men with the crushing responsibility, who had given themselves as a law the task of defeating the Necron, knew for the first time a tender and soothing quietude, which was thus revealed to them. A new flame was born in each of them. They would have liked to carry one of the dancing girls away without delay, and keep her as a delicate treasure.

Sigliaresse, her senses irritated, suddenly left. Her passion for solitude before and after her violent desires was well-known.

More time went by. Now sitting on the floor in the center of the room, the four children were drinking, with crucified expressions, the beverages that Tadée Broun had sent them.

A face appeared, silently, at a hidden door in front of which Vialy was sitting. The face disappeared immediately. Vialy and Manya stood up at went out.

They arrived in a corridor leading to a cubic space with three telephones and a table covered with plans.

The other man bowed.

"What is it?" asked the Chief of Police.

"Unsuccessful attempt on the main cable: a mine in abandoned tunnel 9. The perpetrator caught, taken down to the dungeons. A document found on him."

"Show me!"

The man took out a piece of paper, which Vialy read curiously.

It said: *Six steps directly under transverse gallery found behind former station 21. Cut.*

"That's all?" asked Vialy, with making any comment.

"No. Lighting in sector D cut off. Sounds heard in the microphone indicating work under the former Étoile Metro station."

"Damn! Activate the explosives."

"None of the three mines exploded."

"What!"

"Southern corner of electrocution facing section W of the glacis nullified. Searchlight extinguished. Geocoronium in revolt, although no losses."

"Isolate them…with the major defenses."

"Yes sir. Rumors of attack for tomorrow or the day after. Meetings of ringleaders have taken place. Decisions taken; we'll surprise them."

"Good. Open Omega first. We'll begin by formally prohibiting meetings under Paris."

"Impossible to reach Omega. It's necessary to go through the forbidden tunnel skirting D. I've opened two Necron bombs in D. As for the forbidden, only you can act."

"I'll go," said Manya, coldly.

Vialy made no reply.

"If I don't go into that polypary, it will be necessary to fear a further strike at the cables."

"Go," said the Chief of Police, finally.

As he said the word, the impassive Vialy felt his throat tighten. He did not know why. Manya's action was indispensable, and he, the commander in chief, could not go in person to accomplish all the minor actions of the defense.

Manya went out with the policeman, one of Vialy's faithful agents. The Master of the Police remained motionless momentarily, and then returned to the drawing room. He summoned the Controller of the Defenses and the Director of the Subterranean Workings, and brought them up to date.

"As soon as Manya returns and reports," he said, in conclusion, "have everything swept, to a depth of three hundred meters by powerful emissions of asphyxiating gas. Destroy all the tunnels susceptible to access. Look at the vertical plan in room two in the Wall."

They both went out immediately.

VII. Desperation

Nervous and irritated, Vialy left Tadée's house. The night was still magnificent. In about two hours, the day would dawn. He wandered for ten minutes through the maze of streets linking the luxurious dwellings. He was searching, without knowing why, for an indication of treason, a shadow of treachery within the walls of the city that he was responsible for defending. He would have liked to deflect the wrathful emotion that possessed him with a concrete fact.

Everything was mute and calm. That serenity irritated the police chief. He thought of going on to the footbridges to inspect the bare ground that completed the glacis and sheltered the city of the Thousand from attack

He went down into a secret subterranean passage, and was soon at the foot of the elevator that had brought him down with Pierre Broun from footbridge 14 the day before. He rode up inside the pylon to the fragile metallic bridge, so narrow that it almost invisible in the darkness. Then he started up the mobile apron and allowed it to carry him southwards.

The sentiment of genuine solitude calmed his anger. Far away to the east, the Titanium factories cast a dull gleam into the atmosphere. To the north, the city of the Thousand was asleep in the shadow. To the west, there were the oil-wells, with the enormous plume of smoke that hid the stars. In front of Vialy, beyond the six groups of factories that he could not see, so precisely was their nocturnal activity screened by shutters that encased them in a kind of box, Vialy thought about the immense territory that extended, empty of human beings and possessed by the Necron...

Unless...

He thought about Manya then, going through the forbidden tunnel. At that moment it was as if his heart skipped a beat, like an appeal or a premonition. That deficiency in the rhythm of the powerful muscle that fueled his life was so brief that he did not want to pay any heed to it. What? Manya was not in danger. Then again, who among the Thousand had not been in mortal danger on a daily basis for thirty years?

When she reached the Arc de Triomphe, Manya would activate the mechanisms of retardation and come back immediately. Perhaps she was already on her way back.

He thought for a moment about other dispositions of the subterranean tunnels, which would avoid steps like the one his mistress was taking. But for twenty years, there had been no further underground excavations; they had been content to utilize the ones that existed. If there had not been any treason, no one down below could have attempted to blow up the cables, since only fifteen of the thousand knew their layout.

Meanwhile, the footbridge took Vialy far away from the traces of life. The stars were shining softly in a vast sad and gray sky. In the far east, a kind of vague aurora was beginning to filter, beyond Paris, a slight luminous cloud, which gradually extended. Was it daylight, or some unfamiliar meteorological phenomenon?

The atmosphere was warm and compact. Vialy was not breathing easily. A dyspnea gripped his thorax.

What's the matter with me now? he wondered.

He thought about Manya again. A question occurred to him. *Am I in my place here? In a danger like the one it's necessary to anticipate, shouldn't I be at home, hanging on my telephones?*

For the time being, however, he had a singular horror of being enclosed. He wanted air, and yet more air...

In sum, up here he was like a general surveying the future battlefield.

At that moment, he glimpsed a human silhouette on a footbridge the connected with his a little further on. He was gripped again by his professional concern and accelerated the movement of the apron; then, as soon as he had reached the bifurcation, headed toward the form he had glimpsed—which, in sum, seemed simply pensive.

When he was ten paces away he heard: "I was expecting you, Vialy."

"Were you really expecting me, beautiful Sigliaresse?"

"I have very keen sight. I saw you set off from pylon 14. A silhouette passed over the stars, at the level of the horizon. It could only be you."

"What whim brought you to this remoter spot, Sig?"

"The same as yours."

"It's my job that brought me."

"Shut up!"

"And a muted anxiety that makes me detest enclosed spaces."

"Exactly."

"Is that unique to us?"

"No, Vialy, I saw Ortis on footbridge 5. He said: 'There's something in the air, Sig.' A fault that's about to open beneath our feet."

"Or simply a revolt by those idiots."

"We've put down forty, I believe."

"Forty, a hundred, a thousand—there'll always be more, until the one that drowns us."

"Not this one?"

"No, certainly..." Vialy fell silent. So, his own malaise was affecting various souls, as if it were a mysterious warning.

The woman followed the track of the Police Chief's thought. "It's painful, this impression, isn't it? This malaise is undermining cherished certainties within me. That of omnipotence, for example, and that of our absolute strength. One feels a trifle defeated when one experiences it..."

She extended her hands around her in a smooth sweep. "Oh, Vialy, this warm and soft air, the sky that innumerable eyes have contemplated amorously, the world that surrounds us and yet isn't as closed as our pontiffs claim...tell me, don't you think that it was created for other purposes than the pitiless life we lead here?"

"Yes, Sig, but what can we do? The Necron is there."

"Shut up, Vialy, with your Necron. There are human beings living all around us—your insubordinates. I can see lights by night, from my tower, on hills twenty kilometers away."

"Isolated individuals risking their petty lives, nothing more."

"Oh, my dear, does the role of Grand Master of Police, which makes you a kind of king, leave you an hour of liberty to make a confession to me?"

Vialy remained silent. He was well aware of everything that Sigliaresse was telling him; the tall, voluptuous and knowledgeable woman was echoing his own ideas—but how could he admit it?

"Tell me, Vialy, if the Necron were not to be feared, if one really could wander carelessly around the world, what would you do, knowing that?"

"You know very well, Sig,"

"Yes, I know: you'd stay here, with your burden and your duty. Your role rules you. You're the man who protects eight hundred masters from ten million slaves. Nothing can take away the pride of that responsibility, superior to all desires."

"I protect you as well, Sig. I permit you to find all the subtle joys that make you a sacred magician of Eros. If I relax the yoke that holds the proletariat in place by a single degree, we'd disappear."

Sigliaresse wrung her hands with a despairing gesture. Her bare arms made long pale patches in the darkness in front of Vialy, and her visage seemed to glisten.

"You never read anything but files and dossiers, Vialy. Personally, I read the works that were printed before the Fault, and which are sweet...sweeter than you're able to believe. To think that there was a time when humans were their own masters! They came and went as they wished. They worked, traveled or dreamed in their armchairs. They bred pretty domestic animals and picked sumptuous flowers. They loved one another, or made love to one another, carelessly, at the times that seemed propitious to them, and nothing obviated their caprices, any more than their desires..."

"Yes, Sig, that once existed..."

"Oh, Vialy, how can humans not be mourning for that ancient pleasure, that vanished Eden? The memory alone possesses me like a lover's kiss. And that joy will never be reborn...never... I was born with the Fault, Vialy. I never knew the times for which regret gnaws at me night and day..."

"It also had its miseries and its ulcers, Sig. Who knows whether it wouldn't have inflicted pains and humiliations upon you that ours spares you?"

But Sigliaresse was not listening. She continued: "Vialy, I'm leaving this world. I shall disappear from life. My flesh will soon be no more than atoms mixed in new chemical combinations, and nothing of my consciousness will survive. What becomes of the music when the violin is broken? And I won't have known the moment when life could be savored like a liqueur. I shall die, Vialy, having known nothing in my quest for voluptuousness but the grim shadow of the crushing duties that are incumbent on all of us, the mathematical formulae under which I've spent a third of my life in this world. I'll have been solving quadratic equations while roses were blooming somewhere, roses that only awaited my presence to become the unknown poem of all felicities.

"What are those contacts to me, truly—those female mouths that I've paraded over my body, that I've attached by terror to those parts of myself where I think I sense a frisson arise of the profound joy that always escapes me? I've only done that, you know, in order to recover the physical peace necessary to my algebra. But of gratuitous delights that have been given to me without my strength and my command demanding them, of pleasures that could only be interrupted by the fatigue of enjoyment, I've known nothing. I've run after a plenitude of joy that could only be born in a free mind, indifferent to the miseries of the Necron, to caste struggles, to the poor humanity that death awaits, and which speaks.

"I shall die, and in order for me to be happy before that end, it would have been sufficient for me to go forward without thinking of anything but the pleasure of being, to go into the territory that extends beyond the factories, where free vegetation counsels a life in its own image..."

"Sig, Sig! All human beings before us knew the anguish that's tormenting you. You're pursuing a chimera. Before the Fault, as today, there was talk of nothing but revolt and bloodshed. The history of humankind is a tale of cruelty and ignominy. And yet, Sig, the happiness of which you dream was within their reach then. They didn't find it."

"I would have!"

Vialy fell silent, his eyes moist. Ten million human beings were imprisoned in the gehennas that the Thousand had created, but not one of them thought that the earth, where it was habitable—perhaps everywhere—was waiting to render them happy. They were thinking about killing their masters, not about creating possible happiness. Rancor and hatred alone inspired them, and it was necessary, for that reason, that he, Vialy, could not give way beneath the burden of his responsibilities, nor betray the trust of his peers.

"Sig," he said, "can't you see the chains that bind us? Go, if you want, aboard one of the airplanes we use to drop the Necron bombs. Go a hundred or two hundred kilometers from here. What will you do? Your clothing is made for the city of the Thousand, your arms for amour and not for material tasks. You'd miss your palace."

"Adaptations to be made, Vialy. Amour might be more moving on a bed of dry leaves than my silken sheets. Do you really think that servile labor can't acquire a kind of charm, when they for one's own sake? No, you see; it's necessary to live in accordance with a knowledge and understanding of life. Intelligence, applied to what we've all forgotten, would give a beauty to the meanest pleasure and lighten cares.

"Look at the world that surrounds us! That quietude, that magnificence—what a lesson that gives us! Oh, to understand that life passes and that every hour lost to serenity is an hour of death!

"Is it living, then, to feel restricted by the thousand chains of our duties, and subsist in the barracks of our sovereign power? It weighs upon me...."

In the distance, a bright light suddenly erupted over Paris, spread, and displayed the dentellate roofs and monuments. At the same time, an enormous rumor rose up toward the heavens: a kind of grave and powerful hymn. Then three explosions rang out in succession, and to the south, a response to the grim song became audible in a factory.

"Look, Vialy," said Sigliaresse. "There's the secret of our torment. The phosphate factory will have raw material tonight..."

Above the city of the Thousand, a red triangular jet rose sharply toward the sky, and endured.

"Full-scale defense everywhere. Closure of the workshops and confinement of the workers within the electrocution networks. The day will be decidedly less bucolic than your dreams, Sig..."

Dawn broke.

The two individuals went to footbridge 14 and started the mobile apron. The accelerated movement carried them away. Muffled detonations were audible in the distance.

A broad red stain invaded the east. The hymn was still resonating...

They reached the last pylon and descended into the underground workings. Vialy sealed all the doors and launched the fatal currents.

When they were in the city, Sigliaresse said: "I have an idea that we'll never see one another again, Vialy. Remember that it would only have required a few trivial actions for us to both have been two hundred kilometers away, alone and perhaps destined to be happy."

"Destiny has chosen," said Vialy, somberly.

Hastily, the Chief of Police returned to his house.

As he crossed the threshold, a secretary who was waiting for him handed him a piece of blue paper, without saying a word.

He read: *Telephone one twenty-three a.m. tunnel Z3. Appeal from Manya thus conceived: 'Help. I'm trapped.' Nothing heard since.*

White-faced, Vialy put the paper down beside him.

"What did you do?"

"U 6 left immediately."

"No news?"

"No. Certainly killed. They've infiltrated as far as 1-9."

My turn! Vialy thought. "Pass me the file of orders."

"Here it is, sir."

Vialy signed page one. "Until I return, you'll assume all responsibilities, following the formulated prescriptions. Go!"

The secretary withdrew.

Then Vialy went down into the private tunnel that linked his house to the defenses. He went to the place where Manya had been captured.

Outside, the sun rose on a beautiful spring day. Above the city of the Thousand a red balloon indicated all the powers devolved until the day's end on Syster, the master of massacres.

The enormous popular hymn filed the luminous cupola of the heavens.

VII. Life and Death

Sitting in a corner of his father's drawing room, Pierre Broun watched the guests leaving, gradually. The news about Paris that had arrived by telephone from Vialy's house, where the secretaries were on watch, had not disturbed anyone thus far.

Syster, with his bulldog face, was in conversation with Tadée Broun, who was interrogating him, smiling.

After Vialy and Manya had gone out, B 309 had watched the door for a long time, thinking that they would reappear. Then she questioned Pierre Broun about their prolonged absence, but he was gripped by a violent and irresistible desire for the dancer in the red-bordered stola. He was also suffering because he did not dare manifest that sentiment before his father's mistress.

Meanwhile, the young women had left the room, one by one. Sim Landève, the chemist's son, had taken away the one with the god-hemmed robe. Cold and authoritarian, he had told her to follow him and she had obeyed.

Lucette Broun than took the arm of the one wearing the green hem. The father approved with a satisfied laugh. He liked the fact that, in the city of the Thousand, his blood was the boldest and the most voluptuous.

Biall, the man of aliment Alpha, found himself in conflict with Mairal, Sigliaresse's husband, over the adolescent in the blue-edged stola. Eventually they had gone out with her, wanting to find an elegant means outside of regulating their double desire.

The last contemplated by Pierre Broun with an ardent passion, excited the jealousy of B 309, who divined everything.

She went to Tadée and said: "Would you like us take that pretty child away?"

Tadée agreed. That was very agreeable to him.

Confused and irritated, his heart in tumult and his throat dry, Pierre left then.

Left alone, Tadée stood up then, and the two women followed him.

"Like the petty principalities of two centuries ago, we have four official dancing girls. That will be charming. I'll construct a theater and assemble a troupe of actors. Our life will be entirely sybaritic. Perhaps I was wrong to scorn such things in my youth. It's true that I had other cares then. But now..."

Having arrived at his bedroom, a broad and high-ceilinged room full of cupboards stuffed with files and containing the famous table with handles, albeit invisible beneath a kind of metal box, he sat down in an armchair.

He recalled his past, the years before the Fault, when the engineer Tadée Broun had emerged from the École des Mines. He remembered that astonishing complex and fickle society of the end of the nineteenth century.

Young Tadée had dug oil-wells on the Riviera. He had transformed the center of luxurious life in Europe into a stinking and muddy factory. That had made his fortune, in the time when there were fortunes. He remembered the Fault and his titanic and cruel struggle, the reduction of the masses to docility by terror and, finally, the creation of the terrible new society which, in his mind, the old man judged infinitely more perfect than those of the past.

It was necessary to admit, though, that he had never known love.

He opened his eyes. In front of him, upright and silent, B 309 and the dancer were waiting for orders. Their attitude respired respect, discretion and obedience.

Tadée was irritated by that. He would rather have been a man with whom women were cordial and familiar. He would have liked the caress of an unsolicited hand, a smile that was not on command, even an insolence that remained a testimony of affection.

But he had acquired a power before which, outside the Thousand, no human being could know anything but fear. He had lived long enough to know that obedience is often coupled with hatred.

He spoke curtly: "Show yourselves!"

It was an evident order, but it remained a trifle obscure, in order to leave those at which it was launched the illusion that to understand the two words required a little love.

The two women had no need of love, however, to divine the intention. They were naked in less time than it would have taken a pre-Fault soldier to present arms.

Tadée Broun looked at the two naked bodies. A harsh attention clenched his jaws and caused his sharp eyes to blink beneath the bushy eyebrows. He asked himself, philosophically: what ought one to do in this world—work or play?

The old man almost regretted having sacrificed voluptuousness to creation within the confines to his destiny—but he did not see how his past could have been organized any differently than it had.

He stood up, robust and steady on his strong legs. He would judge, in the morning, whether pleasure, pursued with the same determination as the form of a new society, would leave him a memory as bitter, or sweeter. Then he shoved the two women into the next room, which he reserved for gallant matters.

The telephone rang the major alert, but, with blood in his face, Tadée, for the first time in his life, ignored the appeal and cut off the current. Then he went toward what he thought was love...

It was eight o'clock in the morning. Syster, the chief of the defenses, knew that the attack would take place the following night. This time, there was no question of leaving the underground workings free any longer, invaded as they already were by revolutionary gangs.

He sent the final warning to Vialy, inside the wall, where he had gone at dawn to rescue Manya and had not yet returned, any more than the two secretaries who had gone after him.

At ten past nine, Syster was still hesitating. Killing Vialy and Manya was a redoubtable prospect. He telephoned Tadée Broun in order to obtain the cover of an order from the old chief of the Thousand. When there was no reply, he went to see him.

He went up hastily into the room where the table with the handles was. It was empty. Unmoved, he deduced that Tadée was next door, and knocked.

Again, there was no reply. He went in.

Dead and convulsed, with the atrocious faced of the damned, Tadée Broun was lying to a bed covered in orange silk.

In an armchair, completely naked, two women were, terrified and mute, were holding one another in a tight embrace.

Syster understood. He telephoned Dr. Erhivan, the Thousand's surgeon, and waited, his head in a state of turmoil. By virtue of the disappearance of Vialy, he automatically became the ruler of the world.

Erhivan appeared. Syster showed him the body. The physician examined the pupils and stood up again. "Died at seven o'clock," he said.

"Of what?"

Erhivan smiled broadly and indicated the two women with discolored faces. "The doves ought not to be punished. They had no way of knowing the limits of a septuagenarian physiology departed for the Empyrean of pleasure. He went so far up to the seventh heaven that he won't be coming down again. I'd like to know what his exploit was, whether he succumbed at the beginning of the course, or whether he went around the track a few times."

"Ask them."

"I prefer to put them to the proof, so I'll take the little one away. Come, child!"

The young woman followed him meekly.

Pierre Broun came in. He saw his father dead. B 309, naked and stiff, was standing on the far side of the room.

He went out immediately, torn between opposed and confused sentiments. He was not suffering.

Syster telephone a few people, and then went out, after giving instructions to the loyal Chinaman who was Old Broun's favorite servant.

Now it was necessary to get back to the more urgent problem of the defenses.

As soon as he arrived in his office, Syster gave orders to blow up the subterrains.

Then he waited...

The day went by.

The night passed slowly.

Dawn returned.

At eight o'clock in the evening, the official list of the dead was posted before the imminent attack of the proletariat. There was Vialy, Manya, their two secretaries, three engineers treacherously attacked at the well, a chemist and six members of the powerful society who had been in Paris and would probably be unable to get out.

Sigliaresse had taken over the police in Vialy's stead.

The guardians of the factories and workshops had been allocated barracks underneath the thirty subterranean level under the glacis. In principle, they were not to be utilized in the defense, reserved for the Thousand alone. They had confidence in that many servants in peace time, but in time of war they were mistrusted. The stocks of aliment had been isolated. Inside the wall, preparations were being made to surround the city with an envelope of poison gas. Necron bombs and electric machine-guns were ready.

They waited...

All the factories still functioning were surrounded by electrified fences, in order that the workers would be sequestered there until the revolt was over. Out of a hundred and forty factories, thirty-nine were functioning normally.

They learned, thanks to the report of a spy transmitted by wireless telegraph, that Manya had been captured during the night, wounded, and had been taken to the Messiah's lair. It was thought that Vialy had tried to rescue her, but contradictory rumors were circulating in that regard. In all probability, they had both been killed by the adherents of Diavide, who was directing the revolt.

At ten o'clock in the morning, the attack began. From the district of Paris nearest to the City of the Thousand, an enormous, prodigious, agile crowd suddenly emerged, which rushed the glacis howling. The human stream broadened out, became a giant river, and then an ocean. Hundreds of men were seen to fall and remain lying, electrocuted on the spot, but there were electricians running with the mass. They cut the wires, and the host, still inexhaustible, continued to emerge, dense and furious, extending everywhere, uttering murderous cries.

B 309 went up to the summit of Broun's house. Since she had seen Tadée die choking, while she was aiding him in his furious and intense quest for a pleasure that avoided him, she had had a presentiment of the victory of her own people. She watched those hundreds of thousands of people coming toward her with a profound and powerful joy. She thought that she could divine the Messiah, invulnerable and magnificent, at their head. In an hour, she would be saved.

She thought that she had done more for her own people than anyone had ever done for anyone else. She had revealed to them all the secrets known by Pierre Broun. All that, immediately communicated via the shaft to Diavide's friends, had facilitated the attack enormously, and shielded it. She had also killed Tadée.

If each of the rebels only possessed a hundredth of her courage, this evening...

With eddies, advances and retreats, the mass gradually reached the glacis and launched themselves up the terrible slope.

The machine-guns fired. Thousands of people were laid on the ground, never to get up again, and there was a marked interruption of the progress of the attackers. But

the arriving mass continued to push forward without respite. Dense and wretched crowds were still emerging
from Paris, howling. Leaving countless cadavers in its
wake, the host recommenced its advance.

It drew slowly closer. Those who were carrying the
explosives with which to blow up the wall were clearly
visible. When they fell, others picked up the precious
burdens, and in the end, they were bought into close
proximity with the famous enclosure beyond which they
would have no more to do, they thought, than cut the
throats of the Thousand...

Deafening cries were heard, inhuman howls along
with savage appeals. The concert of voices of hatred and
fury became prodigious.

They arrived at the wall...

A near-naked woman, carrying a heavy packet of
explosives, ran, darting crazed glances ahead of her. B
309 saw her stumble and fall, her body cleaved as if by
an ax. But an agile bearded man picked up the savior
package and continued the run. He too fell, and two
young men rushed forward to seize the inestimable object. They fell on top of one another, struck dead. Then
another woman appeared, young and beautiful, one
would have said. Her belly protruded, swollen by another life. She took the explosive, carrying it above the
child that was living within her, and advanced toward
the wall.

Removed as she was from beneath the execution-
er's blade, B 309 waited expectantly, as if she were carrying death herself.

Abruptly, she felt herself seized by a rude arm. She
tried to turn round, but was immobilized, and could only
catch a glimpse of Pierre Broun.

"Marie," he said, "you killed my father..."

Vibrant, she could scarcely hear. Oh, that pregnant woman who was offering herself and her child to the sacred task of destruction!

"Look, Marie. Look at your people coming and listen to their screams. Listen...'"

He had grabbed her by the hips, and while she learned toward those who were running, he...

The crowd oscillated, came nearer lost ground, regained it, but kept coming...it kept coming...

The cry of the people rose up toward the blossoming sun.

B 309 could no longer contain herself. Nervous and exhausted, she felt a monstrous joy; she wanted to scream...

The tumult was still increasing. The crowd was getting nearer; its cataclysmic howling gave the impression that it was an irresistible force...

In his command post, Syster, who could see everything, turned to his aides.

"Go!" he said.

At a single stroke, as if the earth had suddenly closed over them, five hundred thousand mouths, open a moment, before closed forever...

The immense silence fell, resonating like a mighty explosion.

Panting with horror before the sudden catastrophe, it was only then that B 309 perceived Pierre Broun's embrace.

The hatred toward the man possessing her was prodigious, but her emotion, commenced in fear, was externalized, and transformed against her will, and in the vast silence created by the vertiginous massacre of her people, B 309 uttered, despairingly, a great orgasmic cry.

Part Two: Misery

I. The Passage

Like the lair of some enormous sovereign beast, the long bare tunnel plunged into the chalky soil. Paulin Vialy, a little while before the Grand Master of the Thousand's Police, hesitated before going into the compact shadow; now, he was nothing more than a desperate lover, set forth in search of a beloved shade into the enormous hatred of the people in revolt. Where was Manya, who had come here four hours earlier to accomplish one of the duties of the responsibility that Vialy bore?

Undoubtedly her body was lying, exposed and mutilated, in some refuge where the men of the proletariat would come to seek courage by insulting the corpse of an execrated enemy. But what did that matter to Vialy? He suddenly felt estranged from his own kind. He rediscovered the libertarian soul of the time before the Fault had changed human destiny. What Sigliaresse had said evoked the felicity of being alone, outside the claws of the terrible pincers; Masters and Slaves wandered in his brain. He had the sensation, as he entered the tunnel, of quitting his previous life and going into an unknown and tragic adventure that he could not yet anticipate. But where was Manya?

Behind him, he was leaving the Thousand on the defensive, ready to sacrifice a million human lives to retain their power; ahead, he was going into the land of overheated and ferocious rancor. He did not know whether his mistress was anything more than a debris of dead flesh on the way to dissolution, chemicals returning to mineral nature, but he hoped...

Was it hope, or a sudden disgust for everything, supported by the energy that was his prerogative, leading him by a difficult and redoubtable path toward the ultimate sacrifice of his pride?

With his electric lamp, Vialy examined a copper plate on the side wall bearing the conventional indications. Behind him, there was the lighted tunnel with its guards and its defensive apparatus. Here, beneath this plate, there was a round door like a valve; the dark and stinking opening was visible, in the ground itself, with no masonry or stays. That way, one reached the places to which the rebellious people had taken his mistress.

He opened the metal door and slid into an adjacent hole. He closed it again and disposed wires in a special pattern, the placed a kind of petard on the ground, and went straight ahead. The tunnel in which he found himself had been hollowed out by one of the first boring machines that could drill without debris. It was a curious discovery, without which the Thousand would doubtless have been unable to discover all the chemical treasures thanks to which the defense against the Necron had been organized. Two thousand strands, slanted with respect to the horizontal but eccentric, worked the ground in an oval vertical plane, two meters around its main axis. The digger advanced irresistibly into terrain reduced to dust, but that dust was accumulated regularly around the periphery of the plane of attack, driven back by compression, thus constituting the coating, or rather the surface, of the tunnel. Thus, there was nothing to extract. The machine hollowed out and compacted all along its route a layer of debris as hard as concrete.

The tunnel dated back twenty-five years. No one ever passed through it, because the carapace was crumbling and falling apart. Since its creation, they had learned how to mix the dust of the rubble with a liquid that gave it the hardness of steel. Mobile carpets had been laid along the new routes. Here, collapses and infiltrations permitted the anticipation of the imminent disappearance of the tunnel.

Vialy walked for a long time, Holes appeared in front of him at regular intervals. He stepped over them. The tunnel followed bizarre meanders, and collapsed walls occasionally bit into it. Finally, he stopped at a place where the earth had shifted. The vault bulged there. Inexplicably, a rocky mass protruded from the side wall. Vialy inspected the while, and went to place himself in concave curve. He took a kind of long cartridge from his pocket and placed it against the wall at waist height. Then, with the electric lamp—which contained a small magneto, he closed a circuit.

A spark sprang forth. The earth appeared to dissolve into smoke, and a dense cloud filled the tunnel. With no more noise than the biting of a grinder, an enormous and profound hole was manifest were the cartridge had been placed.

Vialy, who had stood aside, waited for the air to become respirable, and then crawled into the orifice. He went some four meters and then stopped in front of an assembly of stones, which he palpated. Then he began to extract them, one by one, and, passing through the hole, passed into a different tunnel. A strong human odor became perceptible.

He replaced the stones, leaving one of them sticking out slightly, doubtless in order to be able to find the passage again without overmuch searching.

Then, his lamp extinct and carefully groping his way along the wall, he went forward slowly. In his pocket he held on to the butt of his sixteen-shot centrifugal pistol. With that weapon, no sound revealed the advent of death.

The human reek was soon aggravated. The rebel proletariat had been here recently. Vialy sensed a mute emotion. A hundred meters away, at the intersection of two tunnels, was the telephone into which his mistress Manya had said, that same night: "Help! I'm trapped!" Coming from the other direction, his two secretaries had doubtless been massacred in the same place.

Suddenly, Vialy bumped into something flaccid, and yet resistant. He guessed that it was a corpse.

Fearing light, he continued more cautiously.

Five meters further on there is another corpse. Then there are others. He advances one step at a time, very attentive. Now he finds an entire pile of cadavers. That is Manya's defense. She sold her life dearly...

A few more meters. There, the telephone ought to be, by means of which her last words had been heard. Vialy gropes, but finds that the wires are broken. He continues advancing. Is she there, lying amid the cadavers? No. He would recognize her perfume in that reek of the unwashed crowd. They have taken her away, or she is further on...

Suddenly, he stops, his body stiffening, changed into stone. He has heard a sound of breath. His ears weigh up the slight sound. It's a wounded man, still alive. Vialy moves on, bending down. Finally, he finds the body beneath him from which life is exhaling. He bends down and gropes. Here is a face.

He whispers: "Are you conscious?"

An imperceptible voice replied. "I heard you coming. Have no fear; she's no longer here."

At a stroke, Vialy finds himself at the center of the drama that is torturing him. "Who's *she*?" he demands.

"The slut who killed at least thirty of us. You weren't here?"

"No. Did they kill her, at least?"

"I don't know. They took her away to show her off up there. Give me something to drink."

"Was she dead, at least?"

"I don't know. Diavide said: 'To the Permanence.'"

"Which one?" asks Vialy, as taut as a bowstring, anxiously and at hazard.

"The one at Montmartre."

"I'll go and get you some water."

And Vialy goes away...

He follows a long route, still strewn with recumbent bodies. There are more wounded, he guesses, but who cares? He has to get to the Permanence of Montmartre, that's all...

Suddenly, he sees a gleam of daylight coming from an intersecting tunnel. He approaches prudently. It is a vertical shaft dug not long before, doubtless in order to make a quick exit, or to link the system of tunnels to Paris. There is a long ladder.

Vialy retraces his steps. He finds an appropriately dressed cadaver, whose clothing is not bloodstained. He undresses and puts on his costume. He buries his own clothes in a spot whose reference points he notes, and finally, shod in the unknown man's heavy boots, climbs slowly up the ladder.

Now he is in the open air, in Paris in revolt. The shaft opens in the center of the courtyard of an empty building. Having rapidly inspected the surroundings, he emerges.

He finds himself at the corner of the Boulevard Saint-Denis and the Rue Saint-Denis. The Porte Saint-Denis looms up in front of him, an old relic of history. Without attracting attention by virtue of a dangerous curiosity, with the weary expression and curbed back of a brutish factory worker, Vialy heads for the Boulevard de Strasbourg. His gaze darts everywhere and his hand, profoundly plunged in his pocket, grips the butt of his pistol.

A hurried populace, emaciated and suffering, flows around him without respite. The wan faces and skeletal torsos are uniform. There are a great many women and children.

On the Boulevard de Strasbourg an even denser crowd is circulating. The host partakes of two movements, one descending toward the Seine and the other rising toward Montmartre, which Vialy follows.

There is no doubt about it; it is war that all these wretches want. Some are carrying tools similar to the enormous masses of Medieval weapons, others recently-fabricated but obsolete instruments of death.

Vialy passes before a house belonging to the Thousand, where one of his spies ought still to be on watch. He thinks about taking him with him, but discards the idea as soon as it has occurred to him. What would he do with a possibly-unreliable companion? He will be all the stronger alone. He does not know, in any case, what he will do. First, he has to find Manya. After that...

The streets are covered in filth. An intolerable odor emerges from all that. Men and women alike are wearing the taut faces of mystics, and it is obvious that nothing can move these beings, conquered henceforth by some mortal dream, which Vialy knows well.

He wonders, however, where all these fanatics, silent for the most part, are going. When it arrives at the Boulevard Barbès, however, the crowd's route veers westwards. Vialy allows himself to be led. He is in Montmartre, and thinks that he will see the famous Permanence, where Manya's body ought to be exposed. Perhaps these people are going there on a kind of pilgrimage?

Drowned in a human flood that might comprise as many as a hundred thousand individuals, his head heavy and his spine bent, as it is necessary to be, Vialy lets himself drift like a piece of flotsam on the sea. All those around him, long habituated to the exhausting labor and harsh discipline of the wells and workshops, trudge without saying a word. Only the women and a few adolescents chatter in weary and hoarse voices, punctuated with muffled sniggers.

It is an astonishing spectacle, all those ravaged and cruel faces, those clothes in rags, those prehistoric weapons carried by ignorant proletarians deprived of thought. Here is the Place Pigalle, barred by a tight cordon of red-faced louts reeking of alcohol.

Vialy detaches himself from the human conglomerate that is pulling him along and succeeds in stopping. He deduces from the cordon of men that the Permanence is hidden there.

He tries to descend via the Rue Frochot, but the passage is blocked. He takes the Rue Duperré, moving though a motionless crowd that seems to be waiting for the end of the world, singing revolutionary hymns. At the end, however, a further barrage closes off the Rue

Victor Massé. The famous Permanence must definitely be there.

He descends the Rue Fontaine and comes up again by the Rue Henri Monnier. This time, he is able to get through. There is a building belonging to the Thousand, in which a spy is usually on watch. Vialy knows that he will be able to reach any of the neighboring streets through the cellars.

He goes along the narrow winding corridor of the low and narrow house, scorned by the crowd. The secret door which he knows the means to open is there. He goes in.

This time, he has completed a stage, the hardest.

He searches the house, but finds no trace of its inhabitant. He must have gone back to the City of the Thousand, or at least, since he is one of the numbered, to the refuges where good servants can wait without risk until the revolt is put down.

The resident is a careful man. There is no sign of any file or dossier. The three telephones have been dismantled, but their absence deprives Vialy of any possibility—even if the cables have not been cut—of giving any news of himself.

Too bad...

And without delay, he goes down into the cellars.

Five minutes later, having followed a plan marked conventionally on the door of a cellar, he finds himself in a house in the Rue Victor Massé. He dirties himself a little more in order to go out in daylight. The great battle is in preparation...

In spite of the barriers the street is swarming with a strange and varied population whose members look wide-eyed at a shop-front where the famous Diavide, the Messiah, must be at the present moment.

It is there that Manya...

Four men armed with old rifles are stationed in front of a door glazed on the right. They are the first firearms that the Chief of the Thousand's Police has seen. He can be proud of his work. For years he has hunted down rifles and revolvers, and confiscated hundreds of thousands of them. There cannot be many left, and they are really not good models.

Vialy is a decisive man. He does not study the four sentinels for long. He arrives in front of one of them and attempts to go into one of the corridors that must lead to the upper floors. One of the rifle-bearers tries to stop him. With the majesty of a true chief, Vialy moves him aside with a monosyllable deprived of meaning but articulated very affirmatively. No one tries any longer to hold him back.

Here he is at the foot of a staircase. He goes up. On the first floor he hesitates as to whether to commence and inspection of the house, and then thinks that the best thing to do is take the high ground, and he continues up toward the roof.

Now he is at the top. Light is entering in a flood through and immense bay window, and the dull murmur of the street extends like the noise of surf. Vialy is about to penetrate into the first corridor that is on offer when a thickset man armed with a revolver surges forth and raises his weapon.

Among the Thousand, one has prompt and educated reflexes. Vialy's hand is leveled first, the centrifugal pistol shining at the extremity. At the same moment, another burly fellow appears, two paces away. Nothing better! Two silent bullets hit their targets, and the two unfortunates fall to the floor, struck dead.

Vialy thinks that there might be others, and he races straight ahead in order to kill any that appear. He opens a door, weapon raised, and...

Manya is there, tightly bound, inert and seemingly dead, suspended from the ceiling by her wrists...

II. Lost

Vialy cuts the ropes. He catches the light body. Where can he put her, in this bare and inhospitable abode? No chair, no bed...bah! The two cadavers, still warm, will make a passable divan...

Vialy lays the two corpses face down, side by side, and places Manya on top. She is alive, and recovers consciousness.

"Are you seriously wounded, Manya?"

She smiles. "Not badly. How did you find me?"

"It doesn't matter, my darling! I want to know, first of all, how you're feeling, and how soon you'll be able to walk."

"I can walk. A bullet grazed my shoulder. It's nothing."

"You've suffered. How long have you been hung up like that?"

"Not long. There were contradictory orders in my regard. I don't know what they were hoping for."

Vialy smiles, and inspects the shoulder. It is ugly and dirty. He has everything on his person that he needs to take care of it. He cleans the wound with a few drops poured from a minuscule bottle, then spreads a silvery paste over it extracted from a long tube. That immediately hardens to a solid varnish, which gives off a strong odor of bromine.

"You haven't forgotten anything!" she says, smiling.

He does not reply. But massages her forearms and feels the joints, testing each part of his mistress' body in order to discover the exact condition of the physiognomy from which it might be necessary to demand superhuman efforts.

At any rate, he does not know...

A bruise on the hip and grazes on the wrists—those are trivial. He takes out a flat metallic flask and pours a thin trickle of the liquid it contains between Manya's lips.

"Stay lying down for a moment until the tonic takes effect, and we'll go."

"How?"

"I'll think about that while you're resting. What do you think of the bed?"

"Tolerable."

He moves away. Manya remains alone on the two cadavers, which are slowly cooling. She feels vigor reentering in regular waves, her energetic heart and firm head, where her ideas become solidly coherent. *What are we going to do?* she wonders.

On the landing, Vialy is also reflecting.

How can these men of the people, deprived of method and reasoning, hope to take charge of the burden that the Thousand have been carrying for thirty years? Their only rule is ignorance, their exclusive concern fleeing every rule that smacks of discipline, their only love that of the decisions of hazard. I, the most hated man on the planet, have been able to get into the central lair of their activity, release a prey that they held, and kill that victim's two guards. No one knows anything about it as yet. And what are they doing downstairs? What plans are they debating? What major decisions are they putting into action? They're talking and expressing themselves on stupid formulae of hatred repeated a thousand times over. They're drinking, for I scented the famous alcohol they manufacture by fermenting I don't know what filth.

That's all. If these people take possession of our power, what will they be able to substitute for it? Only scientific intelligence can presently permit the perpetuation of Humanity in the conditions in which it lives. They'll die of starvation in a matter of days if they defeat us. But if, by chance...

He hesitated, wondering whether it was necessary to admit that the proletariat might nevertheless be successful... They had already been complaining before the Fault. Where was it necessary to seek the stable rock that would permit reasoning on the matter of happiness?

In sum, he concluded, happiness isn't a positive state but a negative one. It's the deprivation of certain elements of pain. It leads to a kind of quiet serenity that is solely able to take account of the evils avoided. But few judge sanely. Happiness, for those whose conviction is positive, therefore seems like a state that can be pursued and attained. That chimera, merely by its conception, already and irresistibly creates unhappiness.

Vialy was at that point in his thinking when he heard voices on the stairway whose spiral terminated in front of him. He listened. Men were coming up slowly. They stopped in order to be better able to talk. He heard:

"We told him: 'Enough of this waiting. She must die. If not, we're leaving. It's take it or leave it.'"

A thick voice certified: "He said: 'Go do it.'"

Another sniggered. "Yes, but before then, I want..."

A joyful bark rang out: "Of course. A daughter of the Thousand. We have to give ourselves that."

"And to teach her, in our fashion!" exclaimed that one who has spoken first.

The laughter overlapped in the stairwell.

Vialy wanted to know as much as possible and continued listening. Two floors separated him from the "executioners."

"We'll kill her afterwards?" said one voice.

"Of course. We'll cut off her head. It's necessary to display it in the street."

At that moment, Vialy felt a hand touch his. Manya, having got to her feet silently, had drawn closer.

He looked at her passionately, and then murmured: "Shall I kill them all?"

She shook her head negatively, and, with a gesture, asked him to follow her.

He went to the far end of the corridor. There a window overlooked the neighboring houses, giving access to a roof whose slope was edged by a broad zinc gutter.

"Let's go over this roof and reach another building."

He approved, and immediately stepped out into the gutter. If the corroded zinc gave way there would be a descent of twenty five or thirty feet in an accelerating fall, and a crash...

He crawled rapidly, sensing Manya behind him. When another window became accessible, he opened it and went in.

They were in a woman's room, with a mattress and a pair of stockings hanging on the wall. The people had not worn stockings for thirty years. Manya laughed on seeing them.

"Relics!"

He shrugged his shoulders.

Then she said: "They doubtless have revolvers. You'd only have been able to kill them if you didn't give any of them the time to fire; even if the shot missed, which isn't certain, it would certainly have been sufficient to muster the whole street. This way, they'll be astonished, and they'll deliberate until one of them goes down to raise the alarm. There won't be any real pursuit for a quarter of an hour. It's necessary to take advantage of that."

Vialy admired the reasoning, and said, finally: "Shall we go down the stairs here?"

"For want of anything better, yes, but if we can find a practical means of not being seen and choose a hidden route..."

He nodded his lead. "Let's take a look."

They went out on to an empty and silent landing. They went around a triple right-angled corridor and ended out at a bay window overlooking a courtyard two meters wide. There were no windows on the lower floors, but hinged shutters.

"The kitchens of olden times, uninhabitable."

She pointed to hooks riveted to the opposite face. "There's a ladder, if you can carry me."

"I can."

Ever prompt in decision, he leaned over, grasped the first hook and braced himself.

"Climb on to my back."

She did so immediately, and Vialy, thus ballasted, started down. The two fugitives were fearful that their passage might be observed through one of the outlets. The alarm would be raised immediately; although Vialy was dressed as a numbered, Manya's silk dress, still sparkling, and her appearance, like a precious doll, could not deceive anyone.

When they reached the bottom of the wall, and measured the vertiginous descent visually, Vialy uttered a sigh of relief.

They found themselves in a small trapezoid area, strewn with filth.

"Where are we going?"

"We need to get to the Thousand's building in the Rue Henri Monnier.

"Dressed as I am, though, my love..."

They looked at one another anxiously. It was necessary to dress Manya as a numbered. But how?

At that moment, they heard a formidable clamor in the street, which passed fifteen meters away from them. Laughter, yelps and howls mingled in an irritating symphony.

"That's for us," Manya murmured.

Suddenly, a woman appeared, coming to throw something into the small patch of ground. She remained dumbstruck before the two strangers, and her face took on a gray hue. Manya and Vialy, impassive, sensed that the moment of destiny had arrived. Vialy took the centrifugal pistol from his pocket.

The woman was young beautiful and sad. Her hair hung down in disorderly hanks over her forehead. The thin face had a kind of arrogant pride that surprised the lovers.

She spoke first, with a visible emotion in her somber eyes.

"What are you doing here" The voice was not aggressive; on the contrary, it respired a confused desire for love. She added: "It's against you that they're crying out!"

Vialy was about to fire. Manya stopped him with her hand, and took a step toward the young woman. With difficulty, she articulated: "I need you."

The other, her face ecstatic, said: "It's the Revolution. You're all going to die...all..."

Vialy sensed the danger increasing around them. He had to fire. Ten thousand howling voices were hurling ferocious and hilarious cries into the air, in which he perceived his name.

Manya made a decision. "Give me your dress."

The woman did not appear to understand.

"Your dress, yes?" She passed her hand over the numbered's face. The features lit up with a smile. "My dress!" she repeated—and then, abruptly, understood. "Yes! Yes!" she added, putting her hands together: "Run away."

Manya took her hand. "Give me your dress."

The young woman undressed in a trice. Like almost all her peers, she had no vestige of underwear.

Manya put the garment on; it was that of a female textile worker, well enough adapted to her form.

Vialy looked at the thin and weary body of the unfortunate woman, who was standing upright, devoid of shame or concern, her eyes staring.

"Come and find us nearby, in the Rue Henri Monnier: the house with the blue plaque."

"Yes, I know," she said, slowly. "It's said that it's shady."

Vialy bit his lip.

"I'll go," she added. "Go out this way. I'll go get my sister's dress. She's sick."

They went out, clinging to one another.

There was a redoubtable moment when they emerged into a crowd of a thousand faces, whose howling mouths were wide open.

Ten paces further on, they understood the subject of the popular hilarity. An enormous placard was being paraded around, on which, beneath a crude portrait of Vialy, they read:

Vialy and his whore have been captured in Paris. Execution this evening.

The street was full of crapulous bearded faces—the masks of insubordinates, for the workers had to be clean-shaven.

Manya, her face hidden by her bent arm, felt that her fate was hanging by a silken thread, for she had not been able to dirty and humiliate her face, that of a queen among the Thousand. They made haste. But the merriment was so great and the crowd so joyful that they were able to get into the corridor of salvation without incident, and cross the threshold of the refuge.

Outside, people were chanting: "Death to Vialy!"

III. The People in Revolt

Once inside the Thousand's house, Manya and Vialy looked at one another with a strange and confused emotion.

They sat down near the door, waiting for their rescuer, without knowing yet what they ought to do. They were safe. It was doubtless sufficient to wait here. Wait for what? How could they get back to the city of the Thousand? They did not ask that. It appeared to them that the future was heavily weighted in their favor and that this pause was definitive. Outside, thousands of people were howling "Death to Vialy," but what did that matter? When one has just overcome a great danger, one is inclined to believe that one has put an end to all threats.

They did not say anything, being so perspicacious in normal circumstances that their secret was one no longer...

Eventually, Manna spoke in order to break the silence, too heavily charged with felicity.

"What a strange adventure!"

"Yes," Vialy agreed. "Without that woman..."

"Are we still in connection with home here?"

"No, it's all broken."

"Can't we warn them?"

"Who knows how this revolution will end?"

"You don't believe, though..."

"No, they won't go that far, for the good reason that they wouldn't win. But their mystical wrath doesn't seem likely to calm down on its own, nor even by defeat. I don't know what will happen. They're capable of enclosing themselves in Paris and resisting any attempt to force them back to the factories."

"Many are still functioning."

"Yes, but the movement will penetrate them."

"How will they live here?"

"Who can tell whether they won't let themselves die of starvation? It's also necessary to fear that Syster knows the command-post of the revolt. In that case, he'll drown in quarter in asphyxiating gas..."

He reflected as to how they might reach a tunnel that would take them back. Before his departure he had given orders to destroy the all by means of profound explosions that would not agitate the surface. In an hour, the subterrains would collapse, to a depth of three hundred meters. That would be the irremediably closure of all means of return. Had it been done? Would they dare, at present, to risk it, given the danger of finding themselves caught half-way in the grip of the exploded earth?

As for descending to a great depth, they had no way of doing it. To find a shaft that the horizontal explosions had not destroyed might be possible, but where? He knew of a dozen departing from galleries near the surface, of which the people were doubtless ignorant, no matter how frantically they had dug the ground in order to discover the secrets of the surveillance to which Vialy had subjected them for such a long time, but...

Vialy had reached that point in his meditations when someone knocked on the door. He opened it, glad to welcome a recruit who might be useful, but the young woman seemed panic-stricken.

"Get out, quickly! They know back there that you might be here."

"They know?" said Vialy, retaining all his composure. "What does that mean?"

"They've received a communication from your place listing the Thousand's houses, where you might be hiding. They're going to destroy them all.

In the street, the tumult seemed to be increasing, becoming violent and exasperated. Manya went pale.

He looked at the woman, wondering whether she might not have reconciled her sudden affection and her devotion to her own people. She was dressed as she had been before giving her costume to Manya, and her eyes were ardent—with what sentiment, he did not know.

Then the noise of bellowing was heard in the access corridor. Blows sounded on the door, and insults.

Vialy made his decision. He beckoned to them to follow him and went into the next room. The trap-door leading down to the cellars was there. He lifted it up and the two women went through. He lowered the heavy panel again, but before letting it fall completely he pulled back the carpet that concealed it.

Armed with his electric lamp, he preceded his companions into the obscure maze of cellars, which no longer served to lodge much of anything since the disappearance of wine.

The young woman spoke: "They already know, up there, many of the things that happen among the Thousand."

Vialy evoked B 309, Old Broun's mistress. It was that fool Pierre who must have informed the slut. But how could she communicate with Paris?

"What are we doing?" Manya asked.

"I don't have any confidence in the idea of looking for a place that's truly safe and where I can be sure of not being found," Vialy decided. "Our surest means of staying alive is to lose ourselves in the rebel mass."

Manya shivered. "You think so?"

"Evidently. I don't want us to end up at the bottom of some hole with our throats cut. So pay attention! Dirty your face, Manya—we're going out."

They climbed a staircase and found themselves in a courtyard empty except for the sunlight, which showed them a corridor into which they hastened. Through a crumbling porch they appeared in a brightly-lit street. In a matter of seconds, lost in the mass, they became anonymous units: "numbers." They had taken ten steps when Manya, turning round to look for their rescuer and companion, found that she had disappeared.

The crowd oscillated, beat the walls, advanced and recoiled without any rhythm. Irritated bestial reflexes gave it a soul.

For a quarter of an hour, Vialy and his mistress strove to make progress through the resistant and elastic flood. Suddenly, howls burst out behind them. The mass possessing them flowered backwards, and then howled in its turn as a rumor circulated joyfully, transmitted by hundred thousand mouths.

"The factories have just blown up!"

Other news was being shouted:

"The Titanium stores are on fire."

"The underground workings have all been destroyed."

"Vialy is dead..."

An order was passed: "To the Tuileries! To the Tuileries!"

Then the crowd flowed down the Montmartrean slope. Enormous, as invasive as a deluge, it set forth. Gripped by the torrent, Vialy and Manya were obedient to it.

It was an astonishing migration. Filled by an immeasurable flood, every street vomited a human magma, which paused and changed direction at the intersections. At the entrances to narrow side streets it eddies, amid screams of cries for help. Gradually, however, the host plunged southwards, like an irresistible tidal wave, continuing its route amid hymns and multiple vociferations. Everywhere, gaping doorways testified to the popular madness. All the houses were abandoned. Several hundred thousand people were on the move, in fabulous disorder, devoid of weapons, in the midst of an immense racket compounded out of insults, prayers and obscenities.

Twenty paces ahead of Vialy a swaying and dancing placard was advancing, It bore his name and Manya's, with insults and the promise of their execution that evening. Vialy savored the irony of the advertisement, but wondered whether it might be a premonition...

Beside him, clinging to him, his mistress abandoned herself to the human tide. The sun was warming Paris heavily, stimulating the strong odor of all those feverish beings. Vialy watched the sky, dreading the appearance of aircraft carrying Necron bombs.

When the crowd reached the boulevards, Vialy hoped to be able to disengage himself from the tentacular grip of the dense and angry proletariat, and then, once free of the current, reach other streets where he would be the master of his actions and his route. He thought about getting back to the tunnel through which he had arrived at the Saint-Denis crossroads. All the tunnels had supposedly been destroyed, but it might be a false rumor, like that of his arrest, or its anticipation. Perhaps there was still a hope...

On the Boulevards, however, it proved impossible to quit the river of revolutionaries. Issuing from the side-streets, even denser currents became aggregated with the main one, bringing a further impulsion and concentrating the living matter, which entered the streets descending toward the Seine with the prodigious compactness of a block of metal.

Vialy wondered how the Thousand would resist if ten million people hurled themselves at their city with his kind of cohesion. Even the dead, incapable of falling, would keep advancing...

Manya, jostled and shoved, incessantly thrust away from her companion, strove with all her might not to lose him, just as he maintained himself obstinately close to her. The heat and the din were beginning to weaken the courageous woman. Distressed and rigid, she marched mechanically—and all that gave her features the mask of a true factory-worker.

Close to Vialy there was a tall, gaunt young woman clad in rags, who was repeating, with shrill laughter, all the popular phrases. Above all, she delighted herself with insults against Manya, who was marching, without her suspecting it, beside her. The placard was polarizing public opinion in that sector of the crowd.

The behavior of the men was, in any case, markedly different from that of the women. The latter, rendered hysterical by the noise, the heat and their own anger, were all laughing, with an overflow of absurd and lubricious comments. The men retained somber and haggard masks. They sensed that they were being carried away by a force superior to their will. They were obedient without joy to their desire for revolt. They knew that the Thousand would spread death over them as the sun spread light, and that hundreds of thousands of people would be dead this evening or the next day. Living bodies, whose blood as presently beating strongly in their arteries, would be reduced to chemistry and decomposition in a few hours' time. That did not diminish their revolutionary fury, but it did not lessen their anguish.

They arrived at the Tuileries. A long time before getting there, the crowd slowed down. Similar crowds were doubtless flowing from every direction. There was a prodigious aggregation. Finally, their progress stopped. Vialy, holding Manya against him supportively, as many men were doing to any women they encountered, succeeded in reaching a street corner. The mass eddied around the couple without being able to dislodge them from the wall. Soon, everything was compressed, under stress. A kind of silence fell. A colossal sound of respiration was audible. From far away, incomprehensible words arrived in fragments—orders or appeals.

An immense acclamation rose up toward the skies. Five hundred thousand people applauded, with hoarse cries of joy. A dull explosion was suddenly heard, coming from the horizon. There was a second's silence, and then a joyful tumult burst forth again in an apocalyptic racket. Then the words began again, distant and unclear, in vehement bursts.

An admonition went round:

"Look!... Look!..."

Vialy strove to see and to understand. In the west there was an enormous cloud of smoke, spreading like a tree, climbing high toward the zenith. The oil-wells were on fire.

Then the shouting resumed, followed by a word that penetrated every ear like a sworn engagement:

"Death!"

An assent resounded, powerful and affirmative, swelling like a storm, reverberating between the buildings, rolling everywhere: a promise, a desire, a hope, a regret, an expectation and a hope.

Then a detonation rang out, blurred by distance but still quite sharp. A silence followed, filed with a sort of sacred horror, and a desperate clamor went up, with a wrathful and tragic cry. A ferocious anger was born in facial expressions. The lustful women laughed wildly, with nervous movements that made their breasts tremble.

Vialy heard: "We'll die like him..."

"Yes!"

One man howled: "Liberty or death!"

The slogan was repeated; then a woman with a raucous voice declared: "Like him...he's killed himself for us, to prove that life is nothing. We must expect death, and want death, in order to triumph..."

So saying, she brought out a kind of long iron rod, sharpened, and, turning it on herself, in her ecstatic rage, plunged it into her throat. She still had the time and the strength to withdraw the weapon and plunge it in again, lower down, near the heart. Then, vomiting a red flood, she raised her arm to the heavens and collapsed, without falling, wedged as she was by the crowd.

All the women had crazed eyes. A second madwomen snatched the weapon from the one that had just sacrificed herself to the mystical Moloch of the revolt. With an aggravated fury, she pressed the bloody blade to her lips and abruptly plunged it into her own throat, in her turn.

Vialy said to himself: *At that pitch of fury, this crowd is irresistible.*

Two paces away from him was the entrance to a corridor. He wanted to get Manya away from the sanguinary fury that was propagating everywhere, as witnessed by howls of agony that were filing the air. He succeeded in reaching the portal, and went in. Manya followed him.

IV. A Refuge

Manya and Vialy found a dark stairway, and sat down on the steps silently. They wondered what they could do that might be of service to them. The howls of the immense anonymous troop still filled their heads.

"It's frightful," she said.

He nodded.

"What are we going to do?"

"I don't know yet, although I have a plan if the crowd disperses."

"I'm hungry," she said, then.

Vialy did not know what to reply. He liked to make quick decisions, though, and, getting to his feet abruptly, he went up the stairs. On the first floor, he went into three empty rooms where the mattresses of the numbered, made of mineral fiber, were arranged along the walls.

On the second floor, he saw a closed door, and opened it. He was confronted by an old man, seated, who looked at him bleakly.

"Brother, do you have anything to eat?" asked the Chief of Police.

The man raised a hand from which three fingers had been amputated to his face, and articulated, with difficulty: "It's over, then? We're the masters? They're all dead?"

"Yes," said Vialy.

"So much the better," said the old man. "You fought?"

"Yes," said Vialy. "I killed Vialy with my own hands."

Smile cracked the aged face. "You want to eat?"

"I want to."

"Look in that cupboard. You can have that pot. I was keeping it for the day we became masters. They took my three daughters out there."

"Which?" asked the other, curiously.

"The Affielle sisters."

Vialy knew them. Jeanne Affielle, Y 1302, was the mistress of Biall, of the Alpha aliment. She already had the pride of a daughter of the Thousand, for Biall had given her a child. That was one that it was vain to judge unfortunate. The constant misunderstanding of the generations struck the Chief of Police, who almost smiled.

He went downstairs. At the foot of the staircase he removed the lid of the pot that the old man had given him. It was honey, from before the Fault. The gritty transparent gilt of the contents was visible. He held it out to Manya along with a knife.

"Eat, my child."

She sniffed it anxiously. "What is it?"

"An aliment unknown to you, but precious. Orthys had some once. He's the only one. It's honey!"

She tasted the strange paste, hard and sticky at the same time, and then started swallowing the new product. When she had devoured two-thirds of it, she held out the pot to Vialy.

"Yours!"

He finished the strange meal. Then he took out the bottle of cordial, a few drops of which he had given to Manya after dressing her wound, and did the same again. He drank some himself.

"And now?"

"We wait..."

Through the corridor, they could see the crowd oscillating, moving back and forth, decomposing and reaggregating in a thousand ways. From time to time cries rang out, then laughter. The dilution of the immense host was detectable, though. Everyone was going home now. It was hot, and it was midday.

That slow moment continued. Distant explosions could still be heard, which the crowd accompanied by songs against the Thousand.

Finally, the fragmented crowd dissolved. Unappetizing as the alimentation of the proletariat was, since it was constituted by only four comestible compounds—fat, albuminoid, azoic substance and saccharotic substance—mealtimes nevertheless remained important. The cries were attenuated, the circulation became normal.

Vialy recovered hope. "By starving them out, we'll certainly master them."

People came back to the house, who grumbled on seeing the couple sitting in the steps. Vialy did not wish to provoke anyone, and left.

Slowly, calculating their movements to match those of the people whose path they crossed, the two lovers descended toward what had once been the Louvre museum.

After the Fault, indifferent to Art but desirous of conserving the collections, Tadée Broun had isolated the Louvre and forbidden anyone to enter it. In the ardent struggle engaged against the Necron and a host difficult to curb to discipline, the initial orders had been forgotten. In those days the Thousand were thinking of nothing but science, and it would have been a risk of being thrown out of the group for anyone to attribute and importance to the fine arts.

Art was then deemed to be an anti-civilizing force. The Louvre, scorned, like all the other museums, had therefore been abandoned. Almost everywhere else, the populace had gradually taken up residence, destroying everything, but the original order had retained a kind of obscure power here, without anyone knowing why, Doubtless, too, misery is only bearable in familiar and humble places.

Thus, that gilded palace, sumptuous and grandiose, survived, isolated and silent. Many things had been stolen from it in order to be burned, but that was all. Insubordinates had taken possession of it but Vialy had discovered the fact and had them hanged all around the colonnade. That had cast a further fearful discredit upon the monument. It was still employed for meetings between people desirous of avoiding the ears and eyes of strangers, but that was done secretly, without leaving traces, with the result that the Louvre was perfectly suited to the objective proposed by Vialy, who had chosen it for a refuge.

The two lovers got in easily enough. The Chief of Police knew all its secrets. He uncovered a secret door in the courtyard, though which no one had surely passed for thirty years. Although it was stuck, he succeeded in opening it sufficiently. Although there were numerous people around, no one saw Vialy and Manya disappear through the mysterious portal.

When the door closed behind them they found themselves under a somber vault. They finally located a stairway and slowly climbed the narrow spiral. They reached one of the museum's halls. Some canvases subsisted in their frames; others, stripped of their frames, had been thrown on the floor. The floor-tiles had been ripped up and the doors demolished. The windows had all been broken, and thick dust extended everywhere. The atmosphere of the place filled the soul with sadness and regret.

They found another small staircase, as steep as a ladder, which pierced a seemingly-compact wall. They were soon in a cluttered attic, which reeked of damp.

As of old, rolled-up paintings, frames and creates, statues and the debris of worm-eaten wood and canvas, filled the lumber-room. Not only had no one been there for thirty years, but perhaps since the days of the *ancien régime*.

"Make yourself at home Manya."

He ferreted around, found shabby fabrics, curtains and eroded tapestries. He dragged it all into a dark corner, near a round window, which he opened. He made a kind of bed.

"Let's lie down and await events: for those who come looking for us, or those who'll provoke us..."

"This bed's soft," she said, laughing.

"When one's just out of danger, everything is soft."

"I really thought that it was all over," she said, "when we had to obey that inflamed crowd. It gave the impression of an irresistible force. If it had wanted to throw everything into an immediate attack, we'd have had to go with it."

"Oh, we'd have been able to slip away."

"I don't know. I was also scared of falling, I was so tired. Once down, it would have been impossible to avoid being trampled by a hundred thousand wretches. Oh, what a hideous and frightful thing it is, the people delirious with range, who..."

"In three days, docile once again, they'll be working at their customary labor."

"You think so?"

"I'm certain of it. But take a good look at this Louvre palace. You have before your eyes a royal dwelling from before the Fault, such as it was for centuries."

She paraded an astonished gaze around. "Yes, but what are we going to do now, my love?"

He put out his hand and took his mistress by the wrist.

"With all the tunnels destroyed, with no food, we're not in a good position, but first of all, it was necessary to get away from the proletariat. That's done. Let's mark up that point."

"Is it possible to follow the railway tracks?" she murmured. "From the textile depot, we might reach intact tunnels."

"Impossible. It's all electrified."

"The passages connecting the well-shafts?

"We'd have to get out of Paris. That's a redoubtable problem."

"The deep tunnels?"

"I've been thinking about that since I found you, but how do we reach them? We could spend a fortnight searching Paris for a habitable shaft."

"Then I don't see..."

"Evidently. Our own defenses are keeping us out. We didn't foresee that some of ours, gone astray in Paris at the moment of the revolt, might need escape routes. We'll have to organize that."

"You're still hopeful?"

"I think so, Manya. There's no reason yet to despair. Perhaps it's necessary to envisage going outside, but the insubordinates, who are numerous and accustomed to an audacious way of life, could do us a nasty turn."

"I'll go to sleep, my love, while awaiting the big decision."

"Sleep, Manya."

When the young woman woke up, she realized that night had fallen. The nearby window was dark.

She leaned toward Vialy and called out to him.

He was suddenly on the defensive. He had been asleep too. No longer able to see one another, the two lovers reached out to touch one another.

"You're rested?"

"Yes, but I'm still hungry."

"Me too, but I don't know what we can do about it. How's your wound?"

"It itches."

He murmured, in an ironic tone: "I wonder what's happened this afternoon. When have they decided to attack? It's necessary not to let such enthusiasm go cold. It will disappear..."

"Speak more softly," Manya whispered. "This silent but creaky darkness seems suspicious to me. I didn't hear a thing when they captured me in the tunnels."

"You didn't smell them?"

"Yes, but I thought they'd gone."

"Child! They're cunning animals nowadays. But you haven't told me how it happened."

"A banal attack. I was at point 23. I was twenty meters from the turning where the retardation mechanisms are. I tripped over a pebble. At the same time there was a revolver shot behind me. Naturally, my lamp served as a target. I didn't see the fellow, doubtless lurking in ambush in some hole in the wall. I returned fire, then put out my light and ran to the telephone. As I ran I heard noises all around me. I bumped into people, shook them off, and reached the box anyway. I had time to say what was reported to you, and then tried to defend myself. Backed up against the wall, in the darkness, I shot at any sign of life. That lasted five minutes, and I must have killed a good few of them, but they jumped me—about twenty of them—and I went down.

"They didn't want to kill you there and then?"

"There was a debate. They brought me to the Permanence in order to put me on show, alive or dead, to encourage the crowd with the body of a daughter of the Thousand. They'd already killed a few of ours, but I was the first woman."

Vialy kissed Manya, emotionally.

"Just as long, now, as they don't drop a string of bombs on us. If the explosions we heard were made by the rebel workers in the factories there'll be reprisals in the morning on the crowd gathered as we've seen it. The Louvre might be blown up..."

"Are we leaving, then?"

"Of course. We can't stay here forever. On the other hand, my conviction is that B 309, Tadée's mistress, is responsible for all the indications given regarding the veritable state of our defenses."

"How did she obtain the information?"

"Pierre Broun."

"Ah!"

"For that very reason, I'm wondering, if I were able to communicate with our people, whether I ought to do so, because B 309 would doubtless be able to denounce me."

"But how can she communicate?"

"I don't know. You understand that these people, having long thought about it, have ended up finding a practicable means without our suspecting it. Signals night and day...it's even more dangerous if she can receive information and instructions, as well as giving details of our affairs."

"What will you do if you can get back?"

"I'll find Broun and demand that he hand over B 309. If he refuses I'll summon the Council and obtain full authority to seize the girl—but he'll knuckle under. Then again, there are the underground workshops, which I also fear. I've spoken out several times against this mania for luxury, which places twenty thousand numbered in our city, occupied in working on stupid things, pure luxuries, whose are both useless and dangerous. Not to mention that their existence causes ferment among the rest of the people."

"You're a pre-Fault puritan."

"I have responsibilities that oblige skepticism and suspicion. It seems easy to me to live our life, pleasant enough by comparison with the one that so many unfortunates lead, and that ought to be sufficient. Tadée says that the social rules before the Fault were harsher than ours. That's a joke: our power is crushing. It gives us, in addition to all material satisfactions, pleasures of pride that aren't to be scorned—but I don't think we ought to live a hundred paces from our most intelligent slaves—the ones who sculpt, paint, tailor garments, print and wave."

"Isn't it a source of joy for us to hang on to what people thirty years ago used to call the Torch of Civilization?"

Vialy laughed. "In the matter of civilization, the only worthwhile doctrine is of Hindu origin. It counsels moderating one's desires in order to moderate one's troubles. If we'd been able to live with the same simplicity as before, we'd have avoided many annoyances."

137

"Do you think so?"

"There's no doubt about it. This custom of going into Paris, whether to search for books, jewels, furniture or works of art, has put us in a nasty situation. The crowd often sees protective escorts coming to guard the Thousand who makes such raids, and that adds to the stored-up hatred.

Manya went back to his nagging torment. "Provided that B 309 doesn't end up finding out where the cables are laid, and where the klazzites are..."

"Provided, above all, that Broun doesn't let her see the klazzite detonators that Tadée keeps. With that, all of the subterranean mechanisms could be destroyed. It would take three years to restore everything..."

"But the most terrible thing would be for these people to find the deep klazzites."

"That, of course, would blow everything up."

"It would be necessary to leave Paris."

"I've thought about it..."

"And go to live somewhere else, alone."

"Would you like that?"

"With you."

V. The Great Threat

After a pause, Vialy said, eventually: "There's certainly an appreciable pleasure in being a hunted beast, because it gives every minute captured from time and the enemy a color, a charm and a powerful savor. Time breaks down into more numerous units and each unit contains more joy or pain than usual. It is, in consequence, life multiplied, but..."

"I noticed that this morning. My fear was mingled with a subtle joy."

"Yes. In sum, we were in the process of mocking those three hundred thousand individuals who were threatening us with posters ten meters away from the place where we stood, quite safe. I've only just understood something that I've read in pre-Fault adventure stories, which seemed to me to be so bizarre that I refused to believe it. They called it 'the criminal returning to the scene of his crime.' It appears that the policed caught people by the simple method of keeping watch on the place where a crime had been committed. In truth, it's a human impulse superior to caution. It's probable, too, that it's to put more bitterness and sweetness into his sentiment at the same time that a criminal might act in that way. That proves once again that human instinct is more disinterested than it seems, for it there's a gratuitous action, it's surely that only."

"Nonsense! It's a human sentiment."

"I don't know."

"Obviously. It's the action of someone straying from his route when he's urgently awaited."

"Oh. I think that's rather feminine."

Manya laughed. "I like chatting like this, and perhaps the sentiment of the uselessness of all these philosophies helps to give them a more delicate charm and grace. But I'd like to do something. Aren't we too dormant now? Do you really think that we can hope for some saving contingency in this attic in the Louvre?"

"I set out to search for you, Manya, absolutely at hazard, without a plan. I succeeded in liberating you. I'm full aware that if the crowd knew for sure, even once the revolt has been suppressed, that Vialy and his mistress were in Paris, we'd be hunted down mercilessly—and that contingency is still to be feared. But without subtly calculated intentions, for the moment, I'm simply going to allow night to fall."

"Which is as affirmative as a decree issued by the Council of Order. Let's get out of here. I'm bored..."

The couple got up and silently went to the exit from the loft. They went down the wooden staircase quietly, and eventually found themselves in the Museum—but it was difficult to navigate by night. Vialy went astray, and when they reached the ground floor, they were not in the vaulted gallery that they had taken in the morning.

"I no longer know where we're going."

"Bah! One ought to be able to get out of a palace of this size by any of a thousand doors."

On reflection, Vialy decided that they ought to be near a small courtyard. He was not mistaken, but when they started across it they were gripped by amazement. A dense crowd emerged into it at that very movement. In a matter of seconds they were engulfed by the crowd, too abundant for the narrowness of the passages. They tried to cut through it at an angle, but someone whose path they crossed, doubtless thinking that they were looking for an amorous corner, called out to them: "Quickly! Quickly! You don't have time. Come with us!"

They understood that it was necessary, as it had been in the morning in the streets, to follow the hasty company. Clinging to one another in order not to be separated in the dark, they joined the talkative procession.

It led them into a vast vaulted hall, as sinister as a crypt. A lamp suspended in the middle cast a vague light over the distant walls. About two hundred people were assembled there. They slotted themselves in here and there. Under the lamp there was a table. After eddies, scraps of conversation, displacements and searches for friends, everyone eventually settled down and became still.

The two fugitives isolated themselves in a corner. In any case, no one took any notice of them.

A quarter of an hour went by.

Finally, a heavy-set man climbed on to the table and said: "Brothers, you're about to hear the living Messiah. Our dear Diavide will tell us what our duties will be tomorrow. He will reveal to you the decisions made to give us the Victory against the Thousand that will ensure our eternal happiness.

Everyone applauded. Cries rang out, masculine appeals and feminine laughter. An increasing nervousness gripped the expectant and attentive crowd.

"Silence!" said the man. "This meeting is serious. Understand the importance of what you're about to hear; that's why we're holding this meeting. We believe that ten members of the Thousand were in Paris. We've executed six, but one is as dangerous as a hundred. They might be anywhere—except here. Among those we've killed, the famous Vialy and his mistress Manya count for a great deal, fortunately.

A voice said: "Why haven't their bodies been displayed, as was promised?"

The man replied, casually: "We're having them stuffed, and we'll put them at the head when we mount the attack tomorrow."

There was laughter.

A man leaned toward Manya and said, with a expression of savage joy: "It's tomorrow!"

The stout orator continued: "You know that under Paris, to this day, there was a confusion of underground passages sloping up and down, shafts and tunnels mingled and superimposed, with telephones everywhere and rolling carpets. That was how Vialy held us, how he was about to know everything, thanks to his countless spies. Now, it's been destroyed—destroyed by us, and by them."

At that moment a thin form cut through the crowd, emerging from who knew where. She approached the table. The big man immediately got down. The scene did not lack majesty: a subterranean hall, scarcely illuminated, in the center of which, beneath a sparse yellow light, a skeletal man hoisted himself up on to the table.

Falling from above, the light outlined the harsh contours of an ingrate face. The cheekbones lifted up the skin of the face. The orbits gave the impression of two black holes and the unknown. With his hands in his pockets, the man seemed to scan the little crowd proudly.

"Brothers," he said, "I know who you all are. I'm not eloquent. I shall only say the words that ought to be actions for us."

"Revolutionary words," said someone—but the Messiah neither approved nor disapproved. His slow voice continued.

"Our people, my Brothers, are exasperated. They've taken their time, but it has run out; their patience is exhausted."

A woman near Vialy shouted, hoarsely: "Don't reproach them. They were working..."

"They're finally irritated. They're on their feet. The hour has come to die or to vanquish..."

"Vanquish or die!" articulated a man close to Diavide.

"I said die or vanquish," replied the Messiah, in a harsh voice.

A silence followed. Vialy was listening with a passionate curiosity. He did not understand the meaning of the harangue as yet.

The other resumed: "To die or vanquish, you hear? The time for debating and hoping is over. It's necessary to choose between death and victory. But victory is, from now on, the only means of avoiding death."

A frisson ran through the audience, tense and curious. "We'll be victorious," a woman articulated.

Diavide continued: "Brothers, every minute that passes bring us closer, inflexibly, to the moment when the choice will be before us all, for if we cannot vanquish tomorrow, I shall sacrifice humankind."

In the stupor that followed that strange affirmation, a long ripple ran through the audience.

"Are you ready, Brothers?" the voice went on.

Vialy sensed in those words an effort to bind together all the strength of that crowd, to magnetize it and launch it on a redoubtable path. And it was working, for a kind of galvanic current passed through the hall. Gestures could be seen everywhere that participated in the threat and the prayer.

A tumult burst forth.

"We're ready!

"Good, my Brothers. We have, as you know, revolted ten, twenty, thirty times without success. Lack of courage, absence of faith, weakness of will, bodily hesitation. Seventeen times I've come back from outside, where I live, to urge you to revolt. Sixteen times, I've found only hesitation and weakness.

"For fourteen years I have been traveling the landscapes where humans no longer go, and of which the insatiable cohort of the Thousand has deprived you, keeping you yoked to their factories for thirty years..."

He stopped, gripped by a visible emotion.

"Brothers, thanks to them, you're nothing. You're domestic animals, and less: pieces of machinery, Out there, however, beyond the pitiless circle that retains you, there's an immense and fertile land: the divine earth; the place where everything flourishes, everything germinates, where life can expand indefinitely, and where you only have to take in order to possess...

"Brothers, the world belongs to you. I offer it to you. Take it..."

A fury of applause burst forth like a fanfare.

The other continued: "Brothers, the world is there. Do you want it? It's necessary not to think any longer about taking it gently, as before the Fault. It's necessary to crush the Thousand who have forbidden you to approach it. It's necessary to destroy their organization, whose power is immense. It's necessary to raze their city of pride and debauchery, and not to leave a single stone atop another. Do you understand?"

"What about the Necron?" said a voice.

"Shut up! The Necron disappeared more than ten years ago. There's no longer any need to fabricate their Titanium and extract their Geocoronium—work that occupies sixteen hundred thousand of our brethren. Necron has become harmless. And if the Thousand still seem to be struggling against it, that's because they want to hold you in servitude. A few valleys remain where the Necron is stagnating. I've lost a hundred and twelve friends there, insubordinates like me, but on level ground and on the slopes, none remains.

"Brothers, the Thousand have stolen all the joy from your lives. They've stolen the right to be human. They must disappear, in order that free humankind can finally spread out joyfully.

"Brothers, the sovereignty of those masters over your lives, your arms and your women is in its death-throes. Tomorrow, it will be dead. Tomorrow, the Thousand will have expiated their crimes. If you're victorious, you'll rule the world. If not, I shall destroy you along with your enemies, whose disappearance I have sworn.

"If you're sure that they'll disappear, is that because you're certain of our victory?"

Silence fell. All faces turned toward the cold face of the Messiah, who seemed to be meditating somberly. His bald head was shiny. His angular shoulders and rigid immobility made him resemble some kind of scarecrow.

Finally, he pronounced the words of which his previous remarks had allowed the deduction.

"Brothers, we shall vanquish or die, for I know the place where their famous reserve of klazzite is stored. You have heard tell of the power of that explosive. They have made enough of it to destroy all Paris and the factories, for fifteen kilometers around. I've had a shaft dug that extends all the way to that depository. I have three cartridges of klazzite no. 2, without which klazzite, properly speaking, can't be detonated. You can see that

I'm the sovereign master of this world. Tomorrow, I shall press the electric switch that will ignite the K-2 and several thousand tons of klazzite will explode, blowing up everything, just as the Fault caused the city of San Francisco to disappear. Subsequently, twelve millions tubes of condensed Necron will spread their gas over the ruins. If we're vanquished, if our assault doesn't lead us into the city of the Thousand, it will be the end of the world—of this world of misery and crimes—which I have decreed, as a Creator."

VI. By Night

A frisson ran through the audience at those terrible words. It was, therefore, necessary to be victorious! Victory was the sole outcome to the combat that had been engaged, for, when it is a matter of dying, it matters little whether it is by a friendly or a hostile hand...

Vialy wiped cold sweat from his brow,

The man had paused momentarily. In a level voice, he continued: "Brothers, I have said what had to be said. The word here is the act. The two hundred and sixty-seven meter shaft dug by our brother Adamson, whom I see here, has brought us to the point at which we are sovereign masters of human destiny. When our enemies destroyed the underground workings with a remarkable promptitude this morning, they almost caught me in the vertical tunnel, but their appeals to Vialy, whom they believed to be still wandering in that subterranean maze, warned me. I was able to get out. Now the shaft has been repaired and the wires checked. Everything is ready.

"It is necessary to die or to vanquish..."

"We'll vanquish!" cried a hundred excited throats. "We'll vanquish. We'll be alive, we'll have..."

"Peace!" proffered the other, impatiently. "You'll vanquish if you understand that your duty is to attack the Thousand without any concern for dying. Death is everywhere. The only chance of living is if I am sleeping in Tadée Broun's house tomorrow..."

Pride gripped him. "For I am your chief. Without me, what would you be? I am the one who has discovered everything, who has organized and regulated everything. A vile prostitute of our race, B 309, has given us useful information, but I want to prove to you that no one can be redeemed who has given herself to the Thousand. Although her aid has served us, my implacable justice can make no compromise. Whoever has belonged to that abject and filthy race will be sacrificed with them. Know this: if we are victorious there will be no pity for B 309. And let that serve as an example, to prove that Diavide's justice is above gratitude, in the bosom of the most perfect equity!"

"What a cretin!" Vialy whispered in Manya's ear.

"What a brute!" she replied.

But Diavide continued: "I have had weapons and explosives manufactured. Against the aircraft carrying Necron bombs I have special rifles. I have created an entire arsenal, certainly insufficient on its own against the Thousand's defenses, but we have the Numbers that will weigh more heavily in the balance than anything else. It is necessary to reach the defensive wall with the parcels of explosives. The wall breached, you will be able to spread out in their abode, and...

"You know everything, my Brothers; sustain courage and depart with the certainty that inspires determination. Our slavery is over. Go and galvanize the crowd; go to group them and mass them. The final assault is in the morning. My men will set off at the head. The orders will be given to you at the Permanence, to which everyone must go when they leave here, in an orderly fashion."

An approving joy spread. Everyone in the fascinated society swore to die fearlessly.

"Go on then! Let there no longer be any desire in your will, no other hope in your hearts! At ten o'clock in the morning we shall be on the glacis. At four o'clock, if we are not victorious, it will be defeat. Then I shall press the switch that commands the klazzites.

"Die or vanquish! It's ten o'clock; in twelve hours, the battle will begin. In eighteen hours, victory must be ours, or else..."

He fell silent and got down from the table. A kind of desperate devotion was radiated toward him by the entire audience. For a quarter of an hour, the hall was like a company of epileptics. The women, above all, were ardent. Their voices, shrill or sonorous, crystalline or hoarse, mingled violently. A fear also occupied their souls, which no one admitted.

Die or vanquish! Die or vanquish! The phrase seemed to take on a new meaning in their mouths. Near to Manya, a couple started appealing to death. Then the woman took off her garment and offered herself, naked, with shrill cries. Dementia spread. The hollow eyes were no longer content with anything but horror and madness. A flood of incomprehensible words were heard. Vialy perceived squeals and croaks coming from the table where the Messiah had spoken. He was able to see an erotic fury agitating feverish bodies over there. At regular intervals, a woman with a harmonious and powerful voice cried, in a wild tone: "Die!... Die!...."

Meanwhile, men left the hall. Vialy and Manya allowed themselves to be guided by their companions of hazard. Soon, they were in the Place du Carrousel. They directed their prudent footsteps toward the Seine, among other individuals who spaced themselves out. Eventually, they were alone.

The sky was opaque. From time to time, a vague gleam filtered from a house bordering the river, which was splashing quietly as it flowed.

Vialy drew Manya along. "Quickly!" he said. "Every minute counts now/"

They reached what had once been a garden behind Notre-Dame. It was still a garden, doubtless wilder than it had been before the Fault, all trace of order having disappeared.

They both sat down on a stone supported by two others, which must once have been a bench. In those days, mothers had embroidered slippers here for a husband employed in some demanding administration, while children played innocently in front of them.

Vialy took Manya by the torso and said, gravely: "I'm going to let you choose our destiny, my darling."

""Chose it yourself!" she whispered.

"No. Manya, do you want to live?"

She made no reply.

"Do you want to live? That's all that I can say to you clearly, and it's necessary. For me, there's no doubt about it. That man was telling the truth just now. He can blow everything up. Will he tremble at the last moment? It would be imprudent to rely on that doubt. What is certain is that tomorrow, at four o'clock, if he doesn't buckle—and he's as hard as he's full of pride—the rage of his defeat will push him to carry out the great act of destruction.

"So, Manya, I say to you: do you want to live? If you want to die, let's go back to the Louvre and our quiet loft. We'll wait for the cataclysm. In that case, we'll participate in the great sacrifice. If you prefer to live, it's necessary to act otherwise..."

"To do what?" asked Manya, nervously.

Vialy stroked his mistress' body with his palms.

"It's necessary to leave Paris and head eastwards, in a straight line, without stopping, with an inflexible courage, until four o'clock tomorrow. We now have less than eighteen hours, but it might permit us to reach a protected zone. That's at the limit, for it will be necessary for us to cover about forty kilometers. It will be a rude march for you, but I'll help you."

"What will we do then?"

He laughed, silently.

"We'll live."

"But how?"

"Have you read that extraordinary English romance from the olden days about a man named Robinson Crusoe? We'll recommence his life."

"Go on!" said Manya. "But without food, we won't be able..."

"Of course, but I'm going to rob any house that appears that it might contain hidden food supplies. If necessary, I'll rob two, or ten..."

"You believe that we can get out of Paris?"

"Yes. They'll have been able to discover the electrified networks and cut them."

They set forth along the dark and solitary quay. In the distance, to the north, they heard a muffled sound of marching and the massive rumor of a crowd.

"Come on...come on..."

"Where shall we find something to eat?"

"I don't know. Revolver in hand, I'll go into one of the houses that I already know to have contained or created insubordinates."

They arrived close to what had been the Gare de Lyon, with its ancient outbuildings and warehouses situated on the bank of the river. Vialy pointed at an isolated house.

"Sit down here. You need to conserve your strength. Wait for me."

He went at a rapid pace to the invisible door. Manya heard the lock break; then silence fell.

Vialy reappeared ten minutes later. Manya's heart was already accelerating. He came to his mistress promptly.

"It's done. Magnificent haul. They had alcohol, and even eggs. I wasn't mistaken—it's an important house, among the numbered. Here's a glass; I brought a few utensils. Break the eggs into it and drink.

She obeyed silently.

"Drink a little of this liquor, which would have done honor to Tadée."

He chewed something, drank in his turn, and said, laughing: "This glass is the first element of our future Crusoe household. I have more provisions, a sackful. We're going a long way. I even have cloth from before the Fault.

"What did you do to them?"

He hesitated. "I had to kill them..."

Now they were moving at a brisker pace. Vialy was carrying an enormous package slung over his shoulder, attached with cords.

"As we get further away from the center the risk of attracting attention increases. Take this cutlass and keep it open. In case of attack, or even contact with other people, strike without reflection. There's no longer anyone else in the world by two people: you and me. The rest are already dead flesh."

After a brief pause he went on: "The best route to get as far as the defensive zone is to use one of the tracks of the ancient railways. There ought not to be anyone—or hardly anyone—in the miserable hovels alongside them, the lairs of thieves and insubordinates, for those crows must be hoping that the revolt will offer them a feast. There's an enormous area without precise routes, where we can travel safely, save for the risk of an attack—but we're armed. Anywhere else, it would be necessary to fear the guards that Diavide must have posted at the confines, to maintain his people under his law."

They went into the conglomerate of shelters that had been edified a hundred times over and burned a hundred times over, or destroyed by Necron bombs. A new silence reigned over the area. They divined the presence of hidden lives. Here and there, light filtered through the doorways of wretched huts. That helped them to distinguish the roads of that Court of Miracles. Carriages from before the Fault, some utilized or demolished and reconstructed, the conical huts of charcoal-burners, shaky and fragile dwellings succeeded one another without any order or any care for preservation. Sometimes they accumulated in an odious reek of misery and putrescence, sometimes they went through clearings, squares or something akin to crossroads.

Shadows circulated, scarce and mute. Matching strides, Manny and Vialy went on, ears pricked. It was obvious that the cloaca would soon be emptied of almost all its inhabitants, departed in tow with the masses in revolt. Those who were left were mostly women and children, along with old men—who were rare, because the chemical aliments no longer permitted many people to surpass the age of sixty.

Voices, as they passed by, denounced the presence of living beings: growls of anger; insults shouted in a tenebrous argot; voluptuous cries of women taken, or perhaps being murdered...

VII. Flight

As the two fugitives moved alongside a wall of some sort, doubtless ancient, they heard light footfalls following them.

Vialy deduced that their rapid passage through this warren, where haste was unknown, had attracted the attention of the inhabitants. At a dip in the ground he halted and took cover, with Manya by his side. Sensing danger and the futility of words, they remained silent.

The sounds of the pursuit had died away. There were whispers; then comings and goings recommenced. A moment later, the sound of footsteps came closer, moving back and forth, ad as the sky brightened they saw three shadows.

A voice asked softly: "You have the knife?"

"There are two. You take the one at the rear; I'll take the other."

"Right!"

"Where have they gone?"

"They heard us and must have turned aside."

At that moment, some distanced away, the sounds of a dispute erupted. A woman howled indistinct words. The three prowlers ran in that direction.

Vialy drew Manya away. "Quickly!"

They continued their route. Determined to maintain the direction of his march, Vialy, who had a luminous compass, was carefully not to deviate from it. Mute and tense, they marched, their senses attentive, ready to kill anything that they found in their path. But the alarm was not renewed. Soon, they were treading on a more odorous ground, in which one might have thought that a dull heat was slumbering. The atmosphere there seemed compact. There had once been countless huts there, but beneath a sky that was now bright with stars, and into which the moon was about to rise, they could see that they were all broken and collapsed.

"This is the area of the big epidemics. The ten plagues that devastated Paris all emerged from this terrain. We've never wanted to investigate this filthy zone. I've had it drowned with disinfectant gases six times, but in vain. We ought to be safe here..."

The response to Vialy's words was sudden: two shadows sprang forth before them with vertiginous decision. The Chief of Police sidestepped and switched on his electric lamp so as not to miss his adversaries. He fired. Two men fell to the ground with despairing croaks.

"Well, it's not as safe as I thought, this pestiferous region. A society of ten million people obviously furnishes an abundant and dangerous scum. Not that those bandits wouldn't have attacked anyone; they didn't suspect us of being anything other than wretched inhabitants of this miry region—which is to say that their misery must be profound."

They kept marching. A leaden odor was prevalent. The silence was only troubled, apart from the footfalls of the two fugitives, by the noises of fleeing animals.

"To live here! Into what abysm of debasement is it necessary to have fallen?"

"Humans are prodigious animals. Nothing disgusts them."

"What astonishes me even more," Vialy continued, wanting to cheer up the trek, "in our passage through this inhospitable region, is that we seem to be alone in fleeing the imminent slaughter. As you can see, no one appears to fear, not only the revolt, but even its consequences: the Thousand's reprisals and other dangers. I'd have expected to have companions. It would doubtless have been necessary to fight them, but, after all, is doesn't do honor to the foresight of these people. Out of ten millions, there can't be that many fanatics…the rest are tremulous…"

In the meantime, the terrain became bare, and descended along a gentle slope.

"We're coming out of the accursed region. There are houses over there. I know this part of our trajectory. Rails from before the Fault still exist here. Pay attention! If Diavide has posted guards anywhere, they'll be here."

The night was brightening. To the north, a luminous glow appeared on the horizon.

"The moon! We're lucky to have got so close to open country before it became visible. We need to hurry, for in a quarter of an hour, if people are on watch, they'll see us passing by."

Suddenly, Manya drew his attention to a group of motionless men in the distance, outlined by the lunar halo.

Vialy stopped. "That's the surveillance. There are twenty or thereabouts. There are certainly posts set up at intervals. We need to pass between two of them. Let's veer south-eastwards.

They went from cover to cover, from a building to a section of wall, from a hidden corner to another in retreat. They could now hear noisy chatter.

Finally, they got past the group, just at the moment when, to the south, without their being to identify the precise place, they heard voices clearly.

"We've reached the electrified fence. Halt!"

Vialy searched the ground, and waited for a minute.

"Go on!"

They moved forward, supple and prudent. Behind then, now, numerous voices rose into the transparent air.

"The network!"

He had the plans in his mind and recognized the two concrete posts marking the hundred meters of the defended zone.

"To the right of the marker and straight ahead."

Suddenly, he stopped again. In front of them, twenty paces away, another man was fleeing. Seemingly terrified, he was heading straight for the guard-post.

"The imbecile, He'll be captured and he'll draw attention to us."

They started running. The moon was about to appear, and it was already possible to see a long way.

Facile, bare and almost denuded of grass, the plain extended.

"Ah! We're lucky! There's a ridge that will hide us from view. Hurry!"

They ran faster. The terrible electric network was underfoot.

The other fugitive they had seen heard them, and, trying to get away from them, veered northwards. He was almost heading back toward Paris. They could hear him running. Then his error became apparent to him and he resumed the correct route—but it was too late. Cries of pursuit were heard. They were bound to catch up with the unfortunate.

A cry of agony filled the extent.

A slender lunar segment was already over the horizon.

"I can see a curtain of trees, Manya. Run!"

Finally, they reached a kind of trench and descended into it. When they came up on the other side, they had entered a new environment. A thousand vegetables mingled their vital scents there.

"This time, we're out of range of the Messiah's guard-posts. Now it's necessary for us to pass at an equal distance between the Gamma and Delta aliment factories. I'm sure of not going astray. Is anyone still working there? I don't know."

Half an hour later they scented the strong odors of the alimentary chemicals.

"We're almost at home."

Suddenly, however, they heard a clamor of hatred emerging from a monstrous and obscure palace crouching five hundred meters from a bend in the river.

"They're in revolt too."

The cries extended toward the north-west, and a dull bellicose rumor was coming from the distant workshops.

"We'll be in trouble if the defenses let gangs of brigands spread out all around Paris."

"Do you think they'll hold?"

"I'm sure of it. It's inevitable execution for all those who try to cross the excavated zone that forms a ditch round all these factories, for the asphyxiating gases there are renewed every hour."

They continued marching for a long time.

"We're out of the exploited zone now. The oil-wells are a kilometer beneath us, but there are no outlets this far from Paris, so we have nothing to fear. That slight glow you can see to the south must be the explosives factory. That one won't revolt. They never come out of it.

"Now we need all our courage. It's after one o'clock in the morning. Everything we've left behind us will blow up and be drowned thereafter under tons of asphyxiating gases. It's necessary to flee, recklessly. Forty kilometers from here the shock will still be powerful, but not to the extent of disturbing the subsoil, I think. The Necron won't get that far either, without being diluted in the atmosphere. Still, it's necessary to cross that distance!" They went on, with long, measured strides, listening to the quivering night.

Above the horizon, a disk the color of a raw wound cast a bloody radiation over everything.

They were walking along what had been a road thirty years before. The ground, rugged now and laden with broken flints, did not allow much vegetation to grow, except for a light felt that made walking easier.

Manya, to the right and slightly behind Vialy, surrendered to the hypnosis of being drawn along. Around them, a kind of disciplined forest had invaded the terrain. Giant nettles were recognizable by their aggressive vehemence, for the return of the atmosphere to normal conditions had not inhibited the formidable growth of the vesicant plants.

"Do you think there are many insubordinates out here?" Manya asked.

"Surely not. As our factories are much more spaced out here than elsewhere, I have it swept by Necron bombs once a month—with the result that I have, in sum, prepared our flight with that procedure."

"In total, how many insubordinates do you think there are outside Paris."

"There's no way to guess. I believe that about ten thousand have left since the great organization of seventeen years ago. Of that number, patrols have found about a thousand alive and five thousand killed by my bombs or the Necron. About eighty per cent of the rest have probably died from hunger and privation, or been killed in fights with their fellows. That leaves seven or eight hundred who might have lived—but you heard Diavide talking about Necron stagnating in the valleys. We didn't know anything about that. That revelation permits the belief that another two-thirds of the remnant might have succumbed, simply because age-old necessity always leads lone men to go down toward streams in order to catch fish. A hundred or so might have survived, half of whom are now in Paris, having returned by some unknown means to foment the revolt. The remainder might constitute fifty insubordinates, almost all of whom, I suspect have gone a long way from Paris."

"Do you believe that they can multiply?"

"They lack women. Insubordinate women only make up about three per cent of the total number. Five or six might remain in the entire country. Only the hardiest—which is to say, the old ines with masculine characters—can have survived, and they're sterile.

"At present, to tell the truth, there might not be any men or women worthy of the name in the whole of France, except for a domain of animalized troglodytes living around Paris."

The moon was rising slowly. Around the silvery pink disk the sky was a velvety fluid gray. Strict silence reigned. The route extended incessantly before Manya and Vialy, who plunged on indefatigably toward the horizon.

For a while, the road had been encased by high banks. Deformed by the rain but reconstituted by the tenacity of the rootlets, it offered a velvety, mute and elastic surface to the feet.

They marched without pause, sometimes under trees and sometimes in a plain beneath the moonlight. One might have thought that the world had never been so fortunate. A soft silence weighed upon everything; the atmosphere was mild and caressant.

The silent landscape possessed a strange charm full of tenderness. The perfumed animation of the road filed Manya and Vialy with a confused sentiment of liberation and felicity.

"To think that before the Fault there was a violent and feverish life here! Thirty years ago, thousands of vehicles passed along this road every day. Amid the powerful vegetation to the right and the left of us, hundreds of houses were hidden in which humans lived and loved. They must have thought their civilization immortal and were proud of it, believing themselves to be superior to everything that the past had previously abolished. And then..."

"Yes! Paris is as far away today as Nineveh."

"And tomorrow, it will be as far away as the Ark of the Deluge."

"I'd like to visit one of the dwellings that subsist around us," said Manya.

"When we're sufficiently far away from the imminent disaster, Manya, we'll find as many as there are here, and you'll admire them at your ease. This evening, the earth thirty meters beneath our feet, where we're marching now, will be in the air, and the ground on which we're treading will have been replaced...

"But don't think that the dwellings still standing that we'll encounter will retain anything of their ancient beauty. It required four years after the Fault to organize our domination. During that interval, hordes of ferocious destroyers like those you heard applauding Diavide reigned everywhere. Abject brutes, they invariably destroyed everything that could not be of use to them, in order that it could not be of use to anyone.

"It's a popular instinct that is unleashed in great crises: the need to leave nothing that might be useful or pleasant to someone else. That fury lasted for years, and you'll see that human beings more bestial than beasts have devastated everything everywhere, that testified to the comfort, the grace and the tranquil gaiety of old.

"It's necessary to understand that thirty million people have passed over these roads. We sometimes had to destroy them, like rats. I remember one valley near here, further to the south, where three hundred thousand of those wretches died."

"You had them..."

"We had them surrounded by an insurmountable wall of toxic gases. What do you expect? They were partisans of a new religion which they called Adamevism. To please them, it was necessary for only a single couple to live, in order to recommence the creation with a clean slate."

"What happened?"

"They cut one another's throats and drank the blood of the dead. But the horror of that religion, most of all, was the rapidity of its growth. Everything that is bloody fascinates human beings. Adamevism snowballed. It threatened to drown us. They had already murdered two hundred thousand of their companions of both sexes; in their eyes, the selection of the new Adam and his Eve was gradually being made. You wouldn't believe the delirious joy with which women and men aggregated in that madness, in the hope of being the future creators of a new humanity. Each of them believed themselves to be the male or female of the unique couple. We destroyed that, pitilessly."

"What horror! But how do people dare to talk about the sweetness of the life that prevailed before the Fault, with things like what you've just told me?"

"Manya, the charm of the life before the Fault existed—but that was primarily because humans had got into the habit of a certain domination of their most ignoble instincts. And that, as well as the old habitude of familiar cares, was what gave birth to that apparently smiling and esthetic, but superficial civilization, which crumbled so rapidly..."

"All of it was nothing, in sum, but appearance? Which is to say, hypocrisy..."

"Hypocrisy, Manya, is the whole of civilization."

VIII. The Cigarette

"How much ground have we covered, my love?"

"Three hours...ten kilometers, undoubtedly, since the pestilential ground. But I think it would be a good idea to have a rest before dawn. We're following a stream at present. There's the low wall that will serve us as an armchair and table. Oh, Manya, if I dared to make love to you here...!"

They sat down together. Vialy unwrapped the heavy package he was carrying and they ate slowly, without speaking. Around them, the night was tremulous. The leaves were rustling delicately, making a sound like silk drawn over a parquet floor.

They dreamed about the primitive times before civilization, when uneducated humans lived in the forest and established their lairs there. An emotion welled up in them in response to the magical and redoubtable penumbra that flourished in the moonlight.

"I'll go fill this water-bottle with water from the stream," said the man. "I don't think it's expedient only to drink alcohol."

He went to the luminescent flow that was unrolling like a scarf in the moonlight. Suddenly, he heard a cry of fear behind him.

"Help!"

Leaping up the slope with one bound, he ran toward the walk where he had left Manya.

Only the heavy packet was there, beside the stones. The young woman had disappeared.

A second cry rang out, coming from the curtain of vegetation that bordered the wall. With his illuminated lamp in one hand and the pistol in the other, Vialy launched himself forward. With an irresistible violence he cut through the mattress of plants, as dense as a tropical forest. Finally, between two trees, the cone of light that preceded him picked out a kind of human form.

Vialy fired.

"Manya!"

"Here!"

She got up, smiling, still pale with emotion but self-controlled.

"What is it?"

"An ape, I think."

"Not injured?"

"No, nothing at all."

They leaned over the agonized form that was writhing at their feet.

"You've made a mess of it."

The bullet had, in fact, smashed the upper part of the face. Nothing remained intact but a hairy and gaping jaw.

"Truly, yes, one might think it an ape."

The creature was naked and as hairy as a wild beast. Vialy looked at it, and turned it over.

"Bizarre! Has the Necron assisted in the creation of monsters? While we were scheming with our chemistry, was nature transforming its materials? That would be amusing, but perhaps dangerous. Fundamentally, the geological epochs must resemble the affair of the Fault. The atmosphere changed under some influence, and thousands of species disappeared, while others prospered magnificently. Perhaps the elephant is an ancient insect the size of an ant, and the ant an animal that was the size of a twelve-story house ten million years ago."

"You're letting your mind wander..."

"Yes. Let's get moving. Besides which, there might be a nest of these bestial and victorious pithecines in the vicinity. The best thing to do is to get out of here—and the klazzite won't wait. All the same, it would be interesting to see the den of this little orangutan with the aquiline nose and the waist."

"Do you think there'll be many monsters around us henceforth?"

"I don't care, Manya. We'll master them. They're perhaps only monsters in the process of formation. Evolution doesn't move quickly. Perhaps, in fifty thousand years, there'll be original species here, humans with trunks, flying wolves or tigers making honey. The one we've just seen might be an heir presumptive, the *Homo sapiens* of tomorrow. It's doubtless immune to the atmospheric poisons that destroyed us, and won't take more than three hundred thousand years to reinvent the rubble-free digger or Sigliaresse's amour...

"In those days, the last of today's humans, living in some remote and unknown land, will be curiosities like the okapi. Take note that in the modification of vital exchanges by too much or insufficient oxygen, bion or crypton,[11] a protoplasmic form must be generated more plastic and more active than others, which leads is bearer to obtain and advantage over the other animals of the

---

[11] The words "bion" and "crypton" do exist in French, albeit esoterically, the former referring to a vegetative shoot and the latter as an alternative spelling of the krypton, but the author has already reinvented the former term with an idiosyncratic meaning, and presumably intends the other in the same way. The catastrophist theory of evolution suggested here is odd, but has parallels in some other French scientific romances, most notably Han Ryner's *Les Surhommes* (1929; tr. as *The Superhumans*, Black Coat Press, ISBN 978-1-935558-77-4.)

globe. If the Fault has given that transformation an effective degree for the nettle, who knows whether the intelligent being of tomorrow, the one that will rediscover Landève's chemistry, might not be the short-eared owl or the armadillo?

"That ape must have been following us for some time, and with what human precautions! Then it waited for me to go away in order to jump on you from above. All that's almost as strong as Leibnitz's Monadology..."[12]

They were still marching. The day dawned. First there was a bloody strip that one might have thought a bandage of the wound of the sun. The redness erupted all the way to the zenith, and the star finally appeared. It progressed, rotating, above the trees. Bright patches formed and disintegrated incessantly on its red risk, where they were bordered with pale gold.

"What a beautiful thing dawn is!

"Here, Manya, certainly. Nature moves social human beings slightly and rarely. It only touches the individual in the most secret and anarchic parts of the self. Then it exalts sentimental richness.

"Remember that it truly formed humanity, at the beginning of time, with sensations of color, sadness, joy

---

[12] *La Monadologie* (1714; tr. as *Monadology*) is a French version—the first one to be published—of a short text by Gottfried Leibnitz containing a kind of concise digest of his ultimate metaphysical philosophy. The notion of primal "monads"—conceived and modeled in opposition to the Cartesian dualism that divided mind and matter—is sufficiently vague and murky to be extrapolated as the basis of a metamorphic theory of evolution. Vialy's awareness of it, given the circumstances of his society, is almost as surprising as his failure to shoot Diavide, as was his clear duty, when he had the chance.

and fever, stratified in our souls over thousands of years. For thousands of centuries, our ancestors knew and refined the sadness of dusks and the joy of dawns, the ennui of rain and the terror of storms—and it's with those instinctive emotions that we've created beauty and ornamented amour."

"What profundity there is in the word Nature!"

"Yes. That's what permits understanding, because it's the only thing that links aspects and explains them by their intimate opposition. The principle of causality is born of the contemplation of Nature. But to understand is to love, for one always senses that to understand is also, to some extent, to create. Thus, Mother Nature gives us a son: the sentiment that she inspires in us and in which everything human remains enclosed."

Vialy looked at his watch. "Four-thirty. We have less than twelve hours left."

"Have we come a long way?"

"Sixteen or eighteen kilometers, Manya."

"Let's go!"

Midday cast its heavy and compact light over everything.

In a nacreous blue sky the sun piled up its terrible ardor. The heat descended blindly over the groaning earth.

Vialy and Manya stopped in the dense, blue-tinted shade of a plane tree.

"I'm exhausted."

Her face drawn and her back bent, Manya lay down.

"Thirty-five kilometers, my darling. Rest for a moment. We can wait. I'll massage you in a little while, and we'll resume our route.

"Perhaps we're far enough away?"

"No. We need to be on a hill, preferably one made of old rock. Here, we're between two earthen projections, which will smash into one another during the quake. I can see in the distance a gray-blue hillock which might be the refuge we need. It's about twelve kilometers away. We'll make it."

"I'll never be able to..."

"Yes! I might have to carry you part of the way, but we'll be there by four o'clock."

The young woman folded her arms behind the nape of her neck and went to sleep. Vialy went up a slope to examine what the horizon revealed to him of the combat engaged in the distance...

He perceived from time to time the pink cloud speckled with white dot of the powder invented by the proletariat's chemists, specimens of which he had seized on several occasions. The machine-guns were also spreading a gas in the atmosphere that rose up in green-tinted swirls. A kind of frantic agitation of colored layers was divinable, beneath which a great drama was being played out, but nothing was able to reveal the secret of the mortal struggle, the desperate battle that the people were waging against their masters.

On one tiny segment of the horizon, the Thousand's Chief of Police, who was no longer anything but an insubordinate, read just a few lines of the great drama— but time was flowing on, inflexibly.

He went back to Manya.

He drew her into the sunlight, on to the grass, undressed her swiftly, and then massaged her forcefully. He resisted the desire to sink down on that magnificent body, slender, pink and milky, where vigor and softness, elegance and resistance were legible in the tension of the muscles and the flexion of fleshy vaults.

He loosened the fibers and restored elasticity to the tendons of the weary body. He carefully expelled fatigue and restored flexibility to the physical machine. Alcohol then acted on the skin and the flesh that it covered. When he had finished, Manya dressed again with admirable promptitude.

"It's true; I'm better. I can go to the end of the earth!"

Ten minutes to four.

At the foot of the hill designated by Vialy when they had stopped at midday, it was him who as going forward, holding his mistress like a child. She had not been able to walk this far, but he had carried her.

The slope was steep. He climbed it slowly, his face taut and his eyes staring.

Finally, there was a schist plateau where sparse grass grew. He went all the way to the middle, chose a spot, and set Manya down.

"What time is it, my love?" she said.

"Time!"

She shivered, and her hands closed.

He sat down, facing westwards, and hugged Manya's body to him.

"Rest like this. How are you?"

"Tired."

He placed his hand over the beautiful smooth forehead, and looked into the distance. An emotion compressed his breath.

Suddenly, on the horizon, the earth was liquefied. From the distance, where the terrestrial crust was dancing like a river over breakers, a gigantic eddy flowed. Vialy felt the subsoil oscillate, like a falling stone. Then, at a stroke, the line edging the convexity of the world rose up toward the zenith.

On Vialy's extended legs, Manya's body, agitated and swayed, obedient to an unknown force.

Out there, the surface of things changed. Monstrous and frightful, as if a segment of the globe had been detached, a kind of circular satellite rose up toward the sun. In that morsel of night, which expanded slowly, scarlet streaks fulgurated.

Mouth agape with horror, Vialy watched the distant relic of humankind cease to exist.

A tidal wave composed of earth and pebbles suddenly rose up in demented fury, coming from the place where the cataclysm had been unleashed. In front of him, hills were flattened and valleys opened up, from which a hurricane of ashes emerged.

Gradually, the sunlight was extinguished, while the ground underneath Vialy seemed to sink down, like a wrecked ship.

The descending night was striped with chemical fulgurations, monstrous lightning-bolts aggravated by the explosive ballistics of the klazzite, in a rage of oxidizing reactions.

Vialy wondered whether the powerful detonation had reached the deep terrestrial layers where the incandescent metals lay.

Meanwhile, the immense atmospheric depression created a gigantic cyclone. Its titanic fury extended in sheets around the center.

Vialy leaned over Manya's fascinating mouth, which he could still see. He kissed the cherished lips.

Then, rummaging in his pocket, he took out a cigarette and lit it.

Night had invaded the hill. The air was leaping everywhere with the fury of a crazed beast. To the west, however, the luminous jets were becoming rarer. The explosion had completed its work. Now, would the toxic gases, hurled into the atmosphere in millions of cubic liters, the meteorological devastations and the Stygian darkness leave alive the dreaming couple who had escaped?

Scarlet and gilded, the minuscule flame of a cigarette was henceforth the only thought in the world...

KASCHMIR, THE PLEASURE-GARDEN

Preface

Our epoch has enlarged the world. I mean that no one, henceforth, can be unaware that beyond the city, the département, the frontiers—the mental and intellectual boundaries of old—humanities live that are doubtless as useful to the sovereign order of the cosmos as our own: equal in dignity, at any rate.

That sentiment is recent. Nevertheless, it links by threads that are still tenuous, but which time will consolidate, the various qualities and colors of the humans inhabiting the planet.

Where the maps of old bore mysterious patches, everyone now knows that the same desires, the same passions, the same joys and the same dolors reign that surround us. The degrees of applied scientific knowledge that social forms manifest here and there are of scant importance. What is properly human is the depths of souls, and no one can be unaware henceforth that there are souls everywhere agitated by our fevers, our pleasures and our cares.

Already, an entire literature has taken possession of immediately accessible regions in order to set novels there, to analyze psychological idiosyncrasies and to describe delicate or brutal perspectives. In literary terms, Africa is conquered, but America defends itself and Asia remains mysterious. Of the latter, a small fringe has been studied, which does not truly explain the secrets of that immense and powerful continent.

I make no claim to recount Asia here. That would require two centuries and several titans of genius. But I want to offer an original vision of a corner of Tibet that has not yet been polluted by stylographic ink. There is, however, no more illustrious territory than the fatherland of Kaschmir. Since Bernier,[13] who lived in the reign of Louis XIV, visited it, no lover of the moving voyages of yore is unaware of the name of the "valley of pleasure." Many Englishmen of the Gangetic Dominion have also been there in the last century, to care for lungs ill-prepared by the London fog for the atmosphere of the great Indies. No Kipling, however, has yet taken it upon himself—perhaps out of modesty—to relate the mores of the last corner of the earth where gynocracy reigns, where women possess several husbands and the shame-ful word "polyandry" still remains descriptive of social

---

[13] The French physician François Bernier (1620-1688), one-time secretary to the philosopher and mathematician Pierre Gassendi, spent many years in India, mostly as the personal physician of Prince Dara Shokh, the son of Shah Jahan and the Emperor Aurangzab. He published an account of those experiences that was translated into English as *Travels in the Mogul Empire, A.D. 1656-1668* and an essay on *Nouvelle division de la Terre par les différentes espèces ou races qui l'habitent* [A New Division of the Earth in Accordance with the Different Species or Races that Inhabit It] (1684), an important proto-anthropological work that laid the foundations of much later racial theory. His passing assertion that polyandrous societies exist in remote valleys of "Kachemire" is based on a second-hand account of dubious authenticity, backed up by citations from other works that might also be suspect.

mores. That word and the thing that it designates are, moreover, a morality equal to the one that reigns in countries where the relationship between the sexes reposes solely on the mastery of males. There is, however, one redoubtable fundamental difference...

A close family relationship links me to one of the Frenchmen who is doubtless more familiar than anyone else with the Afghan land of Bukhara and the regions stuffed with riches that are coveted by all the nations that border the immense British empire of India. It is from him that I have obtained all the details of this story and the strange romantic tragedy—very implausible, to be sure, for Occidentals like us—that unfolds within it. My imagination, therefore, plays no role in this text, except for putting into literary form a drama that was lived, whose true heroes are resting eternally beneath the luminous and secret waters of Lake Dahal.[14]

---

[14] I have retained Dunan's spelling of this name, although the lake in question is nowadays more familiarly known as Lake Dal, just as I have retained her versions of Kaschmir (Kashmir), Sirinigar (Sirinagar), Jummoo (Jammu), Karakoran (Karakorum), etc.

Introduction

Ethics

There is a conversation between men.

Dramas of amour have been evoked: those which truly happen and those whose novelists imagine.

"The Traveler" (ironically) then begins to speak:

"Certainly, our literature can be reproached for the eternal repetition of the same themes. Adultery has ended up being the basis of all novels. It's too much. It's necessary to admit, however, that adultery retains an importance of the first order in the social existence of the Occident. If romantic situations are indigent, the fault is in the mores that have given a kind of mystical value to two illusory things: the chastity of women and fidelity in amour. All social forces tend—in vain—to protect those two unrealizable entities; by virtue of the fact, adultery becomes the sovereign sin.

"Nothing would be more beautiful than the struggle against the sexual instinct if that were not the very reality of being. Human thought ought not, however, to seek equilibrium elsewhere than its own vital domain. To struggle against fear, against the animal weaknesses of bodies, against the transports of anger, hatred and cupidity is sane behavior. It results in an honest control of instinctive impulses. One is a man, or a woman, of superior moral value when one attain it. But to struggle against amour—what an absurdity!

"Amour is our origin, our reason for being and our finality. It is therefore necessary to consent to follow—controlling oneself, obviously, but following neverthe-

176

less—the pressures of that powerful instinct, or become a kind of monster, a stranger to universal 'becoming,' in spite of appearances: something akin to a book that is well-paginated and bound but whose pages nonetheless remain blank, or a rifle without a barrel.

"Would you admit an intelligence that claimed to explain everything without ever employing the syllogism? A newspaper that never prints the letter e? Thus humans appear to me who have the absurd desire that we should live, think and write without the problems posed by Amour.

"I have said that our moral conceptions in sexual matters, and the prudishness—too often hypocritical—with which we surround them have resulted in the long term with an impoverishment of esthetic elements and literary analyses. That is not to say that we have not delved vertiginously into the psychology of adultery, the universal *deus ex machina*. How many nuances, subtleties, charming and profound finesses, delicate pleasures and graces, however, we could have stored up by overturning the social foundations and studying Amour!

"I am not thinking here about the Thousand-and-One Nights, although, in truth, those incandescent tales might well be an enrichment for ardent souls in the Occident that see so many new arcana revealed therein. I'm evoking the Tibetan regions where the relationship of the sexes is the exact opposite of that which reigns in the Muslim world. Woman alone reigns in those lost regions, populated nevertheless since the origins of the world. She marries as many men as she pleases, and commands them. Can you imagine that?

"Make no mistake: those astonishing mores have their nobility, their beauty and their intelligence. No one can deny that it sometimes degenerates into debauchery, but is it any different in Muslim polygamy and European monogamy?

"In any case, I'm not a moralist. I've traveled a great deal, and nowhere do human beings appear to me to be 'better.' The only certain thing is that polyandry creates astonishing cases of passion, bizarre and monstrous amorous contingencies that overturn all our codes of propriety and social principles. In consequence, one cannot deny, at the very least, that it is very picturesque.

"That matriarchal familiarity has long been familiar to me. It does not fail to offer, I admit, in addition to its ethical importance, a strange and spicy charm to an Occidental stuffed with romantic literature in our fashion. Few writers and travelers, however, have had the courage to recount sincerely what they have seen in the regions where polyandry still reigns. That is because, in principle, such a derogation of the redoubtable principles of male superiority seems to them to attack primary decency. They are stupid. They lack a sense of relativity.

"The superiority of one or other of the sexes is a matter of fact, where it exists. But what state of society, when it establishes an order of relationships between individuals, dos not attract criticism? Let someone cite me a place in the world where no vices, hatred and deceptions are prevalent. Does matriarchy create more that the contrary system? Who knows? As for theoretical deductions, I consider them to be nonsense. Scholars have demonstrated everything at various times: that the earth as flat, that it as the center of the universe, that birds were incapable of fling and that cats were unable to fall on their feet. Estimate the value of their logic in the ductile matter of sexual links and affections!

"But the ethics do not matter. What is worthy of display to the world is their elegance, their emotive power and their décor.

"Now, the picturesque quality of certain situations that I have admired in Kaschmiria is prodigiously interesting. At any rate, in order to illustrate my thesis, I shall tell you about an adventure in which I almost—thanks to a woman with several husbands—drank of the Lethe. Here it is:

I. Voyages

For twelve years I lived in a barbaric land, redoubtable, secret and magnificent. It stubbornly retains the mystery or original civilizations. All the Occidental nations are ambitious to possess its imperium, but the climate, a ferocious and martial mountain, people ardent to defend themselves, and a strange moral purity that does not prohibit debauchery, protect that age-old land. Its Eden is the Valley of Kaschmir.

You have all heard more or less talk of Kaschmir. It is a region whose name is universally known, but which only geographers are able to situate on the map.

West of Tibet, supposedly Chinese, though equally Russian and English, but which in fact still remains independent because it is almost unexplorable, there is a less hostile mountainous massif that extends for several thousand kilometers. England is master there in name, because she possesses, to the south of that extraordinary Alpine block, the famous plains of the Punjab and the powerful Himalaya. To the north are almost-inviolate lands where the Russians and the English have fought for a long time. The man who is most powerful and tenacious is most at home there. Higher up, in Badakshan, which neighbors the famous Bukharia, tribes survive who have preserved the customs of ten thousand years ago, without changing anything. Noble and worthy plunderers, heroic bandits, men resistant to the disease, poverty and fatigue that challenge our civilized bodies, they are doubtless ancestral humanity retained at the stage that preceded the civilization of Halstadt or that of La Têne.[15]

It is, therefore, to the south of Badakshan, that veritable British mastery over that part of India commences. There is the government of Gilgit, which is, as they say "outlying," then Balestan, and finally Kaschmir, below which is found Jummoo, which, with the capital of that name, commands everything west of Tibet.

The English, it must be said, are not very welcoming to French explorers, in those lands of which they have only poor possession. It is for that reason that we know so little in France about Tibet. There are also few Hindus in that India, which is almost entirely Muslim. Because of that, the preaching of Mahatma Gandhi has thus far not had any dangerous repercussions for the British. It might, perhaps, be better if Gandhi attracted proselytes there, rather than Koranic nationalism, which is the most frightening terrestrial fanaticism—which I saw flourishing prodigiously there.

Circumstances had, in fact, attached me in 1920, in the capacity of engineer, to exploratory drilling for oil on the banks of the Chandra. I was in communication with Rufus Isaacs. I had been acquainted with him in London, and he was now governing India in his new quality as Lord Reading.[16] That obtained me a great many facilities of which no one of my race had ever profited. In 1922

---

[15] The former reference is to the "Hallstatt Culture" that thrived in Central Europe in the early Iron Age, between the eighth and sixth centuries B.C. The "La Têne culture," named for a site in Switzerland, developed out of it in the fifth century B.C.

[16] Rufus Issacs, the first Marquess of Reading, was the Viceroy of India from 1921-25.

the drilling had not produced any result around the Chandra, and they were resumed to the east, between the Indus and the Tsaka, near Lake Kyak-Tso, where prodigious mineral fortunes undoubtedly lie. I then took a leave in order to go to see, along with another secret mission, whether there was oil in Gilgit. I had found some elsewhere, between Gor and the Nanga-Parbat, but it was unexploitable, and still on the bank of the diabolical Indus, which describes the most unexpected meanders in that mountainous chaos.

I left Lahore in January with a few robust, audacious and devoted men that I had recruited in Tibet two years earlier and had never left me.

Jummoo is on the edge of a gigantic massif that includes peaks as high as Everest in Nepal. The titan is Mount Karakoran, which is only two hundred meters less than Everest. Nanga-Parbat remains four or five hundred meters below that. In any case, although the scientific methods by which mountains are measured are precise, it must be admitted that the particular gravity of such giants, in a sense independent of terrestrial gravity, has not yet been calculated with sufficient accuracy to ensure the rigor of the observations—which is to say that the theoretical tangent of the marine surface, which serves as a baseline for calculations of height, has been found several times, by observation, to become a secant, because it tends to become tangential to the mountainous mass itself, the latter thus playing the role of a satellite...

But let us leave those problems. At Jummoo I saw the Maharajah, descended from Gulab Singh, the poor devil of a Sikh who constituted a vast empire by chance and crimes under English domination in the nineteenth century. As the prime minister of that shadow of a rajah was a rogue English colonel, however, and pretentious, I left Jummoo without delay in order to go north with, like a companion from my own country, the famous book by the Frenchman Bernier, who discovered the realm of Kaschmir in the Great Century. He had, in fact, arrived there with the redoubtable Aureng Zeb in 1664. I traveled up the course of the river Dawak, sacred like to Ganges and the Chinab. Unfortunately, there was no road suitable for carts in order to go as far as the valley of Kaschmir. The passes there are too high. In spite of recent works, they still remain very difficult even for horses.

Automobiles can pass where horses suffer, so roads can now simply be made wide and flat enough, without worrying about the steepness of the slopes, but those works remain slow and belated. In fact, the Kaschmiria valley only offers esthetic resources. To pay the cost of those beautiful roads they have to lead to places where industry can be enriched.

The road that Bernier followed in 1664, via Rajaori, still exists, but it did not coincide with the trajectory I had planned. That is because my journey also had a geological exploratory purpose. In consequence, I followed a track on which I had various reasons to hope to discover iron. I did not find anything, however, except for an emerald mine. But it is not a mineralogical or industrial story that I am telling you...

II. Sirinigar

I shall therefore skip over the incidents of my slow displacement through the mountains of the State of Jummoo and my passage into Kaschmir. That is the most astonishing voyage in the world. At six o'clock in the morning, you are close to the heavens. The vegetation is then Alpine. You descend into a valley which has flora exactly similar to France; then you enter a plain, and are in the tropics. The next day, you are in the snow, the day after that you go through a forest of cedars like those in Lebanon...

We arrived in Sirinigar, the capital of Kaschmir, after twenty-five days. I was in a very bad mood. I had found nothing interesting in nearly three hundred kilometers, in a country of immeasurable richness, and I had lost one of my Tibetan servants, bitten by a snake in Kirschtvar. But arrival in Sirinigar is an enchantment that would console the gehennas of the old Inquisition. It generates as much astonished admiration as the sea voyage to Venice from the Dalmatian coast. The State of Kaschmir, like all others, can grow or diminish—only circumstances, leaders and the degree of national imperialism are in play in that regard—but the valley of Kaschmir is something limited, which it is necessary to admire in place, in the astonishing capital of the region, the fascinating Sirinigar, the Venice of India.

Imagine yourself in the center of a valley less than a hundred kilometers wide and twice as long. It is the terrestrial Paradise. Summer—a Mediterranean summer but mild and gentle—reigns there incessantly. All the flowers in the world have arranged a rendezvous there, and all terrestrial voluptuousness is displayed there with a delicate ingenuity. Around the valley there is a ring of immeasurable, frightful, absurd mountains, on the slopes of which, on mild sunny days, seated in the center of that immense garden under a cedar, surrounded by roses, one can follow the gradient of seasons and climates with the naked eye, all the way to the perennial snows of the summits. One can clearly distinguish, departing from the peaks, pasturelands, then fields of wheat, vines, and finally the immense floral plantations that produce so many subtle essences, the joy of Asiatic women, and of Europe too, whose most delicate alembics do not produce perfumes as delicate as the gross utensils of the Kaschmirians.

Sirinigar, Queen of Asia, was, as you can well imagine, ferociously disputed for more than a thousand years by the Mongol tyrants. It was a capital hundred times, and burned s many times by invaders. That "Happy Valley" is, therefore, a depository of all the monumental architectures of India: ten centuries have left edifices or ruins there of palaces, mosques, gardens and terraces as admirable as the Ca d'Oro or the palace of the Venetian doges.

It is a kind of aquatic city primarily made up of delightful sculpted chalets, uniformly constructed of cedar wood and extended up to a fifth story everywhere. The river, the Jhetam, cuts the city into two parts linked by seven bridges, and around it, large and small lakes with countless little islands, forming the most original décor in the world. Sriginar has five hundred thousand inhabitants. In a country as well-irrigated, where every rich Kaschmirian possesses his own island transformed into a house of pleasure with a garden, the boatmen, as in Venice, have a considerable importance. They are Hindus who cultivate the singing gaiety of the barcarole.

And now, this is my adventure.

As soon as I arrived at Sirinigar, marling at the admirable country, I sought to savor its grace without mingling with Europeans. I therefore avoided the English hotels and boarding-houses found there in abundance for the use of British functionaries. I eventually succeeded, thanks to the intermediation of one of my Tibetan companions, who had lived in the valley before, in inspiring confidence in a Guebre, the proprietor of a delightful pavilion on the shore of the largest of the lakes, Lake Dahal, and I moved in there.

I found myself a long way from the white colony, and very isolated, but what a delightful spectacle was that of the odorous islets on which svelte chalets stood, with exquisite apartments with concave guard-rails. They had delightfully poetic names: Nasim Bagh, the garden of breezes; or Nichat Bagh, the garden of pleasure. Terraces, fountains and flower-baskets limited my view everywhere while I was daydreaming in my bungalow. The clear water extended all that limitlessly in a subtle play of light and perspectives, all the way to the background, where the city itself stood, and to the far-distant mountains caped with snow.

I had been there for a week, and had even bought some very curious parchments written in old Gujarati, which I was striving to decipher in the quiet peace of a life without incidents. One evening, at about nine o'clock, when the silence was absolute and I was leaning on my balcony savoring the mild warmth, the adventure announced itself; I saw a small boat appear between two islets, in the soft and tremulous moonlight, undoubtedly heading toward me, the sole inhabitant of that shore. It was as narrow as a canoe, and it was being rowed sound-lessly by a white form.

It came to shore facing my chalet. I saw a slender silhouette leap to the ground, almost nude save for a sarong like those Malays were. The shadow approached at a swift pace. At that hour, in the season we were in—the spring—the isles of Lake Dahal are not very busy. That afternoon I had only seen a few female servants and surly men with hieratic gestures: gardeners or domestics. It is only between May and October that well-to-do Kaschmirians come to live in their gardens. At that time, too, English men and women arrive to play tennis. I rejoiced, in any case, in that solitude, without which I would have taken up residence elsewhere. For that reason, the strange and elegant scantily-clad visitor intrigued me prodigiously, and appeared to me as mysterious as a djinni.

A violent and aphrodisiac perfume mingling roses, jasmine and honeysuckle, which grow in Kaschmir as nettles do in France, reached me in regular gusts. I watched the agile form in the moonlight, which was, I was convinced, coming to seek me out.

In fact, the svelte individual leapt casually over the barrier separating my garden from the neighboring property, and approached at a slower pace.

When the shadow was ten paces away I said "Good evening," in a loud voice, in the Dogra dialect—which I speak quite well, and which bears a strong resemblance to the Kaschmirian language, the suppleness of which were not as familiar to me.

The form stopped, and I leaned forward in order to distinguish it better. Eventually, I heard the Kaschmirian formula: "The evening is certainly good."

"Are you looking for me, my friend?" I asked.

I heard laughter. I was questioned, ironically: "Don't you speak my language?"

"No, I can't do you that honor."

"Do you speak Chibhali?"

"No."

"Are you English?"

"No." The dialogue irritated me. "I'll come down," I said, "and we can speak on the same level. Wouldn't that be preferable? Wait for me."

I heard: "Yes, please do, stranger!"

Three minutes later, I was in the garden, and fund myself face to face with a graceful adolescent, extremely effeminate and clad, as it had seemed, in a simple Malaysian garment.

"Be praised," I said to him, politely.

"Certainly, and God," he replied.

"And God," I echoed.

"Come with me now," the adolescent continued, without transition, in the Dogra language. He expressed himself elegantly, but did not seem to like speaking that dialect.

I was familiar with the customs and conversational procedures of the Asiatic races, and I replied: "You give me great pleasure, but will you permit me to ask you where you want to take me in your desire to render me happy."

He laughed again. "Come! I'm only here to fetch you. There will be someone to explain it to you. Each to his office, in accordance with the Law."

The strange grace of that individual of slender form, the European informality of his conversation, his smiling gaiety and something about him that was pleasant and audacious, without anything shady or disturbing, affect-

ed me like an alcoholic beverage. Almost in spite of myself I replied:

"I'll go with you.

III. The Mysterious Dwelling

The unknown was listening to me, his gaze fixed. He replied to my acceptance with a nod of the head; then he raised his arms to the heavens in a gesture of homage, placed them on my shoulders and pronounced some words in Sanskrit. Turning round without further ado, he moved away. As I had said, I followed him. It would have been wise to warn my Tibetans, but some unknown need possesses me obstinately when I travel always to act alone. It's a passion. I'm inordinately fond of risk, of uncertain adventure, unforeseeable circumstances into which I love to plunge.

Thus, I drew away from my chalet without looking back. It did not even occur to me that I had no weapon. The ephebe enchanted me. As in certain pleasant dreams, I was afraid of causing the enchantment to vanish by taking precautions that were too real. I climbed into the narrow little boat.

The adolescent said to me in a feminine voice: "Sit down and don't budge, because your movement might cause us to capsize."

I acquiesced with those sage words. At that moment, the moon was partly obscured by a cloud. The landscape had the silent languor particular to watery regions. A shadow of wind brought us lively odors. On the other side of the lake I could see some of the lights of Sirinigar, and to my left, not far away, the marvelous mosque of Shah Hamadan, the five-pointed bell-towers of which were clearly visible against the gray background of the lunar cloud.

The mildness of the air and the delicacy of the misty spectacle suddenly filled my eyes with tears—I don't know why. Meanwhile, the young man, my guide, paddled with marvelous skill, as the indigenes of oceanic seas do. I scarcely heard the blades of his paddles dipping into the water, or the efforts that he made to propel the frail craft. We were both silent.

After five minutes, I no longer knew where I was. The moon reappeared to inform me, ironically, that I would have considerable difficulty if I had to find my own way home. We went past minuscule islets, then between others vast and perfumed. I saw my conductor describe bizarre meanders, and suddenly realized that he was guiding me in that fashion to prevent me from knowing subsequently were I had gone...

The strange voyage lasted a long time. I strove to make out and file away reference points. Eventually, it seemed to me that we were heading back toward my dwelling. Relative to the moon and the lights of Sirinigar, that was not in doubt. But a kind of illusion subsists, as dangerous as a mirage, which I have often verified. I became more attentive, and my curiosity increased.

"Nourmahal!"[17]

The unknown had spoken that single word. I looked at him, infinitely astonished, and then queried: "Nourmahal?"

---

[17] Nourmahal was a legendary sultana whose story was popularized in England—and probably invented—by a story related in Thomas Moore's *Lalla Rookh* (1817), "The Light of the Harem," that supposedly being the meaning of the name. The story was appropriated by Victor Hugo, who included a poetic version in *Les Orientales* (1829).

"We've just passed her garden," he said.

I was gripped by an emotion. Who has not dreamed of the divine beauty of that favorite of Asia? Nourmahal! The word is magnificent already—it is tender, odorous, caressant, voluptuous, and terminates like a cry of pleasure. Nourmahal! The mistress of the terrible Jaan Guir?

I turned round in order to conserve the memory of the garden where Nourmahal had lived. Then, like a suddenly-cast shroud, the night enveloped me. I thought I had been plunged violently into an icy atmosphere. Looking toward my guide I could no longer see anything. He had made me turn around with an Oriental cunning in order to engulf me in some vault of which no trace would later remain in my memory.

Anger surged within me. "Where are you taking me, dog?"

"Don't disturb me," he said, tranquilly. "We're in a dangerous place. There are caimans beneath us, and I need to avoid making a mistake."

I heard his paddle cleaving and pushing the water.

"Lower your head!"

I ducked. As we advanced further, the passage became colder. A muddy odor developed vehemently. The forward movement went on...and on. By slight impulses provoked by centrifugal force, I thought I divined that we were describing rapid curves. That began to irritate me. I reproached myself bitterly for having embarked so stupidly on an unknown adventure, especially without my faithful Brownings.

Suddenly, the noise of the paddles ceased. The boat followed its momentum for a few meters, and then stopped.

"Reach out with your left hand and touch the wall—can you feel a handle?" said the adolescent in a low voice, with an indefinable emotion.

I leaned over. There was some kind of knocker there.

"Lift yourself up gently, and keep tight hold of the handle. Underneath it there's a space to stand on. Place yourself there."

I could not do otherwise but follow his advice, having no choice between different courses. I leaned on the smooth wall momentarily, and stood on a kind of step. Then I heard the paddle moving the water.

A minute passed. The silence was sepulchral. Evidently, my conductor had disappeared.

I called to him in various languages, angrily: "Where are you, son of a whore?"

There was no reply. I was alone, in that unknown place, with the water of a subterranean lake before me, standing on a stone which, I had verified, really was a step on a stairway-but the stairway went downwards, after did not go up any higher.

I began by cursing violently, and then recovered a sense of reality. After having called myself an imbecile at length, it was necessary to do something.

I had some matches. I struck a dozen of them in order to admire the locale in which I had been disembarked. The vault was at least four meters high. It seemed to be made of heavy blocks of schist: work of the time of the Mogul rajahs.

I was on the top step of a flight that plunged into the artificial river of the tunnel. Behind me, there ought to have been some kind of door, but I could not determine that. The knocker that I had clutched in order to pull myself on to the step seemed to be a simple sculpture. It depicted Siva juggling with his death's-heads. That was cheerful!

Ten minutes went by. I listened carefully for any noise. It appeared to me that something was moving above the vault.

I said to myself: *Two solutions to choose, not three: wait here, or start swimming and retrace the route that brought me here in reverse. Complex as it might be, one must eventually come to an end.*

As I was mulling over that idea, preparing to get undressed and make a packet of my clothes that I could carry around my neck, I heard the partition grate behind me. Then, about a meter to the right, a lighted doorway opened. I called myself an idiot again. I was definitely in decline, for in sum, I ought to have known; the ruse was classic. The door was not directly behind me but to one side.

The unexpected gap had hardly opened when, having become a man of action again, I launched myself forward. I bounded into the beneficent entrance, as if unleashed by a spring. Anything rather than that damp vault!

I prepared myself for various aggressive contingencies, but restrained myself. There was no one there but an old Hangi, in a short boatman's costume. He bowed respectfully before me, closed the door to the vault—he simply pushed it—and said to me in Kaschmirian: "Would you care to accompany me, son of my life?"

Making an abrupt effort to pull myself together, for I know that it is necessary in Asia to act in accordance with slow and calm Asiatic thought, I replied, formulaically: "I shall not fail Father."

He moved away...

IV. Sequestered

I traversed vaulted chambers similar to prisons. Afterwards, I was made to climb three flights of stairs; I was evidently in a vast dwelling. As soon as the first landing, doubtless directly above the subterranean vaults, an extravagant luxury was manifest, which was further exaggerated on the floors above.

Carpets, weapons, incrusted items of furniture, bronzes and ivories were heaped up everywhere, without any order. I had adopted the only appropriate attitude, a strict impassivity, with a great deal of attention and mistrust. I thus appeared not to see anything.

On the third floor, my conviction was firm. I was in the home of rich Hindus, who had connections with Europe, compounded very comfortably with their religion, for alongside Arabic surats, Buddha, Ganesha and Siva, especially, were represented in many precious trinkets set in ritual places. When I arrived in a room furnished in a quasi-European manner—with armchairs, no less— the boatman gave me a sign to sit down and left.

This time, I could wait more pleasantly than down below. Evidently, in such a place, it would be easy to murder me, but in that case, there would have been no need to bring me up so high. Thus, something other than my life was wanted from me. What?

Asiatics have a Machiavellian concept of simplicity. Perhaps my known status as an engineer would lead a Kaschmirian capitalist to unveil to me, in return for guarantees, real and exploitable treasures. Who could tell?

As I was thinking in those terms, sitting in an arm-chair, the door through which I had entered opened. A man appeared. He gazed in silence. Poor, barefoot, with an acetic air about him, he had a magnificent dignity, with his hooked nose and his annulate beard. He withdrew immediately without saying anything.

Suddenly, from one side, very close to me, although I was alone, I heard a kind of rustling. I turned to look. The wall at that place, over an area about a meter square, had been replaced by a metallic trellis like those one finds in Europe in convents of contemplative nuns, in order to isolate them. Someone was moving on the other side, and I heard improbable words pronounced, In English, without any accent.

"Are you not afraid, my adored one?"

I savored the crystalline speech, evidently the voice of a woman, with a profound joy, but I replied with an Arabic or Norman prudence, in Dogra, in order to try to identify the unknown: "Fear could not enter a soul possessed by you, light of my gaze." I employed the Asiatic mode of informal address, in order to see what would follow therefrom.

The voice went on, soft and even, as liquid and harmonious as before, but in Dogra: "What land are you from?"

"From France."

"Aha! I have already married a Frenchman.

I replied slowly, in accordance with a religious formula: "Praised be the Retributor."

The woman went on delicately, with a sort of charming irony: "I gave him to the tigers to be eaten."

I kept silent, devoid of illumination to resolve the enigma posed by the strange conversation. I know that with the inhabitants of Asia and Africa it is necessary to meditate every word, and only to speak judiciously outside the formulae of compliments and politeness. It has been devised precisely for the purpose of deceiving the curious, the hasty and the self-interested.

The woman continued: "I have seen you wandering in Sirinigar for three days. I have been told that you are a master."

I responded, gravely: "I am rather your slave, O Goddess!"

There was a brief silence, and then the unknown spoke: "You are handsome. I shall marry you."

I spoke then like a high-class Kaschmirian gallant. "Apple of my eye, delight of my destiny, may you not renounce that desire, and allow me to realize the task of rendering you happy?"

I heard the rustling multiply then. Someone was standing up. Then it decreased. The woman was drawing away. The authoritarian unknown who wanted to marry me had retired without any further politeness. I then installed myself comfortably and waited to see what would happen next.

An hour later, in the silence, I fell asleep.

I woke up at nine o'clock in the morning. Without thinking about it, driven by the desire to make myself comfortable, I had lain down on the thick carpet had had slept very well. As total silence reigned around me, I set about studying the mysterious abode.

There was no apparent external view. I was illuminated by a primitive lamp seated in the ceiling, the oil in which had been renewed while I was asleep. The walls were solid. Given my arrival by boat, I was evidently on an island in Lake Dahal. But were there any windows in the place? It was necessary for me to verify everything with precaution and celerity. My eyes and ears were in-

cessantly on the alert, for the men of Kaschmir are reputed to be very fastidious and quick to anger when one
treats them with a lack of trust or politeness. At any rate,
in principle, the most normal actions of our European
existence can be profoundly wounding to an Oriental
witness. It was true that I appeared to be in the hands of
a woman, but how likely as it that a woman would be the
sole mistress of that sumptuous dwelling?

Undoubtedly, it was the beginning of an intrigue
such as Pierre Loti experienced and which are elated by
the writers of Persia, Araby or the Indies. A woman
whose husband is traveling permits herself to abduct a
white man glimpsed in passing and subsequently spied
on.

Provided, I thought, the husband doesn't return before my departure from this palace! For, deprived of defenses, I really could not confront, with any chance of
living, the anger of a jealous and outraged husband.

The idea that I was in the hands of a polyandrous
woman did not occur to me; I thought polyandry was
reserved for the lower orders. I searched, however, for a
weapon in the room where the caprice of a twentieth-
century Nourmahal had installed me. There was nothing
there that might serve in combat. That was deliberate.

Shortly afterwards, I was brought something to eat.
There was obviously no reason, as yet, to poison me, so I
had no reason to be suspicious, and did honor to the
complex cuisine of the region.

As I finished my meal, someone came to pick up
the remains.

The servant, a robust Sikh, then said to me in English, like the keeper of some café or smoking-room on
the Strand: "Whisky? Poppy? Hemp?"

I shook my head.

"Sleep, then, for the mistress will not return until this evening. Until then, nothing."

I nodded my head. Not to ask questions but to extract the maximum useful information in the words pronounced before me was the rule I had to follow. Instead of sleeping, however, I investigated my domicile.

The massive oak door opened from the outside. The walls were composed of a very solid kind of concrete. Fundamentally, I was well and truly imprisoned. The floor beneath the carpet appeared to be mosaic tiles, which forbade any thought of piercing it—which I had, in any case, no reason to attempt. An hour of research and methodical examination left me as ignorant as before. Having seen everything, I was about to go back to sit in my armchair when I thought I heard a noise through the left-hand wall, which I had considered until then to be internal.

I drew nearer to it, checked the surface horizontally, and then, climbing on an armchair, I sounded it higher up.

Eventually, I discovered something. Twenty centimeters from the ceiling there was a rectangular orifice about as broad as a hand. It was the relic of a bricked-up window. A little wooden shutter was fitted to its form exactly, prolonging the surface of the wall. I pulled out that shutter, with difficulty and had before me the revelation of the environs. I admired the landscape into the midst of which I had been transported.

The house was on one of the islets on Lake Dahal, of course, as I had been unable to doubt, but it as a long way from my chalet, and I could not get my bearings at first. I was close to the outskirts of Sirinigar. In front of me, bathed in limpid and luminous water, gardens were displayed, and a series of houses drowned in the polychromatic vegetation that characterizes the land of Kaschmir. The solid stone foundations of all the buildings plunged into the lake, and above it, an infinite variety of tapering or flat roofs stretched all the way to the horizon, with the bright green grass that often covered them in the region. Immediately beneath those roofs and terraces, innumerable windows yawned, arched bays prolonged by balconies or corbels like the palisades of the Medieval castles of Europe. There were flowers and perforated woodwork everywhere.

Generous openings permitted me to see into the heart of the houses. Thus, I was able to admire weavers of shawls and workmen carving copper, lamas at prayer, scribes with brushes, jewelers and many others—even dreamers, and also lovers. All of that was before me, exposed in a bright and delicate light. Even the remotest distance did not attenuate the slightest detail. And the emotion of such a landscape, like a subtle and delicate Japanese print, was, for me, akin to a revelation of grace, quietude, beauty and felicity.

V. Zenahab

Subtle vision of Asia, I still find you within me, like a living symbol! I see once again that strange and fascinating paradox, which might represent universal duplicity: the vulgar street offers surly dwellings, and the delicate roofs open on a sincere ingenuousness! Thus it is, doubtless, with everything at which one gazes alternately, on the earth and in the heavens.

Perhaps every verity, similarly, has two faces. Never, in fact, had I imagined Sirinigar thus. Seen from the streets, from the ground, from the lake, everything there seemed closed, as discreet and jealous as the Muslim countries. And now, seen from above, I had the revelation of a city in which nothing is sealed, where life was displayed with the natural and benevolent naivety of which only the inhabitants of Tahiti, according to the accounts of voyagers, seem to have retained the tradition.

I finally understood the country. There was a familiar aspect of the city for Kaschmirians, and another, stilted and secret, for Europeans. I was confronted by the décor reserved for the inhabitants of the Happy Valley.

I gazed for a long time.

Sometimes, thirty meters away, a boat passed by, handled with agility by some tall, nearly naked fellow. In the bow, a kind of curved tent prolonged the prow in a curious shape reminiscent of the head of a porpoise. Within it there was merchandise, or women, or impassive men, dreaming.

Far away to the left, a road described harmonious curves over the verdant ground. It went to a village of which I glimpsed the minaret of the mosque. Then, beyond it, there was the commencement of the aggressive mountain, with its graduated hues, extending from the dark green of a forest of cedars spread over the lower slopes to the rosy whiteness of the summits.

At the foot of a hundred-meter cliff, in a kind of rocky chamber shielded from all gazes—except, of course, mine—women were bathing. They were brown and svelte. A tree hung over them, and I saw them hanging on to the branches in order to play like undines.

Without knowing or caring about such a voluptuous presence, behind that same anfractuosity, an English officer was manipulating geodesic apparatus, with two stiff, cold soldiers who were marching with measured paces.

A boat stopped nearby, probably not far from "my" island, of which I could not, unfortunately, glimpse the shore. Two men were in it. They were talking to other invisible people. They were splendid Kaschmirians, bearded, clad in vast brown robes secured at the waist by a red belt. The hard and staring eyes, the inferior lip, split and heavy, and the arrogant carriage of the head designated them as masters. They were a pure Aryan type, and their speech was incomprehensible to me.

But fatigue forced me to get down from that strange observatory. I promised myself to return to it before long.

I had been sitting down to reflect for a quarter of an hour when the door of my room opened and two tall, lanky armed men came in, wearing supple helmets with leather earpieces, as stiff as soldiers of His Britannic Majesty.

"Come," one of them said to me, in Dogra.

I followed them.

We went through two bare rooms; then, at the door of a third, I was obliged to stop, flanked by the two mute guards. An invisible hand then caused the enormous cedar panel to rotate, and I saw a room prolonged by a flowery terrace. The floor was covered by a carpet. There were no chairs, but an entire furniture of Hindu wealth, with low tables covered with golden trinkets.

I went in. Behind me, the door slammed shut.

Prudence commanded me to expect anything, hope for anything and fear anything; I had, therefore, to measure my gestures and my paces as well as my words. I immediately sat down on the floor, without looking outside, tempting as it was, filled with light, where life was agitating. I was at the foot of a lacquered table.

There, legs folded and mute, I waited, extending my arms along by thighs like a Buddha. Motionless, I must have resembled an inspired Brahmin. The lake extended before me, strewn with its little flowery islets. In that direction, nothing indicated that I was a prisoner, so close did liberty seem—but in the Orient, it is necessary to mistrust appearances.

Suddenly, behind me, without any door clicking, I sensed someone arrive. I rustle of light fabrics approached, very slowly. Without moving a finger or an eye, I remained impassive, but straining nevertheless to perceive everything and understand everything.

A woman brushed me, tall, proud in her gait and perfumed to the point of nausea. She stopped beside me, tapped her foot, and then advanced again. I did not see her mask until the moment when she took her place in front of me, sitting in the Turkish fashion on a prayer-mat. Her face, which I was able to divine as beautiful, was covered with a light gauze, and her body was enveloped in the thousand heavy pleats of countless scarves.

The ensemble remained mysterious, but even more threatening...

Without preamble, the woman said with a cold authority, in very pure English: "You will be my husband?"

I looked at her impassively, and, without raising my voice, attentive to my every word, I articulated: "If it pleases God."

She nodded her head, and lowered the muslin from her face. She really was an admirable creature. She possessed the grave and slightly artificial sadness of the wives of rajputs in India. The nose, however, was Semitic, thin and straight, and the bulging forehead appeared to me to be slightly hollowed at the temples. The mouth, though excessively arched, remained small, tinted with purple make-up. The oval of the face was perfect, but the gaze gave the lie to its apparent youth. It was too sharp and subtly cruel. I read a quality of fixed and bitter curiosity there that I had always thought to be strictly European in origin.

Perhaps the woman was Kaschmirian, but more probably from between Tibet and Punjab. She had in one fascinating ensemble all that each of the Asiatic races counted of the truly beautiful: the skin, in particular, slightly russet, invited kisses. The sclerotics, pale blue, encased strange irises, reddish-brown speckled with mauve. They made one think of those wild beasts that move you like lovers' gazes. Her neck, of a marvelous purity of line, retained the tremulous slenderness of a rush so tempting for scimitars. I could not see her hands or legs.

She went on: "Will you marry me this evening or tomorrow?"

Impassively, I replied: "I want only to satisfy your desire. You shall choose."

Someone came in, and tea was served in a golden cup ornamented with gems, but poorly shaped and monstrous.

"Good. This evening then. Do you know me?"

I looked her in the face coldly.

"God has given me the science of knowing beauty. Thus, I know you."

Those balanced and uncertain phrases have a great value in conversations of which one does not know them meaning or the objective.

The woman retorted: "Do you love me?"

"How could one not love that which is perfect?"

"Look!"

VI. The Severed Heads

She said "Look" and then stared at me with the insolent hardness of a Parisienne at the wheel of an auto
who has nearly run you down. I did not blink, as glacial
as a bronze Buddha. Meanwhile, she leaned over a kind
of low sideboard lacquered in purple, with gilded doors,
opened it, took out something and held it out to me. In
spite of my determination to remain secret and devoid of
visible emotion, I made a gesture of horrified repug-
nance.

It was a man's head, perfectly severed and artfully
embalmed. The skin had retained its luster and the lips
their turgidity. Only the eyes were atonal and empty. I
noticed drops of liquid suspended from the lashes, and
astonishment caused me to lean forward to get a better
view of them.

The woman laughed lightly and said: "He's weeping. I wanted his final tears also to be imitated."

Stupor nailed my tongue. I was still looking at the
severed head resting between the woman and me. But
the harmonious voice went on: "It was the day when I
saw you. I no longer thought about anyone but you. In
order that you would come to love me, I sacrificed him.
Sacrifice is a pledge of happiness."

A chill ran down my spine. But I could still hear.

"He saw you too before extending his neck to the
steel, and he understood, I think, that my joy merited his
death. It was my body for which he wept when I wanted,
in his stead, to reserve the homage of it for you."

I was still contemplating the strange relic. It had
been a man of about thirty, doubtless of the Arabic or

Persian race. The debris retained some of the charm of the beauty of a man doubtless passionate to the extent of offering his life—although those tears...

The woman brought a long, narrow hand with gilded fingernails out of her muslins, and leaned toward me.

"Can you not find words to tell me your thoughts?"

Slowly raising my eyes toward her again, I replied: "Why did you not understand that I would have loved you without it being necessary for him to die?"

She contemplated me with disdain.

"He was the one I loved the least. I cannot have more than four husbands. If I love again tomorrow, it will be necessary for me to be a widow again to acquire the right to love."

I looked at her with a kind of sacred horror. She read my gaze.

"You will remain the preferred for a long time, believe me! For you know at this moment how to be near to me without making gestures, and you understand that it is necessary not to ask me to be naked before the time. Few men of your Occident divine that. They are like crazed beasts..."

She breathed in, unfastened the cloudy confusion of her scarves, and I saw a breast emerge. The nipple had been carmined. She waited for a gesture, a word, an allusion or evidence of passion on my part. I read in her savage and insolent gaze the desire for and the dread of a passionate manifestation. I retained a glacial and sacramental courtesy.

"Yes. It's necessary to know how to master your virility. Shortly, you will be the spouse of Zenahab and you will know those who still are, and those who have been—for, save for two, I still have their heads.

I responded with an inclination of the upper body. "If it please God."

She stood up with a thrust of the legs, and I saw that her muslin robes remained where she had been sitting. Naked from the feet to the breasts, but with the face still veiled, she passed close to me, even more sumptuous in her labored, powdered, gilded, pumiced, ornamented nudity.

She was a woman from the Thousand-and-One Nights.

Her limbs had been rose-tinted at the toes and shins. She wore a blue ankle-ring linked to a similar ring around the thigh by a chain of gold and rubies. Her knees resembled ripe fruits, painted vermilion and gilded. She was rigorously depilated and steeped in perfumes. Touches of color enlivened the folds of her body with traces of gilt and strange jewels. A savor of musk, abusive and irritating, expanded through the room. She went out then, like an idol, but paused beforehand, I divined, in order to contemplate me.

I did not turn round to follow her departure. She finally disappeared through some invisible issue. Certain that attentive gazes were watching me, and that pitiless wills were ready to annihilate me if I accomplished any prohibited act, I did not budge, still meditating on my situation

I finally understood what had happened. When Vaidy Pundyat had warned me, in Lahore, about the danger of Kaschmirian women, I had laughed at the ideas of the erudite but imaginative Brahmin. I had been mistaken.

When Sir Ralph Pelow had advised prudence in gallant matters, I had laughed out loud. They both said: "Beware of falling into the hands of a female vampire.

They exist in Kaschmir. They vigorously maintain the polyandrous tradition on which, in Gilgit, veritable petty republics are constituted."

That seemed comical to me, because for me, polyandry signified poverty and communal life. I had seen such communities in Tibet, where women are rare and men abundant. Four or five men, in consequence, live with a single spouse. She possesses them all. It is quite regular, simple and practical. The men are, in any case, cold and sad. The women only employ that system as conservers of the race, outside of an identifiable paternity, and without passion.

I had lived for a time among the Ladakhis, the most beautiful polyandrous race in Asia. The women there are magnificent, and renowned for their ardor.[18] But what imagination it would have required to establish a relationship between the Buddhist Ladakhis, poor and humble, practicing marriage to five men by a woman because it avoids the division of heritages while limiting the population, and that Kaschmirian of unknown religion, rich, her own mistress, authoritarian, visibly educated in the European manner, and doubtless putting polyandry in the rank of vices. A sacred, religious, sumptuous marital vice...

---

[18] The region of Ladakh in the Indian State of Jammu and Kaschmir is cited by Bernier as an example of a region where polyandry survives, based on secondary sources, and it continued to be cited as such by anthropologists into the twentieth century, although the more conscientious sources are careful to mention the lack of hard evidence of its frequency. Polyandry was formally prohibited by law in 1941, although the necessity of the law is not obvious.

I could not succeed in associating the Tibetans with Zenahab, whose name, in any case, was Arabic. I saw her, instead, as some kind of sacred prostitute in the European manner, merely sanctifying her relationships with her lovers, even keeping her lovers on a leash, or in prison, in order to enjoy them at will and in accordance with her caprices, but ritually.

VII. The Woman Who Commands Males

These reflections, in Europe, are slightly bewildering. At the time when they passed through my mind, I sensed them as needles in the heart of my thoughts. It was necessary, in order for that woman to be able to live in such an extraordinary fashion, collecting men at her whim and putting them to death without having to account for it, that she possessed a quasi-superhuman power in the eyes of the people, since she had servants. It was necessary, too, that the English were either ignorant of her existence, or that they admitted it—which seemed absurd. So many complications and apparent impossibilities.

The fact, however, remained patent; I really was in her hands, at that very moment, with a severed head posed close to my right arm. And that unknown woman had picked me up in passing like a fruit fallen to the ground. She had just quit me ironically, as if to illustrate, one might have thought, the most extravagant hypotheses regarding the reign of feminine lust, sovereign over males.

I posed the corollary problems precisely. It was, therefore, necessary:

Firstly, for me to marry the woman. The comedy as worth playing, and was, in any case, necessary to my security.

Secondly, once having obtained the desired satisfaction, it was necessary to flee, urgently. It was not even necessary to await satiation.

Thirdly, as soon as I was out of that place, assuming that I could escape, it was indispensable to quit Sirinigar and the Valley of Kaschmir. Zenahab must enjoy a numerous and devoted domestic personnel, a considerable authority over the Kaschmirian people, and all the powers necessary to contrive my murder, if the occasion arose, with a gesture of the hand.

With that triple resolution made, I awaited events.

It was six o'clock in the evening. I had eaten and drunk my fill, of foodstuffs brought mutely by somber men. I had not budged by an inch in spite of some weariness of that immobility.

Finally, Zenahab gave me her news. The two armed hirelings who had already accompanied me came to take me away, after having searched me. Had I been armed, the accident would have taken place there and then, for I certainly would not have wanted to renounce my weapons, and would have made use of them instead. It is true that had I been armed I would doubtless have hidden my trinkets in such a way as to avoid their discovery, but having nothing, in fact, I tolerated the intrusion of the two brigands turning out my pockets without flinching.

This time we went down to the floor below, and I was abandoned in a room in which I recognized something hybrid, participating in the mosque and the Tibetan lamasery. A prayer-wheel was fixed to the wall, with a kind of pedal for turning it, and a little bell that tinkled after each complete revolution. Four pillars that were not supporting anything were disposed in a square in the middle of the room. Two lamps were burning to the left and right of the entrance, formed of wicks steeped in sculpted copper bowls, on the sides of which I read Koranic surats. A Buddha must have been buried under a profusion of bright fabrics opposite the prayer-wheel. I divined the multiple arms and the undoubtedly-crossed legs. The blue-painted walls were reminiscent of a little Catholic chapel. It had to be a sanctuary.

I made a slow circuit of the rom. The absence of ornaments did not permit the concealment of the regular holes through which I might be watched, and, if necessary, killed.

An hour passed. I was beginning to miss the carpet that had been lavished upon me thus far, and on which one was so comfortable, lying down or seated, when the door gave passage to a lama in a red woolen robe—the kind known as a chogy—and a red hat embroidered with gold. He wore a tiny prayer-wheel on his right index-finger, and was turning it incessantly with his little finger. That is the Tibetan fashion of telling the rosary.

I knew that the red lamas were from Lhasa. The yellow ones inhabit the Karakoran, much closer to Kaschmir. There was, therefore, a mystery there, but I did not linger over those secondary questions. I waited. The fellow paid no heed to me. He stopped in front of each lamp, struck his forehead with his index finger, placed himself between the pillars in order to articulate three or four barbaric vocables, and went to remove the pieces of cloth—which were not covering a Buddha, as I had thought, but a kind of multiply phallic form sculpted in red stone. Then he withdrew, without even glancing in my direction. According to what I know of the customs of the belief, I must be, from that moment on, married to the mysterious polyandrous Kaschmirian.

An hour later, someone came to fetch me, and I was taken back to the room with the armchairs, the only one where I was at ease. I waited. One tells oneself that, action apart, one must be patient in the fact of no matter what event. One even believes it—but there comes a time when cultivating that impassive and infinite

Touranian immobility becomes to us, extreme occidentals, quite impossible.

I had constrained myself, since my arrival in that place, to a rigid calm. I had now exhausted my stock of patience. My legs were demanding to walk, my arms to act, my head, above all, desired to be occupied with things of the vast world and no longer uniquely with that little corner of Lake Dahal in Kaschmiria.

In brief, I had had enough! It was necessary to put an end to it, promptly, for good and all...

I marched ferociously back and forth in my prison, coldly irritated, calculating how to escape from that place, and...

VIII. Spousal Council

I had racked the old thinkbox but had not found any simple, practical, "industrial" solution to put into operation. I was mistrustful of everything, especially of poorly mechanized actions that could only lead to catastrophes. My mind still taut, therefore, I decided to wait—which is to say that I did not decide anything.

Time was still passing...

It was ten o'clock in the evening when my two indefatigable guardians—did they never sleep?—came to fetch me again and took me to the room where I had had a conversation with the beautiful Kaschmirian. The bay window looking outside had been closed by vast curtains draped over the guard-rail of the terrace. I sat down in the same place as in the morning.

What struck me, from the very start, was a round table placed in the center. A muslin sheet was extended over it, covering objects that seemed to me to be quasi-spherical, but hardly visible. While I was squatting, in spite of the mediocre light of a high-set lamp, I realized what the objects were.

They were six severed and embalmed heads.

I perceived within me, along with the sharp pain of an unarmed man on whom danger weighs, a sentiment of irritated dread against which I had difficulty struggling.

Abruptly, the door opened. A man came in and sat down some distance away from me, without looking at me. He was athletic, and wore the mask of a Greek statue. He was clad in a white Tibetan robe, with felt boots with elevated tips.

The door grated again. It was a European, an Italian or a Spaniard, short, thickset and very alert, his eyes keen and his teeth gleaming, who came in, to install himself to me left—with, it seemed to me, a muted anxiety on his face.

I finally understood: it was the council of spouses.

There was a long interval, and then the last made his entrance majestically. In the context of the interest to which that improbable adventure had given rise in my thoughts, involuntarily, I could not help admiring the newcomer.

He must have been conscious of the effect to be produced, for he remained standing for a minute, and then, as sly and feline as a wild beast, extended himself nervously on the carpet, almost at my feet. He was an African, a Berber, or the half-caste of a European and an Arab woman. He was wearing an extravagant silk turban with red and black squares.

To the right and left of the forehead, attached to the temples, were striped carnations, redder to the left, whiter to the right, and between those flowers, an astonishing face was inscribed. The skin, the color of milky coffee, was shiny, like a nectarine. The eyelids were lowered over invisible eyes, but the nose had the aquiline finesse of an architectural drawing. The mouth—slightly rouged, I believe—offered a raised upper lip, split like a fruit with a kind of feminine sexuality. In the center of the mucus membrane a pale pink line divided the scarlet tumescence. The lower lip, swollen to bursting, seemed sliced like a blood orange. At the corners, in contrast to European faces, a slight swelling added a further camber the limit of the moist flesh, and that closed mouth, thus outrageously displayed, had a strange evocative lubricity. The young man was serious; perhaps there was even a sadness in the stretching of the dermis beneath the cheekbones.

His gandoruah came undone when he stretched himself out, perhaps by virtue of voluntary coquetry. His swollen shoulder thus became visible, with the isolating plan surface. The muscles departing from the clavicle seemed to lift up the taut, attractive and ovoid pectoral, truly reminiscent of a virgin breast, with a broad red medallion at the tip, concluding with a nipple the color of mahogany.

Time passed. Not one of the four men gathered there said a word. An exceedingly old and toothless maidservant served coffee in tiny cups and removed the gauze covering the severed heads. An indescribable embarrassment possessed me. I was pensive, without looking at anything, analyzing a thousand internal impressions: worry, dread and annoyance. I did not feel at all ready to take pleasure in this kind of adventure with several males. I even found everything a trifle grotesque, in spite of the tragic that it remain obligatory to incorporate therein.

Abruptly, a voice rang out in the room.

Zenahab had come in.

The southern European and the Persian turned their heads toward her. The Arab and I did not budge.

She passed beside me. She was dressed as in the morning, in a multitude of light and floating silks. As she brushed past the table, with a shrill laugh, she administered a kick to the pile of severed heads. They all rolled on to the floor. One of them, a blond quadragenarian Englishman, came to rest under my hand. I saw that the man had been killed by a bullet in the back of the neck.

Zenahab extended herself near the bay that continued the room in the fashion of a terrace, presently closed.

She was a long white form on the carpet, from which only the bare feet, head and hands emerged. She laughed, artificially. Finally, she recited verses in Kaschmirian, without appearing to see us. They are difficult to translate, but might be rendered thus:

> I have four happy husbands,
> They rejoice in my body and soul,
> But I would not like to prefer one,
> Because the favorite must be killed.
>
> Preference degenerates into love,
> And love is a slavery.
> The day I become a slave
> I will be no better than a male.
>
> Woman is superior to man;
> Amour does not exhaust her,
> But sentiment exhausts her
> When she has a beloved lover.
>
> I do not want a beloved lover,
> But I want amour itself
> If those I desire are not loved,
> They are nonetheless Zenahab's lovers.
>
> I have four lovers and husbands
> For God commands that one marries
> And that one only belongs to one master;
> A master one must sometimes kill.

She arched her body suddenly, her torso convex, her legs folded, and looked at us all

"Who wants to make love to Zenahab first?"

The southerner replied: "Me?"

She laughed, and articulated with a crafty irony: "There is only a first among several. You are the only one. Thus, you cannot say that you are the first."

"Me!" The Persian or Caspian had risen to his feet, as tense and powerful as a tiger.

Zenahab said: "No!"

She looked at me.

Her voice became caressant in order to speak to me.

"You are the latest to come. Would it not please you to learn the secrets of the joys that Zenahab dispenses?"

I replied, as always when a question is redoubtable: "If it pleases God."

She said: "Close your eyes."

I closed them, attentively.

I heard the woman get up and come toward me. She must have been naked. I raised my eyelids imperceptibly. I was not mistaken. She kissed my head and took it between her knees.

"Look with your hands!"

Meekly, I "looked," but my fingers only sought to satisfy her instruction, without testifying to any ardor. I divined in that extraordinary female a ferocious sadism, ever-ready to realize the unexpected that it was redoubtably necessary for me to anticipate. Finally, she withdrew, and lay down again. She was now lying on a flood of muslin. I gazed at her bitterly.

Oh, to hold her one–to-one and to make her forget, with the whip, if necessary, that European pretention mingled with Asiatic pride! She cultivated her scornful

219

arrogance solely because there had to be armed men, all around us, in the neighboring rooms, on the terrace and everywhere, devoted and barbaric, ready to kill.

Suddenly, Zenahab kicked the handsome Arab.

"Ali ben Dhyian, come!"

The young man stood up.

"Undress."

He let his gandourah fall, with one of those noble gestures that Semites have retained, and which cause one invincibly to think of the beautiful movements described by Homer. I sensed the dangerous juncture approaching, and divined the rotation of the dice on which my destiny was marked.

IX. Drama

What instinct made me search then for some *mise-en-scène* in the mysterious comedy commenced and to anticipate an imminent drama? What is certain is that, at that moment, the gaze that I attached to the astonishing woman saw her hand close upon an object—and I understood that she was holding a slender dagger beneath her, in order...to do what?

She looked at me and said: "Admi Singh, stand up!"

I understood, and stood up, for Singh is trivially ennobling and Admi, in Dogra, simply means "man"—although, in Kaschmirian, man is Manyu, which is a European root.

She made me a sign to approach and pronounced: "Sit down to touch Zenahab, O fortunate husband!"

I sat down beside her, my left leg touching her right knee. Then, her head raised, she issued a command in an unknown language, not addressed to any of the "husbands," which only concerned the mysterious surveillance that was certainly prowling all around us—but I felt a slight frisson along my spine.

Then she gave herself to the handsome Arab.

A sumptuous disgust gripped me while the mysterious woman moaned, her eyes fixed upon my face. Her harsh and cruel pupils searched for a hint of emotion in mine, but in vain.

Finally, without pushing Ali ben Dhyian away, she said to me in my turn: "Undress, Admit Singh."

I could neither recoil nor hesitate. I obeyed her, resigned to submit to anything, but not to make any advance, of which it seemed to me that I was bound—like everything else—to repent, and which, in any case, my body refused.

When I was naked, and it became clear to the lubricious Kaschmirian that I was as unmoved as possible by the spectacle that she had offered me, she shouted two words, as sharp as darts.

Four men leapt from who knows where, leapt upon me and tied me up before I could defend myself. I was carried away, rapidly. A heavy hand placed over my eyes prevented me from seeing anything.

Two minutes later, I was in a dungeon, thrown like a package into the darkness, tied up like a tiger being taken to the dentist. I did not even see how my aggressors departed.

It took a few minutes for me to pull myself together.

The adventure was well on the way to finishing badly. All my efforts at impassivity had come to nothing, or rather, had ended up exciting Zenahab's ire. It is true that if I had shown myself passionate, ardent and virile, there is no proof that I would not have received a perfectly-placed and exactly mortal dagger-thrust in the midst of my gallant demonstrations. I was even convinced that that would have been the case. The woman killed anyone who failed to satisfy her, or who satisfied her poorly. They were two insults. Whoever enjoyed her to the maximum could not fail to inspire in her the desire to immobilize such a sweet moment. Dead again! It seemed to me that she must savor above all else the bitter desire of regret, and obtain an intense pleasure in killing the man she loved.

In every direction, Death was sharpening his scythe.

For me, moreover, Zenahab must, in reality, lack the ardor that she advertised. Was she anesthetized by debauchery, by hashish or opium? There was no evidence of that, for she appeared robust and healthy. In any case, however, I retained the certainty of my impotence—if I had made the attempt—to satisfy her senses, if they were as demanding as her thought, if her mental ardor alone were in question.

The dead men whose heads she showed us had doubtless been similarly incapable of pleasing her. Perhaps the Persian athlete or the southerner, accustomed to excessive exploits, could succeed in creating an appropriate delirium in her—but I, a calm Parisian, for whom mind is a better aphrodisiac than matter, was certainly not the lover of whom she dreamed. Would my throat now be cut, like a goat sacrificed to Siva, and my head confiscated?

It was hot in the cellar, luckily. Otherwise, being naked, I would have suffered. As the time passed without my hearing anything, I thought that it would doubtless be useful to know whether my bonds were well-secured. They had been tied so quickly!

I strove to comprehend their interlacement, and after an hour, the truth—magnificent, in truth—became apparent to me. I had been bound in accordance with a curious Chinese principle. Any effort tightened the cords, simply by virtue of bodily tension, but if I leaned my head forward, and strove to put my elbows together behind my back and allow the cords to relax, my wrists would be able to free themselves.

It took me a long time to understand that and to attempt to free myself. When tied up, in fact, one had a kind of instinctive need to tug on one's bonds. I therefore lay still, without tensing any muscle, and was just about to succeed in liberating myself when a trapdoor opened in the ceiling and two objects descended, rotating.

I understood, and experienced a new emotion. First there was a lamp. Beneath it hung the head of the young Arab who had just possessed Zenahab. It was the beginning of her vengeance.

The trapdoor was closed again, doubtless catching the extremity of the rope, for the lamp and the head remained suspended in the middle of the cellar, and I perceived with astonishment that half of the cell was taken up by a pool of water.

Silence fell again. It was necessary for me to attempt once again, patiently, to escape the tangle of cords. I resumed my efforts. Hup! Suddenly, my right hand was free. I turned in that direction. The left freed itself. I searched for a means of untying my legs. That was quickly achieved. Ten minutes later, a trifle stiff but agile, I was on my feet.

What now?

It had become truly urgent, if possible, to get out of that vaulted cellar. From the trapdoor above, whenever anyone wished, I could be shot without difficulty. Perhaps there was no time to lose.

Let's think, nevertheless, in order not to do anything stupid.

First of all, why is it so hot here, in spite of that pool? I feel the wall. There's doubtless an oven behind it; the stone is very hot. In consequence, there's no chance of escape through that brickwork. The facing wall, however, is solid rock. The other side is impossible for me to reach, because I'm separated from it by a lake—or a bath, or a cistern? Where, then can I hope to flee? It's the expanse of water that it's necessary to explore now. If I dare to think so, that's where my destiny resides.

As I pass under the lamp, a drop of blood falls on to my shoulder from the head that belonged to a fortunate lover an hour before. I rub it away, disgustedly.

Still meditative, my stride nevertheless extends back and forth. Time goes by; I don't know whether it is going rapidly or slowly, but it goes...

Can they see me from up there? If they can, I'm doomed. I listen carefully, but can't hear anything.

Time passes...and more time...I don't know whether it extends over hours, years, or whether the fatal eternity is opening up...

X. Escape

Everything, in difficult circumstances, rests on the exactitude of the interpretative hypotheses that one formulates. I wanted to act, and act quickly, but first, it was necessary for me to understand. That was essential.

So I think hard, examining the ropes by which I was bound a little while ago. I calculate; I meditate; I attempt to scour Zenahab's intentions.

Perhaps she wants to let me molder here for a few days before administering the *coup-de-grâce*. But nothing is less certain. If someone comes sooner, isn't it necessary, since I'm untied, that before the executioners arrive, I've planned my escape...and acted on it? Obviously, if I'm tied up again, that will be definitive. But how to realize my flight...?

On thinking those words, articulating that formula, a nervous laughter seizes me. Realize? I'm naked in a cellar, naked and alone, with a severed head for a confidant.

However—and I continue laughing, without being able to stop—I'm the husband of the woman who lives up above, the monstrous polyandrous Kaschmirian. I'm her husband...

What to do? What to do? My head is seething like a witch's cauldron. Flee... Flee... And I quote Shakespeare, ironically: My kingdom for a horse...

Brutally, a sound interrupts me.

I listen.

There's a slight splashing coming from the facing wall. Then enlightenment penetrates me abruptly, like a blade. That wall borders the subterranean canal by which I was brought here.

It's therefore necessary to reach that canal. It's necessary...

I know, yes—my guide told me there were caimans in it. But there aren't any in Lake Dahal, the most placid lake in the world. The gracious adolescent was doubtless trying to scare me.

I advance toward the pool that occupies half my prison. A stairway descends into it. I follow the steps, which take me to within two meters of the wall. There are seven. By that time, I'm neck deep in water.

Then I climb back up; then, like a good swimmer, I dive, prudently. First I have to make a tour of the aquatic prison. In reality, it occupies more than half of the cellar. The solid ground only extends for three meters, and the water for six. The place is rectangular. It measures four meters in breadth and nine or ten in length.

I dive again, in order to follow the steps, but they don't extend any further than the seventh. The ensuing hole is extremely deep. It must be more than five meters; I can't touch bottom. I climb back up and rest momentarily, leaning against the wall of the oven. Then I go back into the water and feel the facing wall, where I heard splashing.

Ah!

I come up for air, dazed, taut with joy, to the point of lying down full length for a moment to savor my good fortune. Liberty is within reach...

At a depth of three meters, there's a hole in the wall, which doubtless puts my cellar in communication with the canal by which I came, the famous canal that goes to Lake Dahal...and life...

I hurl myself into the water again. I dive. Here's the hole. It's closed by a grille. It's square, a meter each side. Is it solidly fixed? Everything depends on that. Will I be able to demolish that metal lattice, which might perhaps have been underwater for centuries?

I come up again. My heart is beating like a drum. I need to calm down. I mustn't go under water like a child, risking cramp or an accident. I tell myself, trying to hypnotize myself: "Be calm, my friend, be calm!"

Finally, I throw myself into the water. Here are the iron bars. Let's take hold of the ensemble in the center. I brace my feet on the wall, and pull with all my strength, my lungs inflated with air, my cheeks bulging like an Aeolus in traditional illustration. I brace myself...and it come away...

My effort is excessive in fact. I tear the grille away with such force that I turn a somersault underwater without letting go of it. Finally, I let go of the useless item of furniture to which I'm clinging so foolishly, when it's no more use to me, and I hoist myself up to my prison.

Just in time. I feel my head spinning, and collapse on the floor with one desperate thought in my head:

What if they come to cut my throat now?

I faint.

How long am I unconscious? I don't know, and never will.

I finally come round, and I have the terrible sensation, like the residue of a nightmare, of being tied up again. No, I'm free! And I'll be better still. I march back and forth in my cellar, trying to regulate my breathing, to give my muscles their maximum suppleness. I'm preparing myself, like a gladiator before going into the broad daylight of the arena.

Now, let's go! I'm ready!

I descend into the water prudently. I dive when the level reaches my mouth…and here I am at the wall. I insert myself into the hole, the rusty grille of which, reduced to the texture of cardboard, is lying on the bottom. I plunge purposefully into that strange canal.

It's more difficult than I would have believed to make progress there. I should have dived differently, head first. No matter. I get through. For a moment I'm stopped by my braced hips, but I correct the false move, and my torso is now on the other side. I touch the "ceiling" with my heels and my head rises up. Again! This time, I'm there, and with a sudden thrust I climb back into the air.

Just in time!

I breathe in damp and insipid air. It seems delicious. The obscurity is absolute. I make contact with a wall, and follow it. Am I going in the right direction or the wrong one?

I swim slowly, without abusing my strength. I don't know how long that goes on. Are there caimans? There's a bend in the wall. I follow the curve. There's another bend on the other side; I keep following it…

Ah! This time I'm saved…

XI. The Waters of Kaschmir

It is certainly difficult to restore with exactitude the state of mind of a Latude escaped from the Bastille or Casanova, fleeing the Venetian *Piombi*—except that, when one relives an adventure similar to theirs, one perceives the prodigious richness of the pride, the courage, and, of course, the felicity.

I swim through the darkness, attentive to many things of which I ought to be unconscious, when, facing me, I recognize a glimmer of light, a faint gray daylight filtering through the water....

I see that...and my heart leaps, and life seems to multiply within me. I have, however, as a profound quality, a considerable mastery of action. I'm fearful, above all, of the movements of the first surge. When I emerge from my hole, the sight of daylight urges me to act forcefully, to precipitate violent toward the light that, ten minutes earlier, I feared that I would never see again. But I have a completely contrary sentiment. I say to myself: *Now you can believe that you're safe, or nearly. It's not the moment to risk compromising everything without reflection.*

I therefore continued swimming very slowly, avoiding noise, attentive to everything. I drew nearer to the final bend. When I reached it, I finally saw, a short distance away, the entrance to the tunnel, a two-meter vault, very broad, which made the atmosphere seem strangely compact.

My astonishment was great, however, when I saw, three meters in front of the orifice, a vast tangle of vegetation. I emerged into the open and reached that "bush" immediately. Clinging to a dangling branch, I set about examining the whole carefully. Then I understood that the strange canal had been carefully concealed by that obstacle. Without a doubt, I would not be able to get out easily.

I was beginning to feel fatigue, but to remain where I was would have been absurd. I therefore dived into the lagoon open to the air. Five meters further on, there appeared to be no exit, but I perceived a curtain of foliage hanging over another opening framed between two thick walls. I went through the curtain, and this time I found myself in a small lake. Nearby, on a little islet formed by earthy debris, confused and dense vegetation had accumulated. I hoisted myself on to it, certain of not being seen. Everything, in fact, closed around me.

Breathless, I lay down in the thick grass in order to get my strength back.

Meanwhile, I am possessed by joy, and an intimate, albeit belated, ardor toward Zenahab. By the length of the shadows, I believe I can tell that it is five or six o'clock in the evening.

A quarter of an hour goes by. The warmth of the atmosphere caresses me. I feel strong again, but I'm hungry.

And now, entering with rapidity between the two columns that seal the lake, and whose gap can be closed at will, is a boat steered by the young man with the sarong, by whom I was approached at home and asked to come here. An invisible woman is lying in the canoe like a white parcel. It brushes the thicket in which I'm hidden and disappears.

If they close the gap between the columns over there during the night, I won't any longer be able to get of here this evening, but if I slip out now, where can I go? How am I going to remain out of sight?

I continue to wait.

Dusk falls slowly. Anxiety takes hold of me. Unable to resist it, I go back into the water and nervously swim to the "exit." This time, I really am free.

In order not to be seen, if anyone is watching, I go around the shore of the island, following it cautiously. There is not a soul to be seen. In front of me, islets loom up, small or large, but none is very close and none is built up. My "wife" of an evening, Zenahab, knows how o avoid indiscreet gazes. I search for a hiding place or a protection. An enormous cedar extends to the water's edge, and its branches cover more than a hectare. It has grown on a leafy islet on which it seems to be possible to land. Let's go!

Three minutes later, I'm lying among the flowers, scanning the horizon. I finally recognize Zenahab's dwelling. There is no apparent window in this side. Then I search for the location of my chalet. Gauging the distances and the directions, I perceive that it's no more than five hundred meters away. The guide, in order to deceive me, took numerous unnecessary detours the night before last.

Night falls. Shadows cover Lake Dahal. On the horizon, Sirinigar sparkles. This time, it's necessary for me to act quickly and forcefully. When my escape is discovered, the pursuit will be rude. Decisively, I dive into the water in order to go home. I think as I swim that it would be as well to quit the valley of Kaschmir immediately. That Zenahab is certainly dangerous, and seemed to be powerful. The race is, in any case, vindictive. It possesses a thousand secret poisons, incomprehensible traps and mortal contrivances. It is therefore necessary for me to leave. My life henceforth belongs to passers-by, shepherds that I encounter, tradesmen that I speak to, anyone who comes into contact with me. I've just done many things in order to survive; it's necessary now to complete the pride of my escape by rendering myself completely safe.

I come ashore, exhausted, close to my house.

Not a shadow. I creep up to my dwelling; I open the door. It's completely empty. My men have been bought or murdered. I go up to my bedroom rapidly. My trunks have been taken, but a valise made of pigskin—an unclean animal—has been left, which appeared to contain nothing important. It does, however, contain clothing, two revolvers and papers. I get dressed and arm myself. I have flayed feet and my derby shoes are painful, but what does it matter now that I can fight? I eat a forgotten tin of corned beef. Eventually, I go down into the garden and set forth along the shore of the lake. The night is mild. I'm equipped with a blanket taken from the bed. I settle down in a thicket on top of a rock and go to sleep.

XII. The Final Act

The storyteller had fallen silent. There was a brief pause. Everyone was evoking, in his own fashion, the redoubtable abductor of males.

Eventually, the conversation resumed.

"Obviously, it's an adventure of such a sentimental order—if I can put it thus—that Europe can never offer you a similar degree of intoxication."

"I admit that it has the ascendancy."

"And that Zenahab—what a…patriarchal allure!"

"Hush! Is that the right word?"

"In any case, the conclusion is required. What happened next?"

"You were, in fact, able to quit your terrestrial Paradise without further misfortune?"

"Certainly not. I was pursued by ferocious and indefatigable Dogras for a week. I never saw my servants again—murdered, no doubt—and I had to join a company of Sikhs who were going to Yaghestan in order to get away. It was therefore necessary for me to make the return journey through Russian Asia. It took eight months. I wasn't safe until I reached Khagan, where one is in a republic, as in all the lands that separate the 'outlying governments' from the lands where alert Slavs keep watch on the Anglo-Saxons. I came back via Bukhara, where I saw the object of British anxieties regarding the Bolshevik emprise over Central Asia, which is one of the most astonishing social phenomena of today."

"And your Zenahab?"

"I obtained some information about her belatedly, from a spy…I never knew what country he served…"

"How's that?"

"A spy, my lad, is always a man who serves several masters—but which one does he serve with the most loyal application? Only he knows that. The countries to which he reports are generally unaware. They only know that they've obtained 'this' in exchange for 'that.' Who can compare with certainty the precise value of 'this' and 'that'? There are spies who even deceive themselves, and serve their enemy without meaning to, but the importance of a document of espionage is infinitely variable, according to circumstance and timing. My spy, a Hindu, served Russia and England—and Japan too, I believe, and also had connections in China, not without channels of transmission to America. Now, he knew Zenahab.

"According to him, she was the grand-daughter of one of the wives of Gulab Singh, who was burned after the rajah's death—you know that the unfortunate wives of deceased Hindu kings are still burned alive...it's forbidden, but it's traditional In 1843, a hundred and sixty wives were burned simultaneously on the tomb of Soochit Singh. In 1863, to be sure, only thirty-two were burned after the death of Jowahie Singh. It's known as suttee. It's still practiced, obstinately, but in secret, especially in the mountains, where mores are violent.

"In any case, on the death of Gulab Singh, one of the widows burned alive fell off the pyre before the combustion was total and have birth to a child, who was one day to be Zenahab's mother. The child was raise with care, and took refuge at the age of twenty in Lower Tibet. She acquired a notoriety, already justified by the miracle of her birth, as one inspired by Brahma. Shortly thereafter, she became the most magnificent wife of the polyandrous Dispand, had twelve simultaneous hus-

235

bands, every last one of which, it's said, she poisoned, and became very rich. She was also the mistress of an English general, who died and left her an enormous fortune: a thousand lacks of rupees.

"Her daughter Zenahab soon acquired great renown for her beauty. She came to Sirinigar after the death of her mother. She was revered there because of considerable gifts made to both mosques and lamaseries. She lived thereafter with a lavish supply of husbands. To the knowledge of the Kaschimrians, seven men had been dear to her. As she lived very secretly, no one knew what had become of them, enclosed as they appeared to be in a kind of harem-cum-stud-farm. In addition, she was reputed to be a magician.

"The Hindu who told me all that added, sententiously: 'Curiously enough, the men that Zenahab is reputed to have murdered were never those that England regretted.' And he shook his head as he added: 'On the contrary!'"

"I assume, all the same, that your Zenahab didn't continue to pursue you?"

"She certainly did! Having subsequently encountered an Anglo-Indian from Jummoo on the shore of the Aral Sea, I learned that the sorceress of Sirinigar had launched several brigands and Sivaists on my trail, promising them treasures if they brought back my head appropriately severed and mummified, but I don't need spectacles to recognize anyone disembarked from Lower Tibet. I'm able, all the same, to expedite to a definitive nirvana any ill-intentioned Asiatic who gets too close to me. What also protects me is the obligation that my murderer would have to cut off my head and take it with him. Such an operation can't be carried out in the street, or in café..."

"You've encountered your would-be executioners?"

"Yes, three or four."

"And?"

"One of them is still alive…if I missed."

"Will you return some day to that lost land?"

"I'm leaving tomorrow."

METAL

In the compact and heavy night a pale gleam expanded from the Orient. A tenuous muslin seemed to envelop the darkness and dissolve it. The day flowed in ungraspable waves from the luminous wound that broadened in the east. There was a rigid blade, the color of rust, and then an oscillating violet-tinted cloud that wandered toward the zenith.

The world was slowly unveiled by the brightness. First the tumultuous mass of crags and lanceolate peaks sprang forth sharply from the attenuated shadow. Then the brutal grays of granite and schist extended, ascending southwards all the way to the sealed horizon. Finally, the immense blue-tinted forest displayed its infinite pullulation of chlorophylls in the north and the east. The rumor that rose up from it seemed to inflate the enormous cupola of the sky, where enormous ocher clouds were drifting in the ether.

On a rocky peak overlooking the giant forest, on the threshold of a cave ignored by the light, an animal form wrapped in fur pelts was watching. Under the light springing inexhaustibly from the orient, the contours of things became gradually more distinct. The pathways that led to the cavern became clear. Then the form stood up and came to lean on a projecting rock. The view extended from the hostile rocky slopes that formed the slopes leading to the cavern all the way to the blue and green distances where the herbivores were grazing, where rivers ran, and where life reigned in disorder and conflict.

The man gazed.

The veritable beast of that era already possessed an incredible variety of forms. The negro and the negroid with the depressed nostrils, the prognathous Australasians, the yellow and white races, had been differentiated for millennia. Hundreds of centuries of evolution had hollowed out prodigious abysms between the races.

The individual who was surveying the forest at the foot of the chain that would one day be known as the Pyrenees was one of the last survivors of the artistic race that had populated since time immemorial the ground that would later be called France. For a long time, the lowering of the temperature after gigantic rains had driven the herds from the terrain where the Magdalenian lived.[19] The great ruminants had disappeared, and humans, for whom hunting had become harsh and ingrate, had been obliged to quit the prodigious caverns where, for thousands of generations, his ancestors had prolonged their existence. In search of prey, they had gone southwards—but the enormous Pyrenean mass had stopped the migration and the tribe had been living there for half a century.

The man who was expecting the vicinity of the habitat uttered a brief and hoarse cry. Another man emerged

---

[19] The early work on the so-called Magdalenian culture was done by the paleontologist Édouard Lartet (1801-1871), who spent the greater part of his time in caves looking for physical relics and cave art, so his account of the culture put a heavy emphasis on its carvings, especially those in bone and ivory, and its paintings, rather than its crude technology.

from the shadow and both stood there silently, self-absorbed, before the rising sun.

A giant sphere appeared at the level of the horizon, orange and violet, seemingly rotating and throwing off sparks. Its rays came to pose on things like sharp darts. A superabundant life filled the world. The birds were chirping noisily.

The two men were of tall stature, with a powerful torso and short legs. Their faces, hollow and ravaged although they were young, had the expression of meditated dolor that would be an element of beauty a hundred centuries later. An ill-tempered and rapid vitality was manifest in each of their gestures. The obedient muscles possessed the immediate reactivity that only the beasts would conserve when civilization as born. Their garments were clever and comfortable, made of animal skins sewn together with tendons. Their arms were free, and the legs from mid-thigh downwards. Their mobile ears searched for sounds and captured them with precision; beneath the luminous mirror of the eyes, the nostrils were alert, in regular aspirations, to the odors that the wind carried.

Those men were not, therefore, as their descendants would later judge them to be, feeble animals poorly armed and ill-designed for the conquest of the globe. They were admirable machines, intelligent and supple, powerful and despotic, who feared neither felines nor plantigrade carnivores. Only the redoubtable question of nourishment, which would remain the torment of cities twenty thousand years later, confronted them incessantly as a terrible problem. It was necessary for primitive humans, in order to develop their latent humanity, that hunting should be both delicate and facile, so that he would have leisure and that all his activity would not be utilized in vain pursuits. The southward flight of the Magdalenians had obliterated ancient habits; half a century had not yet given these the facility of life without which human being would never have emerged from the great ancestral ape.

For nearly a month now, in that lost and isolated region, between the grim mountain and the deserted forest, redoubtable events had put the very existence of the tribe in doubt. Departed in quest of shellfish from the sea, whose infinite waves broke not far away, two men had not returned. One adolescent claimed to have heard human voices; and finally, the watcher himself had brought back from his last hunt, along with tough and nauseating prey, an object over which the clan had meditated for four days.

It was a dart such as they had been using for millennia; they were launched by means of a curved projector rotating in the hand and presented with the concave curve facing the object to be attained. But the Magdalenian, who knew how to shape flint, diorite and all kinds of hard stone, who knew how to give them the shape of a willow-leaf or the triple projections of a barbed harpoon, did not know the nature of the cold and heavy point, which was not of any known material, and the penetration, the force, the range and the danger of which he had immediately comprehended. In his brain, refined by cares, the certainty as affirmed that that point of *metal* represented a *future*, a power, which renewed human destiny.[20]

---

[20] The radioactive dating methods that allows us to be certain today that the Magdalenian culture did not overlap the early phases of the bronze age were not available in 1925, although

They were a band of six men, come from the austral lands by way of the defiles that skirted the island sea. Outlaws of a kind of Atlantean monarchy, they had fled the hard labor of metal-working, the extraction of the mineral that the priests, with magic words, transformed into terrible weapons thanks to the god Fire. Rebels, they had trailed violent and ambitious souls for long months through what would one day be called Iberia.

They had headed northwards because the negro populations to the south of their native land were possessed of a brilliant civilization had terrified the metallurgists for centuries. Already, exportation was flourishing, with a kind of commercial loyalty, which also included bandits and outlaws. Several of the adventurers had died. Six remained, agile and thin, short and very ugly, according to future canons of beauty. Their arms, hanging down almost to their kneecaps, their concave femurs and bestial faces, powerfully toothed, completed a simian appearance. Their knowledge of art was non-existent, but they knew how to "manufacture" everything that presented itself, and their science of construction and their previously-unknown capacity for working in co-operation had conferred a remarkable power on their company. They were hoping for a durable residence, and for *adventure*. Already, humans had acquired a taste for risking their lives without expecting any calculable benefit. The pleasure of using the most advanced weapons, and of sensing within themselves the aggrandizement of personality that murders and triumph comported, everything that would inspired civilized men hundreds of centuries later to massacre one another—the

the story's account of the origin of metal-working was fanciful even then.

warrior soul, in brief—lived audaciously in those first sons of society.

A few thousand paces from the shelter where the Magdalenians were keeping watch on the horizon, the men of metal had lit a fire in order to cook some meager prey. Their knowledge of fire was prodigious and had never been seen before. They also knew how to avoid the smoke that denounces encampments. A complex system of ventilation, with a kind of filter of branches, caused the treacherous vapors to dissolve. In an isolated hollow, in the shelter of a gigantic rock that protected them on two sides, they were sitting gravely.

Humans spoke little in those redoubtable epochs. Speech aids the disguise of thought, and the vertical beasts only learned to talk when they developed the cunning and guile of felines. Between themselves they exchanged brief ideas in hoarse terms, accompanied by precise gestures. A kind of laughter stretched the skin around the jaws when a pleasant, favorable, fortunate idea prefigured before their eyes the delights of an imminent future.

They had a great hatred of women because feminine tribes, powerfully armed and combative had recently expelled them from a game-rich territory. The women in question were ignorant of metal but they had invented the bow: the dried tendon curbing a flexible and vigorous piece of wood. The precise flight of the arrows launched by the bow had terrified the sons of the forge, but they dreamed confusedly of creating a similar instrument for the copper-pointed javelins. None had yet succeeded in confectioning that instrument.

The sun reached its zenith. The men of metal, crouched around their smokeless fire, listened to the wind and the cries of birds of prey.

The two watchers had come down from the cavern and were prowling in the forest. Up above, the rest of the clan—three adolescents, three women and two children, were working flints, and making shafts for javelins with packets of branches. One child was scraping a fresh bear-skin. A haunch of meat, piles of shellfish and an as-yet-unskinned herbivore constituted the clan's alimentary resources. Of the three females, one was very old, rude and desiccated. She was in command in the absence of the men; another, a half-breed of two tribes, had troubled and firm facial features. Only one would have been beautiful, even in the eyes of those who were to live ten thousand years later. Her nose was almost straight and her inferior jaw flat. Her eyes glaucous, her torso advancing and her hips rolling, she had not been taken by any man, for beauty did not have the meaning then that it was later to acquire.

The humans who were to come later, exhuming what they called derisively the Venus of Brassempouy, did not imagine that they possessed the Aphrodite of their Magdalenian ancestors. With short legs, abrupt hindquarters and a rectangular thorax, the ideal female of those laborious epochs gave no hint of the masterpieces of the art to come. Thus, the women who possessed rhythmic lines, the incessantly rolling and unrolling spiral that constitutes a beautiful gait, the slenderness and sphericity of forms, adapted in ungraspable contours—all that constitutes beauty for the humans of our time—were scorned as ill-formed and unformed. It required elegant and ancient peoples to be fused with others, brutal and ugly, but new, for a comprehensible tendency toward grace finally to be manifest in the variety of growing forms.

The metallurgists, ignorant of art, had an admirable desire to be initiated, to know, to assimilate. The Magdalenians themselves seemed to have exhausted their natural delicacy. By virtue of having sculpted, polished and engraved stone, they had acquired, along with the knowledge fused with a labor that would henceforth become unnecessary, a sort of indifference for their artistic endeavors. The admirable visions of animals leaping, running and browsing that they have bequeathed to us were no longer, for them anything but amusements and games. Thus the torch-bearers were succeeded.

It was at the foot of the rock where the men of metal were resting that the first anxiety was born that gave birth to war. The Magdalenians were wandering without any precise goal. They had discovered strange odors, one of which was the reek of fire, and that had excited their fears, but their sense of small, habituated for centuries to dry atmospheres, had never been able to control and discern precisely the musty and mingled odors of atmospheres charged with water vapor. Then again, they had a strange self-confidence consequent on the fact that the sun had been visible that morning, when for so many years only the rain and the clouds that contained it had constituted their horizons.

One of the metal-workers suddenly stood up, smoothly and without making a sound; the other five imitated him. He seized a spear lying by his side, arched his back violently backwards, pivoted on his left leg and straightened up like a cranequin stretching.[21] The spear flew, plunged with a rustling sound into the leafy mass and struck a hard unknown object with a dull thus. Three

---

[21] A cranequin is a kind of crossbow.

other men imitated that gesture simultaneously, each with a particular weapon: a dart, or a metallic mass launched by the thrust of an arm. All of that followed the spear, and silenced fell again.

Then the men of metal split into two groups without saying anything and ran to the left and the right. They ran toward the human emanation perceived by the first of them.

Three metal-workers suddenly found themselves confronted by one of the two alert Madgalenians. The later reared up, brandishing and enormous flint ax with an immense oak-branch for a shaft, and brought it down in the first assailant. In spite of the rapidity of his reflexes, the other did not have time to avoid the impact; his club with metal spikes quit his fist, and his atrociously crushed face became a bloody mass. He collapsed, unconscious.

The man following him set his foot on the tree-stump behind which the Magdalenian had placed himself, and rose up in his turn brandishing a pike with a shiny tip—but he suddenly collapsed. The second Magdalenian emerged from the thicket had hurled a spear into the assailant's side. The point penetrated with the sound of a hammer striking a rotten branch; the shaft trembled like a taut cord. With a gasp of agony, the man fell. The last of the metal-workers remained in the rear, on the defensive, but, hearing other sounds, the two Magdalenians, with a brief cry, hurled themselves into the wood, one of them carrying away as a trophy the club with the metal protrusions employed by the vanquished enemy.

A chase began. Of the men of metal, four remained, tenacious and violent; they launched themselves in pursuit of the Magdalenians—but the latter had explored every corner of their habitat during the previous two years. They split up, came together again, crossed a stream at a ford, drew away from their cavern, and eventually, after a long detour, came back toward the rocky slopes where the forest ended. Their abode was some way off, to the west. They sat down in a cleft where bones were rotting. The odor of carrion, they knew, disguised and hid human odors.

In any case, they had an issue behind them, which led to the harsh paths of the mountain, where they had sometimes pursued agile and mistrustful animals. The peril averted, their essential concern was the strange club. Fragments of copper and iron pyrites were driven into the wood, hardened by fire. That made the weapon heavier, rendering it more dangerous. The simple club, the flint ax, and all their other weapons, were only effective in direct impact. In the case of a weak blow, or a glancing impact, the blow was absolutely innocuous. With these pieces of metal dotting the knotty wood, a wound would always be serious, and the Magdalenians understood vaguely that with the discovery of that hard, massive, cold and hostile substance, war would take on an unknown and redoubtable aspect. They foresaw the infinite cruelty that the centuries would bequeath like an entitlement to glory. The men of flint passed curious and fearful palms over the asperities of copper and iron; their astonishment was both horrified and admiring.

Nothing was moving any longer in the forest. Rain began to fall. The strangers must have gone back to where their two dead comrades lay. Perhaps they would render them a vague honor, the beginning of an as-yet-indecisive religion. What was certain was that they had renounced, for today, the pursuit of the conflict. Hazard had served them poorly. The men that had encountered thus far had been shorter in stature and less immediately violent in their reactions. The Magdalenians, sons of an exhausted race, displayed a miraculous muscular vitality.

It was necessary for them to put the ancestral abode beyond the reach of the strangers and find out how many enemies there were, in order to overcome them. Such were, at least, their ideas, although they did not take any methodical and certain form. Their already-abstractive minds conceived plans of defense, but they floated nevertheless between confidence and doubt.

The men of metal prepared their war as clearly as a mediocre power of imagination permitted. Their thought-processes did not include either hesitation or worry; as a wild beast seeks incessantly for an exit from a cage, they would not renounce crushing the hostile men whose resembled them so little in physical terms. They had, in sum, the ferocity of adventurers and the spirit of enterprise of nomads.

Dusk was falling when the Magdalenians returned to their shelter. They had not brought back anything comestible, and the sharp eyes of the inhabitants had observed that, anxiously, a long time before their arrival, while they were slipping prudently and smoothly through the rocks and plants. The strange club with its shiny shards also attracted the curiosity of the tribe at a distance.

They had arrived at the foot of a winding path that extended in steps over a sheer mass of schist, when a shearing noise caused the ears of the victors to twitch forwards. A heavy mass struck the rock noisily and rebounded on to one of the men, who uttered a kind of dolorous yelp. There was no doubt about it; their enemies, lying in ambush, were expressing their hatred.

The man's wound was slight, but the weapon was nevertheless astonishing. It was a disk, swollen at the periphery and pierced with a hole in the center. One caused the disk to spin around a slender branch until centrifugal force conferred an enormous momentum upon it, thus increasing it range its range, and specified its direction with a flick of the wriest. The men of that era even achieved murderous effects with such disks on large mammals at a hundred paces, utilizing the index finger as an axis of rotation.

They were only to get back to the cave by complex routes that were permanently sheltered. The incident, which left a bloody bruise on the forearm of one of the Magdalenians, was not repeated, and the metal disk brought yet another rare aliment to the curiosity of the clan.

The club and the disk were passed from hand to hand while the night extended its immense velvet over the mountains and the plain. There were true speeches of thirty or forty words inspired by the unfamiliar objects. The intelligence, keen but devoid of certainty, the vague and instinctive religiosity, mingled with pragmatism and impatience, which were characteristic of the declining race, did not give those humans efficacious means of investigation. While their enemies were methodically planning a means of attacking the cavern and killing its inhabitants, their artistic soul was dreaming in confrontation with the miraculous objects, come from lands of which they had sometimes heard mention, long ago.

Only the old woman expressed, in shrill onomatopoeias, phantasmagoric memories of a man of her family who had come back after many years from an exploration of the lands of living weapons, and she said with conviction that the metal disk was an extremely ferocious and dangerous animal.

The rare low clouds floated in the scant lunar light. The cavern was at rest. One of the men was on watch, in the glacial damp, raped up in stinking pelts. From the corner where he was placed he collected the sounds, the odors and, when the moon appeared, the sights of the declivity over which the paths leading to the cavern snaked. In the shadow, the abode resonated with violent respirations. The old woman and the children were sleeping at the back, near an orifice communicating with the mountain.

The men of metal knew the way to the Magdalenian lair. They had prowled around all evening in order to delimit the area of defense and attack. Hidden in the bushes nearest to the slope they had seen numerous faces appear up above. Endowed with little imagination, they could not see anything particularly beneficial in the possession of such a dwelling, since the terrain was not rich in game.

Desirous as they were to continue to wander toward unknown Edens, it nevertheless seemed to them that it was necessary to kill the humans inhabiting that repair. Their metallurgical science was scornful of the art of shapers of flint, and in spite of the morning's redoubtable example, they believed that they were armed in a fashion to triumph without difficulty.

It was at dawn that the men of the old race sensed the necessity of doing battle in order to continue to live. A sky the color of ash was gradually revealed. Bitterly cold north winds were sweeping the swollen clouds toward the snowy summits of the mountains; the rain and the mist formed a gray magma around blurred realities. One of the Magdalenians advanced some distance from the cavern. His sense of smell picked up the scent of humans nearby.

By means of a kind of natural staircase that rose up in the midst of sparse and spongy grass toward a neighboring peak, he reached the edge of a torrent, and came back toward the forest shielded by a steep canyon. It was then that he saw one of the strangers creeping cautiously along a rocky ledge overhanging the cavern, invisible to the watcher. He was too far away from the enemy to reach him, but he decided to get closer, and set out hunting in his turn.

And that is how, on rounding a giant spherical boulder, he found himself face to face with another enemy. This one was butchering the leg of a herbivore, doubtless killed in the course of the investigation of the Magdalenian dwelling. Armed with a shiny, sharp and slender blade, he was slicing through the red flesh.

The two men, unexpectedly brought into confrontation with one another, were subject to the reflexes of war. The Magdalenian snatched a pike from his side, raised his arm with a powerful gesture and threw it abruptly. The long-armed man did the same with a bright-pointed spear.

The Magdalenian had the advantage, a brain that commanded with more precision and power, and an advance of a tenth of a second in muscular reaction, and the pike was three arms' lengths from the enemy's body when the latter hurled his spear. The Magdalenian ducked; the blade of the spear passed by, the shaft striking his head solidly—but the man of metal, hit beneath the right nipple, oscillated. His face creased with pain and his mouth opened in a gasp. He tried to put his hand to his hip, where a long dart was hanging, but the other, back on his feet and braced, brought down his flint axe on the enemy skull, and the metal-worker collapsed without uttering a cry.

Anthropophagy was rare in the Occident in the Magdalenian era—not that any moral concern inhibited the humans, but human flesh was not really appetizing. Cannibals have always been intellectual degenerates. Furthermore, numerous diseases increase their virulence in passing from human to human in that way. It was the hygienic reason that banished anthropophagy from very start in races of superior intellect. The Magdalenian nevertheless took account of the fact that the fine prey might aliment the entire clan for several days.

Up above, however, the stranger on the protruding rock would soon be close enough to kill the inhabitants of the cave without having been seen; it was necessary to go toward him.

It was on hearing small stones rolling that the man of metal realized that he too was being tracked. Turning round, he saw the Magadalenian some distance way, climbing through the strata of schist. Both were in awkward and dangerous situations, but no concern of prudence held them back. They arrived in close proximity and launched their assaults. As before, the two weapons departed simultaneously, the stranger's a pyrite disk, the other's a short harpoon.

The harpoon missed its target, but the disk struck the Magdalenian's forearm. A bloody wound was immediately manifest, but only irritated the injured man. Without any prudence, he immediately scaled a steep slope, ran along the ridge where the other stood and attacked him.

The duel was brief; a javelin launched by the stranger was deflected by the club, and the club, raised in its turn, came down on the metal-worker, who staggered, attempted to throw a short, sharp blade taken from his fur garment at his enemy, and fell to his knees. He got up again, as tragic as a wild beast in agony, and finally lost his footing, falling from the narrow ridge on to the path that ran beneath it.

Up above, in a gap in the clouds, a blue light expanded over the forest and the rugged mountains. Nature, misted by water vapor, had the discolored aspect that humans, many centuries later, would call melancholy.

Death reigned, however, over two bodes that had been exuberant with life a few seconds earlier.

There was also fighting in the cavern.

The Magdalenian crouched down in order to gaze at his panting enemy from a distance. Around him, there was a softness in the vague light. Perhaps he was sensible of that, at a moment when the destiny of his race was reaching its accomplishment. A bitter determination, however, expended his consciousness. The sentiment of having vanquished the enemy added to the euphoria of the quietude succeeding the emotion, the pulsing temples and the dolorous sanguinary traces of the battle. He felt stronger, more powerful, more divine, and thought he had established a kind of mastery over the blue-tinted spaces that extended to the pale horizons. His throat strangled a cry of joy, resonant with hoarse appeals.

Suddenly, he heard the sounds of collision and combat beneath him in the cave. He wanted to run there.

It was necessary for him to go down as far as the agonizing body of his enemy. As we went past that blood-flecked face, that torso stuck to the ground, those legs twisted and broken by the fall, he saw the wild eyes staring at him bitterly. Pleading? Fearful? Challenging? Who could tell? The victor passed by; bloody foam oozed between the lips of the dying man with each movement of the thorax.

Finally, the Magdalenian climbed the slope toward his dwelling at a hasty, anxious but triumphant pace. The entanglement of pathways, slopes and bends succeeded one another, and then came the stiff final ascent.

Here is the lair. The low archway opens its portal, in a shadow the color of deep water. An appeal resounds in the breast of the victorious man...

A massive body springs from the vault, a spear extended forwards; the victor feels the barbed metal harpoon in the warm flesh of his shoulder. He rushes upon the one who has taken possession of his lair. His club extracts a brief cry of pain from the other. The two men collide, wounding one another.

In that struggle, the Magdalenian has time to see: the children, skulls split, are lying on the ground; the old woman, disemboweled and decapitated, is at the back; she has defended herself like a man, and her hand is still holding a flint ax. One of the men of metal, his face horrible crushed, testifies that they have not forced their way into the dwelling of the men of flint without a fight.

The heir of the marvelous artists of an epoch already dead, he has the sentiment that he remains the last of his race in the fact of this enemy.

All of that precipitates through his mind torrentially. He fights.

The cavern is deep, but narrow at that point. He has already struck the other with terrible blows, but now the metal-worker makes a lightning gesture with a hand equipped with some sort of bright blade. He sees, has seen, that unknown weapon coming toward him. His torso recoils, collides with the all, the arm carrying the club seeks the impetus to strike again.

Too late. The luminous dart reaches him. He is aware confusedly, of the pelt that resists, then cedes; his retracted flesh tries to repel the slender and inexplicable weapon; the blade plunges in.

The Magdalenian feels a glacial gleam penetrating him. A dolorous ring circles the weapon embedded in his torso. The pain increases, enormous and immeasurable, drowning consciousness and will within him. He tries to draw another breath, to inflate his breast with oxygen, but in an atrocious belch, a jet of blood spurts from his gaping mouth.

The metal has vanquished.

In the bloody cavern, filed with the reek of dead flesh, the man of metal has approached the last living being: the woman who prefigures the beauty of the times to come. Terrified and rigid, she is backed up against the wall, in a corner. He is bloody, and his rage is calm. Undoubtedly, he is the only surviving male of the two battling clans. Perhaps the pointlessness of those murders is haunting his low brow and sharp eyes.

He draws nearer, the blade shining in his hand that has just sacrificed the last of the Magdalenian men: the first sword, the first perfected instrument of assassination. And now the raw soul of his metallurgist ancestors is vibrating within him. Art is not, for these men of the South, enslaved by taxing labor, a customary and age-old usage all of whose secrets have been explored by ancestors. Before that slender and curvaceous body, scarcely clad in a worn and limp animal-skin, he senses the mystery of feminine grace. He perceives in the pulsation of his arteries the possible infinite expansion of the admiring sentiment that animates him.

He stops in front of the woman. They contemplate one another in silence.

Finally, the knife falls from the hand of the man of metal and his hand sketches an amicable gesture.

She has read in the enemy's eyes his power and his future. She abandons the cold granulation of the stone at her back, where she thought she would die, steps over the body of one of the dead men, and another cadaver. The man backs away from her, breathing heavily.

Here is the daylight, the forest extending to infinity like a somber carpet, the silent mountains where the wind alone groans as it scrapes the granite. The sky extends its cupola the color of pearl between the four horizons.

They are now a couple.

Their children, vagabonds, laborers and artists, will be able to unite science and dream. They will conceive beauty. It is thanks to some of their descendants, headed toward the Orient, where the sweetness of living lies, that a barbaric people of the Aegean Sea will know iron *and* art. That people, thus fertilized by the blood of Atlantis and that of the Magdalenians, will acquire immortal glory under the name of Hellas.

SF & FANTASY

Adolphe Alhaiza. *Cybele*
Alphonse Allais. *The Adventures of Captain Cap*
Henri Allorge. *The Great Cataclysm*
Guy d'Armen. *Doc Ardan: The City of Gold and Lepers*
G.-J. Arnaud. *The Ice Company*
Charles Asselineau. *The Double Life*
Henri Austruy. *The Eupantophone; The Olotelepan; The Petitpaon Era*
Barillet-Lagargousse. *The Final War*
Cyprien Bérard. *The Vampire Lord Ruthwen*
S. Henry Berthoud. *Martyrs of Science*
Aloysius Bertrand. *Gaspard de la Nuit*
Richard Bessière. *The Gardens of the Apocalypse; The Masters of Silence*
Albert Bleunard. *Ever SMalher*
Félix Bodin. *The Novel of the Future*
Louis Boussenard. *Monsieur Synthesis*
Alphonse Brown. *City of Glass; The Conquest of the Air*
Emile Calvet. *In a Thousand Years*
André Caroff. *The Terror of Madame Atomos; Miss Atomos; The Return of Madame Atomos; The Mistake of Madame Atomos; The Monsters of Madame Atomos; The Revenge of Madame Atomos; The Resurrection of Madame Atomos; The Mark of Madame Atomos; The Spheres of Madame Atomos; The Wrath of Madame Atomos* (w/M. & Sylvie Stéphan)
Félicien Champsaur. *The Human Arrow; Ouha, King of the Apes; Pharaoh's Wife; Homo-Deus*
Didier de Chousy. *Ignis*
Jules Clarétie. *Obsession*
Michel Corday. *The Eternal Flame*
André Couvreur. *The Necessary Evil*; *Caresco, Superman; The Exploits of Professor Tornada* (3 vols.)
Captain Danrit. *Undersea Odyssey*
C. I. Defontenay. *Star (Psi Cassiopeia)*
Charles Derennes. *The People of the Pole*
Georges Dodds (anthologist). *The Missing Link*
Charles Dodeman. *The Silent Bomb*
Harry Dickson. *The Heir of Dracula; Harry Dickson vs. The Spider*

Georges Le Faure & Henri de Graffigny. *The Extraordinary Adventures of a Russian Scientist Across the Solar System* (2 vols.)

Gustave Le Rouge. *The Mysterious Doctor Cornelius* (3 vols.); *The Vampires of Mars; The Dominion of the World* (w/Gustave Guitton) (4 vols.)

Jules Lermina. *Mysteryville; Panic in Paris; To-Ho and the Gold Destroyers; The Secret of Zippeliu; The Battle of Strasbourg*

André Lichtenberger. *The Centaurs; The Children of the Crab*

Listonai. *The Philosophical Voyager*

Jean-Marc & Randy Lofficier. *Edgar Allan Poe on Mars; The Katrina Protocol; Pacifica; Robonocchio; Return of the Nyctalope;* (anthologists) *Tales of the Shadowmen 1-11; The Vampire Almanac*

Xavier Mauméjean. *The League of Heroes*

Joseph Méry. *The Tower of Destiny*

Hippolyte Mettais. *The Year 5865; Paris Before the Deluge*

Louise Michel. *The Human Microbes; The New World*

Tony Moilin. *Paris in the Year 2000*

José Moselli. *Illa's End*

John-Antoine Nau. *Enemy Force*

Marie Nizet. *Captain Vampire*

C. Nodier, A. Beraud & Toussaint-Merle. *Frankenstein*

Henri de Parville. *An Inhabitant of the Planet Mars*

Gaston de Pawlowski. *Journey to the Land of the 4th Dimension*

Georges Pellerin. *The World in 2000 Years*

Ernest Pérochon. *The Frenetic People*

Pierre Pelot. *The Child Who Walked on the Sky*

J. Polidori, C. Nodier, E. Scribe. *Lord Ruthven the Vampire*

P.-A. Ponson du Terrail. *The Vampire and the Devil's Son; The Immortal Woman*

Georges Price. *The Missing Men of the Sirius*

Edgar Quinet. *Ahasuerus; The Enchanter Merlin*

Henri de Régnier. *A Surfeit of Mirrors*

Maurice Renard. *The Blue Peril; Doctor Lerne; The Doctored Man; A Man Among the Microbes; The Master of Light*

Jean Richepin. *The Wing; The Crazy Corner*

Albert Robida. *The Adventures of Saturnin Farandoul; The Clock of the Centuries; Chalet in the Sky; The Electric Life*

J.-H. Rosny Aîné. *Helgvor of the Blue River; The Givreuse Enigma; The Mysterious Force; The Navigators of Space; Vamireh; The World of the Variants; The Young Vampire*

Marcel Rouff. *Journey to the Inverted World*

Léonie Rouzade. *The World Turned Upside Down*

Han Ryner. *The Superhumans; The Human Ant*

Pierre de Selenes: *An Unknown World*

Angelo de Sorr. *The Vampires of London*

Brian Stableford. *The New Faust at the Tragicomique;The Empire of the Necromancers (The Shadow of Frankenstein; Frankenstein and the Vampire Countess; Frankenstein in London); Sherlock Holmes & The Vampires of Eternity; The Stones of Camelot; The Wayward Muse.* (anthologist) *News from the Moon; The Germans on Venus; The Supreme Progress; The World Above the World; Nemoville; Investigations of the Future; The Conqueror of Death; The Revolt of the Machines; The Man With the Blue Face*

Jacques Spitz. *The Eye of Purgatory*

Kurt Steiner. *Ortog*

Eugène Thébault. *Radio-Terror*

C.-F. Tiphaigne de La Roche. *Amilec*

Simon Tyssot de Patot. *The Strange Voyages of Jacques Massé and Pierre de Mésange*

Louis Ulbach. *Prince Bonifacio*

Théo Varlet. *The Golden Rock. The Xenobiotic Invasion; The Castaways of Eros; Timeslip Troopers* (w/André Blandin); *The Martian Epic* (w/Octave Joncquel)

Pierre Véron. *The Merchants of Health*

Paul Vibert. *The Mysterious Fluid*

Villiers de l'Isle-Adam. *The Scaffold; The Vampire Soul*

Philippe Ward. *Artahe ; The Song of Montségur* (w/Sylvie Miller) *Manhattan Ghost* (w/Mickael Laguerre)

MYSTERIES & THRILLERS

M. Allain & P. Souvestre. *The Daughter of Fantômas*

A. Anicet-Bourgeois, Lucien Dabril. *Rocambole*

A. Bernède. *Belphegor*; *Judex* (w/Louis Feuillade); *The Return of Judex* (w/Louis Feuillade); *The Shadow of Judex*

A. Bisson & G. Livet. *Nick Carter vs. Fantômas*

V. Darlay & H. de Gorsse. *Arsène Lupin vs. Sherlock Holmes: The Stage Play*

Séamas Duffy. *Sherlock Holmes in Paris*

Paul Féval. *Gentlemen of the Night; John Devil; The Black Coats ('Salem Street; The Invisible Weapon; The Parisian Jungle; The*

Companions of the Treasure; Heart of Steel; The Cadet Gang; The Sword-Swallower)
Emile Gaboriau. *Monsieur Lecoq*
Goron & Emile Gautier. *Spawn of the Penitentiary*
Paul d'Ivoi. *Around the World on Five Sous* (w/Henri Chabrillat)
Rick Lai. *Shadows of the Opera: Retribution in Blood; Sisters of the Shadows: The Curse of Cagliostro*
Steve Leadley. *Sherlock Holmes: The Circle of Blood*
Maurice Leblanc. *Arsène Lupin vs. Countess Cagliostro; Arsène Lupin vs. Sherlock Holmes (The Blonde Phantom; The Hollow Needle); The Many Faces of Arsène Lupin; The Island of the Thirty Coffins*
Gaston Leroux. *Chéri-Bibi; The Phantom of the Opera; Rouletabille & the Mystery of the Yellow Room; Rouletabille at Krupp's*
Richard Marsh. *The Complete Adventures of Judith Lee*
William Patrick Maynard. *The Terror of Fu Manchu; The Destiny of Fu Manchu*
Frank J. Morlock. *Sherlock Holmes: The Grand Horizontals; Sherlock Holmes vs Jack the Ripper*
Jean Petithuguenin. *The Adventures of Ethel King*
Antonin Reschal. *The Adventures of Miss Boston*
P. de Wattyne & Y. Walter. *Sherlock Holmes vs. Fantômas*
David White. *Fantômas in America*
Pierre Yrondy. *The Adventures of Thérèse Arnaud*

Victor Margueritte. *The Bacheloress; The Companion; The Couple*

SCREENPLAYS

Mike Baron. *The Iron Triangle*
Emma Bull & Will Shetterly. *Nightspeeder; War for the Oaks*
Gerry Conway & Roy Thomas. *Doc Dynamo*
Steve Englehart. *Majorca*
James Hudnall. *The Devastator*
Jean-Marc & Randy Lofficier. *Royal Flush*
J.-M. & R. Lofficier & Marc Agapit. *Despair*
J.-M. & R. Lofficier & Joël Houssin. *City*
Andrew Paquette. *Peripheral Vision*
Robert L. Robinson, Jr. *Judex*
R. Thomas, J. Hendler & L. Sprague de Camp. *Rivers of Time*

NON-FICTION

Stephen R. Bissette. *Blur 1-5. Green Mountain Cinema 1; Teen Angels*
Win Scott Eckert. *Crossovers* (2 vols.)
Jean-Marc & Randy Lofficier. *Shadowmen* (2 vols.)
Randy Lofficier. *Over Here*

ART BOOKS

Jean-Pierre Normand. *Science Fiction Illustrations*
Raven Okeefe. *Raven's L'il Critters; Rave's Faves*
Randy Lofficier & Raven Okeefe. *If Your Possum Go Daylight...*
Daniele Serra. *Illusions*
Randy Lofficier. *Over Here*

HEXAGON COMICS

Franco Frescura & Luciano Bernasconi. *Wampus*
Franco Frescura & Giorgio Trevisan. *CLASH*
L. Bernasconi, J.-M. Lofficier & Juan Roncagliolo. *Phenix*
Claude Legrand, J.-M. Lofficier & L. Bernasconi. *Kabur*
Franco Oneta. *Zembla*
L. Buffolente, Lofficier & J.-J. Dzialowski. *Strangers: Homicron*
Danilo Grossi. *Strangers: Jaydee*
Claude Legrand & Luciano Bernasconi. *Strangers: Starlock*
Thierry Mornet & Juan Roncagliolo. *Guardian of the Republic*
J.-M. Lofficier, M. Garcia, F. Blanco & J. Pima. *Strangers 1: Strangers in a Strange Land*
J.-M. Lofficier & Others. *Strangers 0: Omens & origins*